Submissive Beauty

Submissive Beauty

By Eliza Gayle

Resplendence Publishing, LLC
http://www.resplendencepublishing.com

Resplendence Publishing, LLC
2665 S Atlantic Avenue, #349
Daytona Beach, FL 32118

Submissive Beauty
Copyright © 2011 Eliza Gayle
Edited by Michele Paulin and Juli Simonson
Cover art by Kendra Egert, www.creationsbykendra.com

Print format ISBN: 978-1-60735-316-4

Print Release: December 2011

There are many great writers who suffered through this book with me. It's not always easy to write a book and we rely on our friends and fellow writers to push us through when we need the extra motivation. I only hope I give enough back.

My special thanks go to Jessica Lee, Dee Carney and Lissa Matthews. They offer their ideas, critiques and extra support when I most need it.

Last and certainly not least I want to thank my editor. With her insightful comments and dedication to detail she makes my books much stronger.

Chapter One

Gabby turned in her chair to stand and bolt for the door when the room lights flickered out and the spotlights on the stage in front of her lit up. The sea of strangers chatting around her immediately ceased their conversations and sat riveted, waiting for the demonstration to begin. If she left now and hurried, she might still make it home before *NCIS* started...

Or she could stay and watch the show alone. Curiosity about the infamous Sanctuary got the best of her and kept her butt in the chair. What would a few more minutes matter anyway? Gabby tugged at the hem of her skirt for the umpteenth time since she'd arrived.

Before she could change her mind again, a platinum blonde, petite woman, scantily clad in a tight, red latex dress that left nothing to the imagination, ambled onto the stage in four-inch spike heels.

"Good evening, everyone. Welcome to tonight's demonstration of the violet wand with our very own Master Thomas." Light applause broke out among the crowd. "If you will please hold your comments or questions until the end, I'm certain all will enjoy what he has in store for us."

With that she walked from the stage. For a long, silent moment, they all waited for more. Gabby swallowed hard. This was not the time to make a spectacle of herself and try to slip out.

"Welcome, everyone."

Gabby heard the voice over the microphone before she ever saw the man. The dark, rumbling tone cascaded down her spine alongside an involuntary shiver. Goosebumps erupted along her arms and legs. Wouldn't that be a voice to come home to every night?

A shadowy figure on stage caught her attention from the corner of her eye, and she strained in his direction to see what he looked like.

"For tonight's demonstration, the lovely sub Linda has volunteered to be my subject."

Lights flashed, the curtains parted and a lounging table appeared in a bluish spotlight. A curvaceous, dark-haired woman stood next to the table, dressed in a cute pair of ruffled panties and nothing else. She took her place on the table, lying still and compliant. The eerie glow of the lighting gave the scene an ethereal touch—mesmerizing actually. Any remnant thoughts of leaving dissipated at the sight of Master Thomas and his willing submissive. The lovely woman waited motionless for him to approach her from the opposite side of the stage. Gabby, on the other hand, fidgeted restlessly in her seat, fear and anticipation warring in her mind.

When he stepped into the blue spotlight, Gabby was struck by the sheer size of him. He towered over the scene laid out in front of him. The low lighting made it difficult to make out the details of his face, although it was obvious he had thick dark hair—the kind she longed to thread her fingers through. And the memory of his incredibly commanding voice still whispered across her exposed skin even while he wasn't speaking.

As Master Thomas began to explain the technicalities and safety issues to consider when using a violet wand, Gabby watched the way he paced around the table, the little touches he gave the woman and the serious expression that never wavered from his face.

Beads of moisture trickled along the curve of Gabby's neck as the demonstration proceeded. Her palms began to sweat. Had the temperature in the room ratcheted up, or was she the only one this affected? Although the arousal wetting her panties was a dead giveaway, her reaction had nothing to do with the room and everything to do with the man on stage. Curious and a little mortified by her body's response, she tore her gaze from the scene and glanced around the room. To her relief, it was too dark to make out much more than silhouettes around her. If she couldn't see them, then they couldn't see her. Still, Gabby had chosen a seat in the back corner not far from the door, so she could leave quickly if she needed to.

A sudden buzzing noise filled the room, and a slight gasp among the club goers had her swinging back to Master Thomas and the girl lying next to him. In his hand was a black tube with a clear globe on the end that crackled with alternating zigzags of blue and purple light inside. It was like one of those electric toy spheres in the specialty stores she'd seen at the mall. Gabby had no inkling what that would feel like against her skin and, at the moment, wasn't too keen on finding out. But with Master Thomas wielding the wicked little toy, the scene instantly took on a train wreck effect, and Gabby couldn't look away now if she tried. She desperately wanted to see what happened next.

"The most important thing is to take it nice and slow when starting out and stay completely tuned into the sub you are playing with." He squeezed the woman's knee then, and she rewarded him with a shy smile.

A sharp stab of longing speared through Gabby, and her stomach clenched. What would it be like lying there at his instruction and waiting for him to give and take as he pleased? The all too familiar question she'd pondered over the years was brought sharply into focus by a single voice in a darkened room.

His hand moved, and the wand dipped to the sub's shoulder—a quick testing tap that caught her off guard. Her body jerked in response. A few murmurs sounded in the crowd as he touched her again, this time stroking a few inches down her arm. Amazingly, she remained still, except for the closing of her eyes and the muscles of her face going slack as she relaxed into the experience.

"Depending on the level of voltage you're using, each touch has the potential to bring a sharp jolt of pain." Thomas turned the knob on the base device and touched the implement to Linda's stomach. Her gasp shattered the quiet of the crowd. "Or a simple buzz of tingle." He turned the dial once again and placed the device perilously close to her pussy. The resulting moan of pleasure sent a shiver across Gabby's skin along with a fresh wave of heat building between her thighs. "It all depends on what you as the Dom prefer and what you know your submissive can tolerate. I'd suggest starting out very low."

With little pause, he began stroking Linda everywhere from her arms to her legs to her belly and even a quick kiss to her thinly covered pussy. He covered every exposed inch of her flesh and then some. Her legs twitched, and her head swung from side to side with the most amazing expression of bliss curling at her lips. When she began to moan, Gabby noticed her own bra and panties suddenly drew tight, the sensitive tips of her nipples rubbing against fabric. The absolute need to strip out of her restrictive clothing clawed at her gut.

"Once you have your girl or boy ramped up and on the verge of begging, you can switch to this handy little attachment called the body contact." Thomas pulled the wand from the base machine and set it aside. He replaced it with a small metal attachment that fit snugly in his palm. "With this in your hand, you effectively become the wand. Now when you touch her, *you're* directly delivering the current the wand did." He pinched one of Linda's nipples, her back arched and a low, sultry wail filled the room.

Watching the sub and her reactions to the way Master Thomas teased and tempted her with an increasing pattern of more electricity affected Gabby more than she anticipated. The look of sheer pleasure on the other woman's face cried out to her on a level she couldn't suppress—the side of her that she'd kept hidden for ten years until her husband had walked out eight months ago.

Master Thomas grabbed the woman's legs and pushed them gently apart. Gabby held her breath in anticipation, knowing that neither she nor the sub would be able to control their reactions. She leaned back in her chair and let her legs fall apart, the sudden desire flaming through her far more than she'd experienced in a very long time. Gabby wanted more. Grateful for the darkness of the room, she rubbed the inside of her thighs, inching closer to her now soaked cotton panties. She'd never before considered whether she was a voyeur, but judging by how wet she'd become, it would be hard to deny it now.

The moans from the sub were now constant and growing louder by the second as Master Thomas stroked her inner thighs and pussy almost nonstop. Her body twisted and thrashed around the table. Soft pleas fell from her mouth. Thomas whispered into her ear the entire time. Gabby could only assume it was reassurances or commands that heightened her pleasure.

"Please, Sir. Please may I come?" Linda begged.

On the verge herself, Gabby slid her fingers underneath the soft fabric of her underwear and pushed through the sopping folds of her pussy, straight to her throbbing clit.

Her eyes focused on Master Thomas. The sharp intensity in his gaze, even from this distance, told her he took great pleasure in seeing a girl twisted up and on the verge in front of him. Or maybe it was way he held his lips, slightly curved at the edges that clued her in to the enjoyment he derived from the scene. She wondered if Linda, the sub, belonged to him... Would he make her beg to come or had he already given her permission earlier.

Gabby flicked her swollen nub over and over with the tip of her finger as her own need for release teetered on the edge. In her mind's eye, it was her not Linda on the table with Master Thomas driving her to the brink. Never in her wildest dreams had she thought she'd enjoy a public scene like this. Yet her fear of discovery dissolved a little more with each passing second. Her mind swirled with Thomas' voice. Everything he asked she yearned to give.

The pressure behind her clit teetered on a painful edge.

Please. Oh God, please.

"Come for me, girl. Come for me now."

Her pussy squeezed.

A ragged scream tore from the sub as she came in hard racking sobs. Light flashed in Gabby's vision as his command triggered her, as well. She bit down on her lips to keep from crying out while her muscles clenched and spasmed in pleasure. Long minutes later, Gabby opened her eyes and sat there in a daze trying to figure out what exactly had happened. Her hand was between her legs, her lungs screamed for air and tears stained her cheeks.

The stage lights winked out, and Master Thomas and the girl disappeared behind the curtain.

Gabby managed to pull down her skirt before the lights in the auditorium came on, but that was the extent of movement she could handle at the moment. As the club members filed out and moved to the adjoining bar, Gabby remembered the question and answer segment of the night's session would be conducted in the other room. She struggled to find her composure, but a light spacey feeling she'd never before experienced surrounded her. The overwhelming sensation felt so good she didn't want it to stop, at least not yet. She couldn't ever remember feeling this good.

A rustling sounded next to her as someone took the seat beside hers. Gabby froze in place and stared straight ahead. Mortified by her behavior, she couldn't turn and face whoever had sat down. Hot blood flooded her cheeks as shame bubbled inside her. What had she been thinking? Somehow, someway, she needed to refocus and pull herself together enough to drive home. She was going to kill Angel. Her best friend had talked her into attending tonight's meeting of the local BDSM club then had pulled a no show.

"Are you okay?" That voice. Right next to her.

Oh God, did he see her? Did he somehow know what she'd done during the show?

Gabby squeezed her eyes against fresh tears threatening to fall. She gulped for breath, trying to fight back the sudden wave of panic threatening to consume her, not to mention the fog in her head.

"Sit still and concentrate on your breathing, sweetheart. Let me get you some water."

She grabbed his arm when he turned to leave.

"I'm fine."

"I'm sure you are, but you still need some fluid. You're pale and shaky. Don't worry, I'll be right back."

Gabby watched him disappear into the bar area then scanned the seat next to her and the floor for her purse. She had to get out of here before he returned.

After hooking her bag on her wrist, she popped up from her chair and swayed to the right as the room began to spin. What the hell? She grabbed onto the back of the chair in front of her to steady herself but to no avail. Much more of this and she'd find herself pitching forward into the rows of chairs.

"Whoa, what are you doing, young lady?" Master Thomas hooked her around the waist and pulled her against him before easing her back toward a seat. That quick moment of her body pressed to his flooded her with renewed desire. Even the subtle scent of his cologne turned her on.

"I-I'm…"

"Yeah, yeah, you're fine. I heard you the first time. Except you nearly took a header before I grabbed you. So sit down, and let me give you some water." His silky tone had turned gruff, which did little to turn her away or settle her mind. Her butt hit the leather seat once again, her skirt riding up as she sat. Her brain warned her to adjust her clothing, but she was simply too out of it to care. With Thomas still touching her, it was impossible to think long about anything other than his contact. His heat.

"So what happened to you? Do you have any medical condition I should be concerned about?" He stared at her intently, looking right through her as humiliation burned up her throat and cheeks. "That's not it is it?"

Gabby shook her head. She didn't know what to say, but she certainly didn't need him calling for an ambulance or anything crazy like that. "I'm not sure what happened." To her mortification, her voice came out a broken whisper. Something about this man had her flustered and unsure, and she'd behaved like a woman who didn't know how to handle herself out in public. It was damned embarrassing.

"Here. Have some water, I think it will help." He held the water glass up to her lips and tipped it up as she drank greedily. After a few swallows, he moved the tumbler away, and she relaxed into the chair. "I'm Thomas, by the way." He held out his hand, and she glanced down at his long, strong fingers with neatly trimmed, blunt nails before sliding her own hand lightly into his.

"Gabrielle. But everyone calls me Gabby."

"Why?"

She puzzled at his question. "Why do they call me Gabby?" She'd been called by the nickname for so long she didn't even remember when it had started. "I'm not sure. I can't even remember a time when anyone called me anything else."

"That's a shame. You look more like a Gabrielle to me. An intelligent and curious woman who may be in over her head at the moment, though." His assessment caught her off guard and might have offended her if she wasn't feeling so loose and relaxed. In fact, the dizziness had faded and been replaced with an unexpected serene calm.

"I'm not sure what to say to that." She pulled her hand back and fidgeted with the hem of her skirt.

"It wasn't meant as an insult, merely an observation." He stilled her hand at her thigh by covering it with his own. "Do I make you nervous Gabrielle?"

God, she loved the sound of her name rolling from his tongue. It came out exotic and sexy. And hell yes, he made her nervous. He was a Master in a lifestyle she craved but had little practical experience in—not to mention he'd gotten her off just from watching him on stage, and she had a sinking feeling he knew it.

"Can I have some more water?"

He smiled at her obvious avoidance and handed her the crystal tumbler of cold water. She gulped down several more swallows before handing it back.

"Thank you for the water and the attention. I shouldn't have skipped dinner this evening, and the heat in here must have gotten to me. I think I should probably head home now and get some rest."

The grim set of his lips and the narrowing of his eyes told her that he knew she was lying, but she wasn't about to spill the truth to a stranger. Gabby still had to walk out of there, and she didn't want to do so in shame.

"You're a beautiful woman, Miss Gabrielle, and would certainly give a Dom a run for his money I'd bet. You should stay for a while longer—meet some of the other members."

Hope shot through her at his words. To hell with the implication that she'd be a challenge; he had called her beautiful. She rose from her seat, and Thomas did the same, offering his hand again. He certainly knew how to be the perfect gentleman.

"Thank you again for you help, and it was a lovely demonstration you gave to the group tonight. I've never seen that piece of equipment used before. It was very educational." She again grabbed her purse and let him lead her toward the front door.

"I'm glad to hear that you enjoyed yourself." He lifted her hand to his lips and pressed a kiss to the tips of her fingers. "Do you need an escort home?"

Was he offering? Her nipples tightened at the naughty images that popped into her head. This man in her townhouse, taking charge of their encounter, giving her the experience of a lifetime.

Stop that, Gabby. He's just offering you a ride home, not a fucking lesson in BDSM.

"Thank you, M-Mas—"

"It's just Thomas, sweetheart. The club insists on calling me Master, but honestly, I prefer only my sub to do so and only when she's ready."

His sub. So he did have one already. Of course, he did. A man with his talent, intelligence and a voice that could easily make a woman come on demand would not be unattached. "Thank you, Thomas, but I really do feel back to normal again, thanks to you. And I only live a few miles from here, so it won't take me long to get home."

"You live here on the east side or uptown?"

"Uptown in the fourth ward. I love it there."

He smiled. "I can imagine you there already." They reached the door, and he held it open for her. "I hope you'll come back. We do meetings and demonstrations every month. It's always educational and sometimes a little fun, too." He winked at the last, and she knew for sure then. He'd somehow seen her masturbating to his voice as he'd touched and encouraged the beautiful Linda.

Gabby rushed from the door without another word, afraid to look back. She shouldn't be so embarrassed by her behavior; Thomas certainly didn't seem to mind. But she'd been caught off balance and didn't know how to read the mysterious Dom who'd helped her.

She fished her keys from her purse, hurriedly unlocked the door and jumped inside. She should have never come, yet she'd learned a little, experienced even more and she didn't regret that—not really. She was, however, still going to kill Angel tomorrow when she got a hold of her.

Chapter Two

A banging noise in Gabby's head roused her from a deep sleep as she blinked her eyes against the bright sunshine pouring in her room. She'd forgotten to close the drapes again. Unable to settle down after returning home from the meeting, she'd grabbed a book and snuggled under the covers to read. That was at one in the morning. Now as her vision focused on the digital clock on her nightstand, she saw that it was after seven.

"Come on, Gabby, wake up and open the door." Her best friend's muffled voice sounded through the front door carrying all the way to her bedroom. Gabby flung the covers and rushed to open it. She didn't need Angel standing out there making such a ruckus. Next thing she knew, her neighbors would be complaining about the noise.

"I'm coming, I'm coming. Quit making so much damn noise." She flipped the locks and wrenched the door open to find her petite friend smiling at her.

"Finally. I've been banging out here for five minutes, waiting for you to drag your lazy ass out of bed."

Gabby stepped aside, ushered Angel inside and shut the door behind her. "My lazy ass, huh? This from the woman who left me hanging last night."

"I know, I know, I'm in so much trouble for that."

"Trouble? What do you mean?" Gabby stifled a yawn behind her hand.

Angel tossed her purse onto the chair and stalked toward the kitchen, chattering all the way. "Well...I got myself in a bit of a predicament last night with Master and ended up in punishment for the night."

Gabby laughed at her friend and the sparkle in her eye when she turned back to face her. "I'll just bet you did. Somehow, you manage to do that more often than not. I can't believe Jeff hasn't caught onto your antics yet."

Angel rolled her eyes. "I have no idea what you're talking about."

"Uh huh."

"Anyway, I feel awful for not showing up last night so, as soon as Jeff left for work this morning, I hightailed it over here to check on you."

"You could have just called."

Angel reached into the refrigerator and took out the orange juice then grabbed two small glasses from the cabinet. "Yeah, I could have, but would you have answered?"

"Of course, I would have." Maybe.

"You are such a terrible liar."

They settled around the kitchen table, and Gabby twirled the glass between her fingers. The events of last night still clouded her mind, and she couldn't forget how wonderful she'd felt during the demonstration.

"So...are you going to tell me?"

"Tell you what?" She knew where her friend was headed, but she wasn't ready to share the full extent of what had happened, not even with Angel.

"Come on, Gabby, spill. What did you think of the meeting? How was the demonstration? Did you talk to anyone? Meet anyone interesting?"

"Damn, Angel, slow down." She shook her head and stood. She had nervous energy to burn, and she needed to do something. Today would be a perfect day to play in her garden. Work she could do later after it grew too hot to be outside.

"It was awkward being there alone. I didn't want to stay, but when the lights dimmed and the demonstration began, I decided to give it a try. And I can admit I found it very educational."

"Awesome. I wasn't sure what you'd think of the violet wand. You'd be surprised how incredible it feels."

Gabby turned sharply too her friend. "You've experienced it?" She held her breath, so curious.

"Yes, I have. Jeff loves to push my limits when he can, and that was one of the things I was most afraid of so he convinced me to try it."

"And?"

"And it was the most incredible thing I'd ever experienced. It heightened everything. Perception, arousal, all of it. I experienced the most incredible orgasms of my life, and that night realized just how much I really trusted my Master."

Gabby's stomach jerked at her friend's words. She could hear the love and trust in her friend's voice, and her heart ached for that kind of experience. That kind of need and satisfaction flowing through two people was a rare and precious gift indeed.

"The sub last night was really into it. Her emotional and physical response to the scene was off the charts." She couldn't tell her friend how the desire in the room had rushed over and through her until she'd been compelled to touch herself. Just thinking about it now had her panties dampening in desire all over again.

"Who conducted the demonstration last night?"

Gabby hesitated almost afraid to say his name. "Master Thomas," she whispered.

"Oh my God, really? This is perfect. Gabby, he's the one I've been telling you about. The one who I think would be perfect to introduce you to the lifestyle. He's a wonderful teacher."

Gabby nearly joked on her juice. Angel had to be kidding. Either that or she'd lost her mind. Thomas would never be interested in someone inexperienced like her. Besides he'd mentioned a sub last night, and she was definitely not looking to get in the middle of someone else's relationship or share a Dom with someone else. Baby steps.

"You aren't really serious?"

"Of course, I am. I wouldn't joke about something this important. I already talked to him about you last week, and he seemed interested. I had planned to introduce you to him last night."

Gabby's stomach cramped painfully. This could not be happening. The one saving grace for her last night was knowing they were complete strangers and would likely never see each other again. She reached for the chair and sat down with a hard thud.

"Gabby, what's wrong? You're pale." Her friend reached out and felt her forehead. "And clammy. Are you sick?"

Only sick of embarrassment. "No, I'm fine. Not enough sleep is all."

"Well then, back to bed for you, young lady. You can sleep a few more hours and still have plenty of time to get whatever you need done."

"No, Angel. I'll be fine."

"Then at least let me fix you something to eat. That should help." She hopped from the chair and headed to the fridge for supplies. "Finish up that juice, and I'll get you some more. And then you can finish telling me about last night."

Gabby didn't think she could eat. Her stomach felt like a heavy weight had settled in. "Angel, what did you mean you talked to Thomas about me? What did you say?"

"Oh don't worry, hon, I didn't tell him that much. Jeff and I have known him a long time so I kind of know what he likes. Trust me, you are just what he's looking for."

"I got the impression last night that he already had a sub." She spoke quietly and evenly, trying to sound as if it didn't matter. Because it really didn't.

"Nope, it's been at least a year or more since he's had a regular sub. He comes to the parties and plays here and there, but so far, he hasn't connected with anyone. It's as if he's waiting for something...or someone..." Angel's voice drifted off in an odd wistful tone that confused Gabby.

"I find that hard to believe." Her sarcasm caused Angel to swivel and look at her.

"Did something happen you haven't told me about?"

Gabby cast her eyes downward. "What? Why would you think that?"

Angel walked over and sat down at the table again. "Oh yeah, you're definitely holding out on me. ' Fess up. What happened?"

"Nothing. I told you I watched his demonstration and found it fascinating."

"The demonstration or him?"

"Both I guess." She squirmed in her seat, continuing to avoid Angel's too inquisitive gaze.

"Did he talk to you?" Gabby groaned. Her friend was far too perceptive.

"Yes, for a few minutes after the demonstration right before I left."

"Well, damn." Now, Angel sounded disappointed.

"Why? What's wrong?"

Angel returned to the stove and flipped the sizzling omelet onto a plate and grabbed the bread from the toaster.

"It's nothing."

"Now, who's holding out? Come on, spill it." Her friend set the plate in front of her and handed her a fork.

"Only if you eat your breakfast." Leave it to her friend to coerce her with a bribe.

"Fine." She scooped some of the egg onto her fork and shoveled it into her mouth.

"Thomas is an incredible Master and a very good man."

"But…"

"No but. I'm serious. He and Jeff have been friends for a very long time, and I've gotten to know him well over the years."

Oh God, please don't let her tell me she'd played with him, Gabby wasn't sure she could handle that right now. She didn't want to jump to that conclusion so she exhaled a slow breath and waited for Angel to tell her the rest. "Go on."

"I know what you're thinking, and you couldn't be more wrong. I don't play with him." She paused. "He has a hard time finding serious subs who are willing to serve to his fetish."

Oh no, this did not sound good. If it had Angel hesitating, she couldn't imagine she'd be able to handle it at all. "Jeez, Angel, just tell me what it is."

"He has a thing for setting up scenes that will throw a sub way off balance. He digs to finds their weaknesses then challenges them with what he calls risqué type scenes."

Gabby drew her brows together not understanding. "I don't get what you're trying to say."

"He gets inside a girl's head, picks out what her fears are and starts chipping away at those with scenes designed to face them. It's both intense and exhilarating, but it's not for everyone. He could explain it much better than I can."

"Is he a cruel Master?"

"No, not at all, but sometimes, he comes across that way. It really is hard to understand without seeing or experiencing it. One thing I do know is that he is a great Dom, and when he claims the right sub, she will be lucky to be owned by him."

Gabby ate a few more bites of her food, trying to process what Angel was getting across. One thing didn't make sense. "Why did you seem disappointed that I'd already talked to him?"

"Another one of his quirks is his first meetings. He's a little unorthodox with a new girl he's interested in. I guess you could say he likes to perform a test of sorts so he can find out if she'll be receptive to his kind of training."

"What kind of test?" This conversation was getting stranger by the second.

"One designed to see how obedient you are as well as set the tone for the whole relationship."

"I take it you don't mean going out for dinner or coffee to chat then."

Angel laughed and grabbed the used dishes from the table then carried them to the sink. "Not hardly. When he's ready to get together with a girl for the first time you can bet it will be a situation that will make you squirm."

"Like what?"

"That's all I can say. It would be wrong for me to divulge Master Thomas's activities, and if I thought corner time for hours last night was a rough punishment.... If Jeff found me discussing another Dom like this, I'm certain my ass would hurt for a week."

Gabby nodded. "Yeah, you're probably right about that. You're one lucky woman, you know that?"

"You will be too, Gabby. You just have to get out there and look, unless of course you met him last night." She winked and headed to the door.

"Where are you going? Leaving already?"

"Yes, Jeff has plans for me at lunch, and I have to go and get ready. Punishing me gets him very worked up and the next day is always well worth every second of discipline."

Gabby held up her hand to stop her friend. "Don't tell me. I don't think I could take it."

Angel laughed and walked outside. "Don't worry so much today. We'll reschedule our get together for another one of the group meetings, and this time, I'll pick you up so you don't have to go alone."

Gabby groaned. After last night, she was in no hurry for a repeat. "Maybe."

"Just because the thing with Master Thomas didn't work out like I'd hoped doesn't mean I'm giving up on helping you. I've got plenty of ideas up my sleeve."

Gabby rolled her eyes.

Angel walked down the sidewalk and hopped into her car. Gabby watched her friend drive off and wondered more about what Angel had not said. She'd chosen her words about Thomas carefully, yet Gabby had heard the conviction in Angel's voice about what a good man he was.

Oh well, water under the bridge. It didn't matter anymore. Her behavior at the club hadn't been appropriate, and she'd never see him again.

Chapter Three

Gabby soaked in the warm sunshine while sitting in her favorite Adirondack chair in her garden, reading a book. It had been two days since her foray into the local BDSM social scene. She still flamed with embarrassment when she remembered the details, and she'd thought of little else since that night.

Even concentrating on her work had been a challenge, although she'd managed to muddle through the rest of the workweek. Now, it was Saturday, and after working in her yard all morning, she'd showered and curled up out here with every intention of escaping into some fiction. Except, ever since the demonstration, something had shifted inside her and she couldn't seem to turn off the need brewing inside. She'd even dressed differently this afternoon with a simple halter-top, no bra and the shortest skirt she'd found in her closet. Oh yeah, and no panties.

Gabby laid the book aside and spread her legs. She didn't have to worry about anyone seeing her bare pussy since her garden was protected by a privacy fence and sat back away from the house. It was truly her refuge from the world.

Warmth spread from her toes to her thighs and into the folds of her sex until her clit began to throbbed from a combination of heat and need. She wanted to touch herself to the point it drove her crazy, but the voice in her head—

Thomas's voice—wouldn't let her. Told her she had to wait. Her hands grazed her inner thighs from her knees to her hips until her body shook with desire, but still, she couldn't get the picture of him out of her head or stop his voice from admonishing her to behave.

She ached to know what he would do to her if he were here. Would he touch her or make her touch herself in front of him? She'd never done that in front of someone else. The thought frightened her as much as it turned her on. The farther her mind slipped into the fantasy the less she cared about anyone seeing or watching anything she did to the point she wished someone could see her.

She grew wetter by the instant and moisture trickled through her folds. For a quick second, she traced the path with one finger and gasped from the pleasure. She was so wet and horny she contemplated going inside to retrieve her vibrator. It wouldn't take long.

But she hated that thought.

She wanted to spend long hours at the mercy of a Dom, not a battery operated boyfriend. Not just any Dom, though. She wanted someone she connected with beyond the play. Someone looking to take complete control. Gabby sighed. She was looking for the impossible and damn well knew it.

Here like this, she could still hear her ex-husband Scott's last words in her head as clear as the day he'd said them.

"Are you really leaving me to become a slut?" Gabby winced at the memory of Scott's nasty question. In the past, she'd tried every which way to explain to him how she felt and why, but time and time again, he'd called her need to submit to a dominant either stupid or sick.

Relax, Gabrielle. Thomas's voice was in her head again. He and Angel were right, she needed to relax and do what felt right. Her ex was gone, and no one was here to make her feel incomplete or worthless. She deserved every second of pleasure she found.

Gabby relaxed the tense muscles in her neck and let out a long, slow breath. If she longed to serve a Master, so what? She needed to get past society's hang-ups and let herself live the way she needed to. Gabby allowed her thighs to fall wider. She let go of the hang-ups holding her back while she massaged her way toward her hungry pussy.

In her mind's eye, she still saw the girl on stage while Thomas worked her over with the violet wand. Every time the girl jumped or Thomas issued an order, her own clit pulsed and throbbed. Gabby gave her nub a quick touch, and her body arched into the exquisite pleasure that simple move gave her. God, what wouldn't she give for Thomas to be standing in front of her watching...directing her?

She dragged the tips of two fingers from her clit to her anus creating a stab of lust that clenched low in her belly. A soft sigh escaped her mouth as she relaxed further, allowing herself to enjoy her own touch, not to mention the illicit thought of being outside, wishing someone saw her. She wanted *him* to see her.

At an excruciatingly slow pace, she eased a finger through her slit, grabbing onto the chair for support. Her head swam with the sizzling lust of the night at the club, the atmosphere, the girl on the table, the buzzing of the wand in the deathly quiet room and the man she still craved.

She pushed another finger alongside the first, and her muscles squeezed, sending a sweet current of sensation along very sensitive tissue and nerve ending. If she angled her fingers just right, she might hit her hot spot that would send her over the edge. Gabby shifted her arm and hand until...

"Oh yes." Her breath hitched. She moved her fingers in and out. The need to come for him again overwhelmed her. After only a few strokes, her release hovered precariously—

A shrill noise sounded next to her chair nearly, sending her flying into the grass.

"God damn phone." She couldn't stop now. She was so close.

The phone rang again. "Damn it." She had to answer it. She'd been expecting Angel to call all day, and she didn't want to miss her.

Take the call and keep going. The voice in her head urged her to obey. *No one has to know.* Could she hide from her best friend the fact she was lying outside half naked with her hand buried in her pussy?

Gabby grabbed the phone with a shaky hand. She'd managed to go this far outside her comfort zone, why not keep going?

"Hello," she answered, doing the best she could to calm her voice but knowing she still sounded breathless.

"Gabrielle?"

Gabby's muscles tightened, frozen in shock at the sound of the voice at the other end of the line. Why the hell hadn't she checked the caller ID?

"Thomas?"

A low chuckle sounded at the other end. A soft sound that pulsed through her body and straight to the clit she'd been about to massage. Oh God, she was masturbating. Guilt surged through her.

"You recognized my voice. I like that."

"It's very distinctive." And seductive.

"Your friend, Angel, gave me your number. She thought you wouldn't mind. Have I caught you at a bad time?"

You have no idea. She cringed at her thoughts but didn't move her hand, too afraid he'd hear her.

"No, no, it's fine. I was just taking a break." Her voice shook when she spoke, and she prayed he wouldn't notice.

"You sound out of breath, like I've interrupted something." He paused. "Actually, you sound just like you did at the club the other night."

No, no, no way could he know what she was doing when he called. Gabby closed her eyes and willed her body to calm, but just hearing his voice made it worse. She wanted to fuck so bad now she almost told him so.

"I was outside reading a book. I had to run for the phone."

No way could she admit her actions. Not only was he a stranger, but she'd be mortally embarrassed to be caught.

"Gabrielle, are you telling me the truth? What were you really doing?"

Damn it. Busted. He wasn't going to let this go, and she had no idea what to say.

"It's nothing really. I was reading a book—"

"Uh-huh. You're as breathless as when we met, and you weren't reading a book then."

No, she was masturbating to his voice. Exactly the same thing she'd been doing when the phone had rung. He was far too perceptive for her own good.

"Where are you Gabrielle? Are you alone?"

"I'm outside in my garden, and yes, I'm alone." Her heart raced at his questions. Embarrassment warred with need, resulting in the ache to move her fingers. To rub her clit while he spoke to her. Did she dare? She moved her hand a fraction, careful not to make a sound.

"Gabrielle, why are you holding your breath?"

She exhaled slowly, trying to stay calm. "Nervous, I guess." Her voice shook.

"You have nothing to be nervous about, although I do expect the truth. What were you doing exactly when the phone rang?"

She chewed on her bottom lip at a loss for words. She was actually considering telling a practical stranger that she'd been touching herself, that she still was.

"Answer now, or I'll hang up."

Fear punched her gut. No, she didn't want him to go.

"I was...I was..." She couldn't get the words out.

"It's okay to tell me. You have nothing to fear from me." For some unknown reason, that calmed her. He calmed her.

"I'm embarrassed."

"Gabrielle, you're a sexual woman, a submissive, being embarrassed is never important. Obeying is all that matters. Now, tell me."

Fine, embarrassment be damned. She'd just do it. "I was touching myself when you called."

"Was that so hard?"

"I guess not," she ventured. "Sir," she added as an afterthought.

"Did you stop when you answered the phone?"

Her breath hitched, and her face flamed, but she'd let him take her this far so why stop now? "I stopped moving my hand, but I didn't remove it."

"You fingers are in your pussy now?"

"Yes," she breathed.

"Yes, what?"

"Yes, Sir." Oh hell, the more he talked and demanded answers the more she wanted to succumb, to give in to her own desires as well as whatever he might ask of her.

"Touch your clit with your thumb for me, Gabrielle."

"But—"

"Gabrielle," he interrupted. "Since we've been talking, your breathing has grown heavy, your voice shaky, and your resistance has faltered. I recognize the sounds of your need."

"Yes, Sir," she acquiesced. Gabby shifted her hand and moved her finger over the hard little nub. The gasp she tried to bite back fell from her lips. This close to her release it wouldn't take much, in fact, if he tried to make her hold it she might fail her very first task from the one man who haunted her every waking moment.

"Now, just hold still like that for a few minutes and tell me why you are outside playing with yourself? Can anyone see you?"

She shook her head. "No, this is a private garden that I've created. No one can see me unless they come in through the gate." Her breathing accelerated into short, hard pants as she tried to talk and not think about the clit pulsing under her thumb or the fingers being covered by more of her juices.

"You're a naughty little girl this afternoon. That pleases me. I'm intrigued."

Her stomach jolted at his praise. The phone began to slip in her hand, and she tightened her grip to maintain her hold. Shifting back into place, she grasped it closer to her ear.

"You want to come, don't you? You want me to tell me you to come." His voice rose, louder and deeper than before. "Go ahead. Ask me. Now."

She hesitated only for a second. "May I come now, Sir?"

"Fuck your pussy first. Let me hear how much you need it. Convince me."

She moaned on his words, her control threadbare. Still, she followed his instructions. She moved her fingers and moved them fast in an in and out motion that created increasingly more friction.

"Mmm, I can hear you. You're nice and wet, aren't you?"

"Yes...yes, Sir." She couldn't hold back, sensations swirled through her body. Her nipples tightened, and her muscles clamped.

"Please, Sir. I'm going to come. Please."

"Then come, Gabrielle. Come for me. Now."

She flicked her thumb once...twice and everything exploded around her. Her body shook, knocking the phone from her hand, and she screamed out her pleasure. She fucked herself hard, adding a third finger as she rode the wave after wave that crashed over her. "Oh fuck. Yes. Yes. Yes."

Minutes stretched out as the pulses continued until finally she slumped back into the chair and eased her hand from her sex. Never before in her life had she come this hard. Master Thomas did this to her. *Incredible.*

Oh crap...the phone.

Gabby searched the grass and found the handset lying where she'd dropped it. She scooped it up and pressed it to her ear as quickly as she could. "Thomas, I'm so sorry. Are you there? I didn't mean to drop the phone."

He laughed. "I understand completely, sweetheart. I like hearing the sounds you make when you enjoy yourself. Now, before you go inside and clean yourself up, I want you to find a pen and paper. Can you do that for me?"

"Yes."

"Yes, what?"

"Yes, Sir." It wasn't easy to remember the "Sir" every time he addressed her. She twisted to the little table where she'd lain her book and grabbed up the small notebook and pen she always kept by her side no matter where she went. She liked to journal a lot, and there were always little things here and there that she didn't want to forget. "I have a pen and paper."

"Very good. Prepared—I like that, too. Write this down. 310 Franklin Street. Tonight at 8:00 p.m. sharp. You've piqued my interest, and I'd like to spend some more time with you. I also called to speak with you about a job."

"A job?" That threw her off track. He'd called her for some other reason than personal? Fresh heat crept up her neck and face.

"Yes, Gabrielle, a job. But I believe, now, that we need to spend some time together beyond that. Which changes my requirements for tonight."

She stilled, her friend's warnings running through her head.

"If you want to get to know me on a personal level, and I think you do, you will have to do so on my terms. So tonight, you will come dressed in a skirt with no panties. When you arrive at that address at eight sharp, you will let yourself in. Proceed to the living area at the end of the hall where you'll lift your skirt and bend over the end of the couch. You will not move or speak until you are instructed. Do you understand these instructions?"

Gabby sat there open mouthed and speechless. She barely knew this man, and he expected her to walk into a strange house that might or might not be his and bare her bottom for God knew what?

"Gabrielle, I know we're barely acquainted, but I like what I've seen so far, and I think you're attracted to me as well. It could very well be worth the exploration, and the small dare I ask you to make. You don't know me well enough to fully trust me, but what about Angel? Do you trust her?"

"Of course, I trust her. She's my best friend."

"Then ask her if you should come tonight. However, these are my non-negotiable terms. I hope you will come, but if you do not, then I will wish you well in your search and hope we can become friends."

"What about the job you mentioned?"

"We shall see after tonight. Goodbye, Gabrielle." The click sounded in her ear, telling her he'd disconnected from the line before she'd had a chance to say another word. Despite that, she sat there stunned and unmoving for several minutes.

Was he serious? Really serious? She would have to be crazy to put herself in a position like that. Right?

Gabby eventually put the phone down and attempted to fix her skirt. She still sat exposed with the fresh air and sunshine beating down on her and now she desperately need to talk to Angel. But first, she wanted a shower and a chance to recover from what had happened in her quiet and usually boring garden on an otherwise average Carolina sunny afternoon.

Twice now, she'd gotten off to a voice that left her shivering in pleasure with a wicked desire to obey him. How had that happened? And should it continue? Angel's warning from the other day struck her then.

She was right. I do worry way too much. This was about letting go of the past and becoming who she craved to be.

Can I do it?

Chapter Four

Gabby turned her car down Franklin Street, and her anxiety soared to an all-new level. She'd gotten dressed per instructions and rushed out the door. A glance at the dashboard clock said ten minutes until her deadline, and she still wondered what the hell she was doing. Every possible scenario she'd imagined led to nothing but more questions.

What would Thomas do to her if she went through with this?

Surely he would touch her, but how far did he intend to push her in one night? Her mind raced with myriad possibilities as fear gripped her so tight she found herself strangling the steering wheel.

Get a grip Gabby. This is what you've been waiting and wishing for, isn't it? A gamut of emotions coursed through her; fear, excitement, arousal, curiosity, and...her arms trembled...more fear. A bark of nervous laughter pressed through her lips. Angel had assured her repeatedly that nothing bad would happen to her, and that Thomas could be trusted with her safety.

She'd learned that he held a considerable position in the community and commanded a generous amount of respect from the members of the club. Those assurances had been enough for her to get this far, but as she searched the numbers on every mailbox, she considered giving up and returning home.

No one would think less of her if she wasn't the right type for Thomas's unorthodox demands. Who could blame her for wanting to get to know a man before letting him dominate her? *Yeah, too late for that Gabby. Whether you like it or not, he's been dominating you since you first heard his voice.* Gabby sighed.

She spied the number three hundred and ten on a black mailbox encased in brick and quickly turned to the right into the drive. A wrought iron gate stood open as if awaiting her arrival. She slowly drove beyond it and up the winding drive. The house loomed in front of her, large and old. If this was indeed Thomas's house, he had very expensive taste. She'd guess the stately brick home was built in the late 1800s and had been restored sometime in the last decade.

The few gaslights that were lit out front did little other than cast shadows across the footpath that led to the front door. Compared to her modest uptown townhouse she was way out of her league. She parked her car close to the walkway and strained to see through the inky darkness. No other cars were in sight. She shook her head and banned the negativity from her mind. Just because she didn't see any other vehicles didn't mean they weren't there. These houses typically had hidden garages around back.

Gabby took a deep breath and rested her forehead on the steering wheel for a minute, releasing the air one short puff at a time. If she didn't calm down, she'd be shaking like a leaf by the time she got inside.

Get a grip, Gabby. You decided you're going to do this so buck up already.

She stepped from the car and carefully balanced herself, wondering once again why she'd worn ridiculously high-heeled shoes. *Because they're pretty, that's why.* She walked to the front door and automatically reached for the doorbell. Lucky for her, she caught herself in mid-air seconds before she pressed it. He'd said to enter the residence unannounced and proceed instead of waiting for an invitation to come in. She struggled with her social conditioning as she complied with his directions. Nerves jumped in her belly at the thought of walking into the wrong house and finding herself in more trouble than she could handle.

She opened it noiselessly and peeked through a crack in the door, afraid someone would catch her. Just inside she spied a long narrow foyer leading to what she presumed would be the living area. Gabby crept through the door and quietly closed it behind her. She tiptoed toward the back of the house, trying not to click her heels on the hardwood floor.

The room opened up into an inviting space filled with comfortable furniture and a large screen television as the focal point. Where she'd expected expensive antique furniture, she found a comfortable space that looked lived in, especially the large overstuffed couch that dominated the center of the room.

Gabby glanced at her watch and realized she had about thirty seconds to get in place, or she'd be late. She hustled over to the coffee table, set her purse and keys down and stepped to the end of the couch as instructed. Her body curved around the large rolled end as she wiggled into place—head down, ass up. Nervous didn't begin to describe how she felt. She took a deep breath and lifted her skirt on the exhale. Cold air swept across her naked bottom causing goose flesh to erupt across her skin. Gabby squeezed her eyes shut and tried not to be afraid. She'd followed his instructions to the letter despite the fact entering a strange home, where she now had her bare butt and pussy exposed to anyone who walked into the room, was by far the craziest thing she'd ever done. She prayed it would indeed be Thomas who found her.

Minutes ticked by. She squirmed and fidgeted against the sofa, beyond restless and antsy. If she had a lick of common sense, she'd leave. Go back to her own house, her safe life and reconsider why this had seemed like a good idea. She should have her head—

A large, warm hand caressed her right butt cheek, sending a hard shudder up her spine. Gabby sucked in her breath. Her adrenaline spiked. She bit at her lip and strained for some sign that it was indeed Thomas who stood behind her and not a complete stranger or even a crazed maniac.

"You have one of the most spankable asses I've ever seen, Gabrielle." The dark, smooth timber of his voice poured over her like the finest scotch splashed into a glass, fluid and loose.

Her butt clenched.

"Relax sweetheart. You're safe with me. You have my word on that."

His hand continued to move across her flesh, warming her as she did the best she could, under the circumstances, to stand still. She had so many questions on the tip of her tongue and had almost blurted out some of them several times, before reminding herself that he'd warned her not to speak until given permission.

"I understand you're nervous, Gabrielle, and I'm so proud of you. You took the chance I needed you to and for that I am grateful."

She smiled at his words as warmth spread through her. His praise alone helped her relax. She eased the breath she'd held between her lips and sighed into the couch.

"But…"

Uh oh. She hated the sound of that one little word.

"We need to lay some ground rules for our time together. Are you listening?"

"Yes, Sir," she whispered, grateful he'd not chastised her for speaking out of turn.

"Good girl." His hand swept down the back of her thighs to the crook of her knee, which tickled. When her leg jerked, he laughed softly behind her. "A soft spot I see." He strummed his fingers a few times over the sensitive area before heading back toward her bottom. Thomas worked his strong fingers over her muscles better than any masseuse she'd ever been to, and she melted a little more into the cushions.

"Now, about the other night at the club..."

Gabby sucked in a breath.

"You were in sub space when I found you."

Was he asking or telling? She didn't know what to say.

"While it was pretty obvious, you still should have told me the truth when I asked. You were alone in the middle of a lifestyle demonstration, masturbating, without a Dom of your own in sight to look out for you." His voice had changed from the soft rumble to a stern, forceful tone, and his hands were now still on her buttocks, reminding her of the calm before a storm.

"I...uh...um..."

His touch disappeared for a few seconds before a hard blow landed on her ass, sending pain and shock coursing through her. She'd considered he would spank her, in fact had been pretty sure about the likelihood of it, but *owww*.

Another smack landed on her backside stinging more than the last. Pain and heat suffused her, but it was the familiar tingle of arousal vibrating along her clit that surprised her. Gabby rolled onto the balls of her feet in an effort to show him she wanted more, but he didn't respond.

"When I called your house and asked what you were doing, I had to coerce the truth from you. You will not do that again."

Humiliation flooded her with heat almost as much as her burning bottom. "I was embarrassed and...and afraid."

"That is my point, so listen well, little one. I guarantee if we proceed beyond tonight you will no doubt journey through myriad emotions, and I have to know that you'll be honest with me—always."

Two more quick, powerful swats sent more fire burning through her. Tears welled in her eyes as she tried to focus on what Thomas had said and not the pain and pleasure brewing inside her. His expectation for her to tell him everything, whether she felt comfortable or not, seemed reasonable, albeit hard as hell to execute.

"Do you think you can do that? If not, then I'll stop now and send you home. We'll be friends."

Oh God. Yes, stop. No, don't. She couldn't think straight with her ass on fire and tears dripping down her face. But she did know she didn't want to leave.

"Yes." It was all she could manage.

"Yes, what?" Clearly, he had no intention of making this easy.

"Yes, Sir. I'll be honest."

His hands again caressed her sore cheeks, switching from one to the other, soothing her throbbing skin. The combination of the pain and desire mixed with the new pleasure of him kneading her muscles was a heady sensation. The hot, wet tears streaked down her face as something changed. Her earlier fear gave way to an unmatched arousal building inside her.

"Stop putting so much of your focus on your fear. Instead of thinking about all the different ways I could hurt you, think of the many things I can do to bring you more pleasure than you can bear."

She squirmed against the couch, eager for Thomas's touch as his fingers inched lower. Soon, he would discover this ordeal had her wet and ready despite whatever emotions unsettled her. Her guard faltered a fraction more as she opened to the idea that being here with him didn't seem wrong at all no matter how crazy it sounded in her head. She wanted nothing more than to spread her legs wider and let Thomas have his way.

"Do you like being spanked, Gabrielle?"

"Yes, Sir." How could she possibly deny it when her pussy ached with the need for him to touch her again? Right here, right now, she would give anything for this man to pleasure himself with her body. To fuck her.

"Does your ass hurt?" he asked softly, his voice so full of seduction she wanted to melt.

"Yes, Sir," she whispered.

"Do you want me to stop?"

She shook her head violently into the pillow.

"I can't hear you, beautiful."

"No, Sir. Please don't stop." If he left her this close to the edge, she wasn't sure she could handle it.

His hand delivered another quick, sharp blow. This time she cried out as the flames erupted along her skin and traveled straight to her swollen bud.

"We haven't even discussed a safe word for you yet, but I don't intend to push you too far today. I'm just making sure I have your attention. But if you want me to stop you just say the word, and it's done. Do you understand?"

"Yes...yes, Sir," she answered; gasping for the breath she needed to ask for more instead.

"Have you ever stood for an inspection before, Gabrielle?"

Her mind reeled with his implication. She'd done enough reading on the subject to know what he was talking about but...

"No. I...uh..."

"You don't have much real time experience at all do you?"

Gabby tried to concentrate on his questions, but it was hard with his hands still roaming her ass and the backs of her legs.

"No, I don't." She whispered the words, embarrassed to admit that at her age, she'd done very little to explore her submissiveness over the years.

"Why not? No, don't answer that now. We'll discuss it later. We'll get to a full inspection in the near future, but for now, I'm going to take a quick look while you hold absolutely still without a word. Is that understood?"

"Yes, Sir."

She held her breath waiting, imagining the any number of things could happen next. Thomas trailed his thick fingers between the cheeks of her ass before grasping them firmly and spreading her wide, exposing every inch of her intimate self to his perusal. Gabby's stomach dropped, her cheeks flushed hot and, somehow, she swallowed the protest that automatically bubbled up. The moan, she couldn't hold back.

"You'll have to get used to this, sweetheart. I won't allow you to hide anything from me—ever." His thumb tapped at the tight entrance of her ass, sending shivers racing along her spine. "And with me, there isn't any part of you that won't get used."

Gabby inhaled deeply, letting the air out nice and slow. She'd only been taken there once by a man, and that had not gone well. Fortunately, through experimentation with plugs and other toys, Gabby had discovered just how erogenous a zone that was for her. Now, with her ass heated from his hand and her brain fuzzed up, she throbbed more than ever between her thighs.

"It makes you wet to hear me talk about it."

It wasn't a question, so she remained silent, determined to follow his instructions. But his fingers were on the move again and so close to touching where she ached, Gabby wanted to scream. Instead, she sucked her lip between her teeth and bit down to keep quiet.

"Damn, woman. You are so wet." He slid through her moisture, grazing against every sensitive nerve ending she possessed until her legs quaked with the effort of holding herself up. She wanted to die of embarrassment almost as much as she wanted to beg him to fuck her.

Almost.

Being this exposed, this open to a man like him, had more of an effect than she'd expected. Gabby couldn't breathe. Thomas' touch had broken through her reservations and gone straight to the needy woman inside.

Her legs began to shake. Arousal flared so hot inside her she fought not to cry out. To beg for him to make her come.

"Do you want something?"

Oh God, now he taunted her with his questions. She heard it in his voice. He knew exactly the effect he was having. Thomas trailed his fingers down her right hip, teasing her with an all too light touch. More like torturing her.

"Touch me."

A quiet chuckle blew a puff of warm air across the flesh of her buttocks as she realized his mouth hovered close to her skin. "You definitely don't give the orders in this relationship, beautiful. I decide when and what to give you, and you happily take whatever that may be." He pushed two fingers through her wet slit a moment before plunging inside her.

She moaned at the delicious friction he created against her sensitive tissues. Dear God, she was going to die. His movements stilled with his fingers still filling her. Gabby wiggled her bottom willing him to move.

"Remain still. You will not move until I say so. And don't even think about coming without permission."

She wanted to scream in frustration. "Yes, Sir." Although how she'd control it she had no idea. Failure was imminent.

Thomas' talented fingers pulled from her clasp and trailed her juices down the inside of her thighs. Gabby's heartbeat raced along with her accelerated breathing. Every touch of flesh to flesh drove her closer to the edge until she'd become one giant ball of aching need. With his fingers once again probing at her entrance, she felt more of her control slipping away. The fact he eased inside her one inch at a time did nothing to stop the pressure building behind her clit.

The first thrust lured her so close to the danger zone, she whimpered. Gabby balled her hands into tight fists and pressed them against her mouth as a scream built inside her. Those wicked fingers of his pushed and pulled harder and faster as her release continued to rise no matter how hard she fought it. Moans and sobs alternated from her lips until she knew it was too late. No way could she stop the impending release.

"I know, Gabrielle. I can feel it. You need to come baby, don't you?"

"Yes," she whimpered.

"Then ask me for it. Convince me you need it."

"Oh God. Please Sir. I can't hold it back. Please let me come for you."

His thumb pressed hard against her clit, and Gabby shot forward on the couch over the added sensation.

"Then come, sweetheart. Let me feel your release on my hand."

With little encouragement Gabby cried out and came, her muscles clamping down on his fingers as her body shuddered around them. She begged him to not stop as she rode out waves of the most exquisite pleasure she'd ever experienced. Thomas had given her the permission she craved and taken her to new heights. He'd given her the first taste of what true sexual freedom meant to her. She was never going to be the same again.

Minutes later, she sank into the couch cushions, burying her face in the pillows. He remained behind her with his fingers still filling her. Now that her lust had been sated, Gabby's embarrassment had returned, as well as the desperate desire to cover her exposed body parts. Her natural tendency to hide within herself warred with the woman he'd momentarily unleashed. The side of her that had been fighting for control for a very long time.

"Can you stand for me, Gabrielle?" His question came out a husky whisper that smoothed over her senses and reminded her that he'd not found the same release as her. He'd given her this gift first. Would he fuck her now? Fresh butterflies erupted in her stomach at the thought of him taking her like this, filling her from behind.

He wanted her to stand, though. Confused, she worked on focusing on his request. She nodded and pushed on her arms. They trembled underneath her weight, but she somehow managed to get herself to her feet. Her hips swayed to the side, and his free hand grabbed her arm, steadying her.

Only then did his fingers ease from her now aching pussy.

"Turn around, please." She did as he asked while avoiding his eyes. Instead, she focused on a spot on his chest and waited for what came next. Would he ask her to leave? Did she not please him?

He swept his fingers across her cheek. "Can you get on your knees for me, sweetheart? Are you steady enough?"

She nodded and slid down, settling her knees into the soft plush carpet that cushioned her body. It was far easier than being on her feet at the moment. Automatically, she bowed her head and clasped her hands behind her back, just like she'd learned in her studies. This was considered a standard pose of respect and submission.

"Such a good little submissive you are." He lowered his hand to her face—the hand he'd used to fuck her. His fingers still glistened with her juices. "Open your mouth and clean my fingers, please."

Gabby did as he asked and opened wide, catching his gaze as she looked up at him. His intensity seared into her as she took his offering into her mouth. Tentatively, she lapped at his skin with her tongue, recognizing her own tart flavor as it exploded across her taste buds. Riding on the euphoria of her release, she didn't bother to examine how she felt about this, but the pleasure that lit his eyes while she did as he asked was all the encouragement she needed. He seemed pleased.

"Damn. You are incredible like that. On your knees, cleaning me like a good little girl." With a hiss, Thomas suddenly withdrew from her mouth and grabbed her shoulders, pulling her to her feet. He unzipped his pants and shoved the material from his hips. His cock sprang free and Gabby's eyes grew wide at the size and breadth of it. No wonder he was so coveted—as if his powerful presence wasn't enough. Without thought, she grabbed him with both hands and stroked his thick length. When a slick bead of pre-cum formed at the tip, she slid her thumb across it with the intention of massaging his head. Thomas grabbed her wrists and pulled her hands free. He clamped them behind her back and held them secure with one hand.

"Did I tell you that you could do that? Did I give you permission to touch me?" he growled. When she didn't answer, he continued, "Do not try to control your time with me. It will not work. If this training relationship is to continue then you must accept my direction. If you want something, then by God, you'd better learn to ask for it first."

Before she could respond his mouth captured hers in a searing kiss. Lips and teeth moved together as his tongue plunged deep, seeking more heat and moisture as their tastes mingled. His was as dark and smooth as his voice and something she never wanted to end. Thomas' free hand curled in her hair, holding her tight against him, eliciting a whimper from her.

Want and need suffused. Her heart sped up and her mind raced until her knees buckled, and Thomas had to tighten his arm around her waist to steady her. This was no ordinary kiss. He consumed her with a combination of hunger and passion. She moaned into his mouth, and he deepened the kiss.

Thomas pressed her hands into her back, moving her forward until the hard length of his erection nestled between her thighs. The thin fabric of her skirt did nothing to hide the heat coming from both of them. In fact, when the crown of his cock nudged at her clit, her need for him spiked. Gabby fought his hold, her only thought of getting her hands all over him. His tongue fucked into her mouth much like she imagined his dick sinking into her pussy. Those images certainly didn't help. Helpless to stop him or urge him on, she whimpered once again. He shifted his stance, brushing his chest across her hard nipples. With the beat of arousal pounding through her blood, she thought of little else than getting him inside her.

Never in her life could she remember an edge like this, an arousal so tight she hovered on the line between pain and pleasure. He nudged her clit twice more, nearly sending her flying from the ledge again then eased his mouth from her. A soft cry of disapproval fell from her lips. He was going to torture her; she just knew it.

Their gazes connected—his dark with power that told her in no uncertain terms he was in charge, something not to be forgotten. Gabby tried to catch her breath and find a calm that evaded her. Not possible with this much need swirling inside. The only thing that made her feel marginally better was the harsh breathing she'd picked up from him. She was not the only one in the room affected.

The skin around his warm eyes crinkled when he smiled down at her. A smug smile if she'd ever seen one, but she had no smart retort when her body tingled from head to toe and her pulse beat steadily in her clit.

"How do you feel?" He spoke with concern, but the smile still played around the corners of his mouth. He was far too pleased with his effect on her.

"I'll be fine, Sir."

He released her hands and took a step back. Before she knew it, he had his pants refastened and his clothes rearranged as if nothing had happened—except for the thick ridge of his erection outlined in his pants. Seeing it almost made her giddy. Knowing that Thomas desired her meant more than she'd expected.

"Good. Then when you get home, I want you to think this through. What happened here tonight is minor compared to what you'll have in store for you tomorrow night and the nights after." He pulled her into his side and wrapped his arm around her shoulder. "I'm not always an easy man, Gabrielle. You need to be sure."

"But I—"

He placed two fingers across her lips. "Your need to argue is cute to a point. Go home. Take a warm bath. Get a good night's sleep. You'll need it. If you decide to continue, then I'll expect you here tomorrow night at the same time." He scooped up her belongings from the coffee table and handed them over.

Gabby stood there in a confused stupor. He wanted her to just go home? Now?

"Don't look so surprised or disappointed. This isn't any sort of punishment. You've been amazing tonight." He pressed a soft kiss on her lips in front of the door. "If you have any questions I can help you with, I'm only a phone call away."

Before she could utter another word, Thomas led her out the door and down to her car. He opened her door and ushered her in. Apparently satisfied she was all set, he backed away and waved goodbye before slipping back into his mysterious house.

She stared at the red brick façade with its neatly trimmed hedge.

What the fuck had just happened?

Chapter Five

Thomas walked into the media room in the back of his house and took a seat in one of the plush chairs located in front of the big screen television. The idea of returning to the living room cramped his stomach. Instead, he needed some space and time to clear his head after the scene with the enigmatic Gabrielle. The potent combination of her fear and bravado pulled at him even now. Talk about a conundrum. Surprisingly, he'd been only moments away from taking things too far too soon.

He stared at the blank black screen in front of him as he replayed the evening with Gabrielle in his mind over and over. He'd barely expected her to show up let alone go through with everything he'd asked. Under his hand, she'd begun to bloom with only the barest of encouragement. Sure he'd sensed apprehension, but the underlying need had fought for dominance and won. Now, his mind raced and his dick throbbed with a desire for this woman that worried him. He couldn't afford to let anyone get under his skin. That knowledge didn't dissuade him from acknowledging his need for a submissive. Some things could only be ignored for so long.

It had to have been her eagerness to please that got to him. So many of the submissives he met these days were jaded beyond their years. The needs that so often brought people to the lifestyle were often consuming, and it was the many players that often left women like Gabrielle broken in their wake.

"Here. You look like you need this."

Thomas stared at the tumbler of amber liquid his friend and houseguest David held in front of his face.

"Thanks." He reached for the glass and swallowed the shot. The rich smooth alcohol began to warm his throat and insides immediately.

"So that was the woman you told me about? The one looking for a Dom?" David dropped into the chair next to Thomas and extended his legs in front of him, his feet resting on the coffee table.

"Gabrielle." He loved the way her name rolled from his tongue. He'd listened to Angel refer to her as Gabby more than once, but he refused to acknowledge the nickname. He loved the lyrical sound of her full name being pronounced not to mention it suited her far better than the girlish abbreviation.

"She's beautiful," David sipped at his glass before he continued, "and from the sound of things, very responsive. I really enjoyed her screams. My dick's been hard since the first one."

Thomas smiled despite the tension surging through him. "I know what you mean. She was more than I expected. Although, she's possibly a little on the naïve side. It's obvious how much this means to her, but I suspect the emotional aspect will be intense. I'm not sure she's the right candidate for us."

"Who's emotions are you really talking about?"

Thomas turned sharply to meet David's gaze. His friend had every right to ask the hard questions, but that didn't mean Thomas had to like them.

"Haven't you always said how it's impossible to separate the emotions from a Dom/sub relationship?" David asked.

Thomas relaxed into the leather chair once again. "Which is exactly why I can't take this lightly. The goal is not to get her attached to me."

David swirled the liquid in his glass. "Or for you to get attached to her, right? Maybe it's time to rethink your position."

Tension arced between them at David's insinuation. No. Nothing had happened to change Thomas' mind. His intentions were to not get too involved. Attachments were for the David's of the world not him. "It's not going to happen. You asked for my help, and I'm happy to give it." Thomas traced the etched groove of his glass as he remembered the smooth expanse of Gabrielle's ass. An overwhelming hunger threatened his mind. God, he'd wanted to take her so bad he'd nearly lost it.

"And in the meantime?"

"In the meantime, nothing."

David swallowed his drink and stood. He crossed to the small bar, and Thomas listened to him pour another drink. They were both in trouble.

"You don't think she's in the right place?"

"Oh, she's in the right place all right. In fact, she'd be prime picking for a less scrupulous Dom." An unsettling thought. The idea of her being broken tore at his mind.

"Then it's settled. Tomorrow night at dinner, we spell out the terms for her and see where things lead. Hell, she might say no." David returned to his seat and flashed his trademark devil-made-me-do-it smile.

"She won't."

David held up his glass in salute. "I do admire your confidence, my friend."

"I'd call it more instinct rather than confidence." His gut was telling him far more than that. They definitely needed to proceed carefully with her. But as much as his head told him to walk away, his mind filled with the image of her at Sanctuary. The innocent rapture across her face had mesmerized him from the first moment he'd lain eyes on her. Her ability to get caught up in a scene she wasn't even participating in astounded him.

He'd been determined to learn more about her, and Angel had been more than willing to fill him in on her situation. Freshly divorced and desperately in need of a good Dom to teach her was how Angel had described her friend. She'd been right about the "in need" part. He'd felt that first hand. Angel had assured him her friend would be open to an arrangement of his liking. So then why was his stomach tied in such severe knots it would take more than a bondage expert to get them undone?

"You are going to explain the situation to her when she comes for dinner tomorrow night, right?"

Thomas didn't like the tone of David's question. Of course, he would. And he'd do whatever it took to get her to accept. Any other option made pain throb behind his right eye and forced him to imagine her with someone else learning what he ached to teach her. She was clearly on a quest that suited her well. If he and David didn't intervene someone else would.

Thomas gripped his glass tightly until his fingers ached. It wasn't the knowledge she'd seek from another that motivated him. No, it was the events of the last hour that stuck in his brain, sinking deep into his pores. From the exquisite flesh she'd eagerly bared to him all the way to the fear waiting in her eyes, she frankly appealed to him on a level he'd not felt in too long to remember. And this wasn't exactly his first rodeo.

The image of his fingers in her mouth was now burned into his retinas. The fantasy of her lips stretched by the width of his cock instead would likely drive him to jerk off before the night ended.

Somehow, her scent still tickled his nose, and the desire to taste her overwhelmed him. Oh yes, tomorrow night would prove to be very interesting indeed.

"Earth to Thomas." David waved his hands in front of Thomas' face to catch his attention.

He lifted his gaze and frowned.

"Where'd you go, man?"

"I was just thinking." Obsessing more like it. What the hell was happening to him? This lack of control bothered him.

"I gathered that. Are you sure you want me in on this, Thomas? I can bow out now, and you and Gabrielle can examine whatever this is." David waved his hand in the general direction in front of him.

"What? No." Thomas blew out a hard breath. "Nothing's changed. This isn't about just me. Tomorrow night, we'll discuss it all with her and see what she has to say about it."

"Uh-huh." David looked unconvinced.

Thomas wasn't about to invite any more discussion on the matter, so he attempted to change the conversation.

"What's going on with my illustrious accountant?" Thomas moved to the bar and poured another drink.

"My guys are still working on the full background check. Nothing out of the ordinary has popped yet. A few parking tickets, a penalty payment to the IRS a couple of years back for not paying enough quarterly tax payments, but nothing to set off any alarms. So far, he's pretty ordinary."

Thomas scoffed. "Other than his appearance, I doubt that. I've had a gut reaction to the man since I took over, and I'm telling you, something isn't right."

"Did you talk to Gabrielle about the job? We need something more official than your gut to pursue."

"No, it didn't come up. I was a little preoccupied."

"I know. I heard."

Thomas sighed. Another thing to taunt him tonight. The mewling sounds of Gabrielle nearing her orgasm as well as the full-blown screams he'd driven her to with his fingers. His body tightened with the brutal force of intense desire. Next time, it would be his dick buried deep inside her, torturing her ruthlessly.

"Just find some information to nail the little prick to the wall, and I'll take care of the rest." He'd hire Gabrielle whether he needed to or not. He wanted her. And if having her would slake the mind-bending lust gripping him by the balls, then that's exactly what he'd do.

As if it were that simple.

He didn't just want her. First, he needed to figure her out, peel back the layers that made her tick, reveal her darkest desires and possess them and her right along with it.

"I hope you know what you're getting into with this one," David muttered.

"I always know what I'm doing before any relationship begins." And he wasn't about to start changing the rules now.

* * * *

The long, never-ending day finally came to a close. Thomas breathed a sigh of relief when the bright sunshine dimmed to the comfort of twilight. David had spent the day at his office, and Thomas had opted to work from home instead of going into Sanctuary. With so much going on with the changes he'd begun to incorporate, one day of peace and quiet had sounded damned good to him. It gave him a chance to focus on the accounting mess he'd discovered. He'd sifted through bank statements, cancelled checks, credit card statements and invoices until his eyes crossed. All to no avail. He suspected the financial answers he sought were right in front of his face, but for some reason, he couldn't see the forest for the trees.

Thomas pushed the last of the paperwork into the file folder and shoved it into his desk drawer. A glance at the clock informed him that Gabrielle would be arriving shortly. The caterer had arrived a couple of hours ago, and he needed his mind clear and on his guest when she knocked on the door.

He closed the office door and quickly proceeded to the kitchen. Part of his inability to focus on the problem at hand had been thanks to a certain untrained submissive who'd lingered on his mind all day long. The vision of her draped over his couch with her ass in the air would not soon be forgotten. His muscles tightened at the memory, and his dick thickened. Not like he hadn't been half hard all day anyway.

He surveyed the kitchen from the doorway not wanting to disturb the preparations. Pans of food simmered on the stove, and the aroma reminded him he was hungry for more than sex.

Professionally, he had some serious knots to untangle, but privately, he had high hopes for an exciting evening. He had a date with a certain gorgeous blonde who tempted his every need. Movement from the corner of his eye caught his attention. He turned and focused on the view from the bay window just in time to see an expanse of bare leg emerge from her small car. Tasteful sandals were strapped to her small feet, and when she full disengaged from the vehicle, he discovered an elegant but short black skirt hugging her lush curves. She'd swept her hair up on one side leaving her neck bare and perfectly lickable. Mmm... Like last night, no jewelry adorned her neck or ears, leaving her simple beauty to shine on its own. He breathed deeply, remembering the fragrance of her body. She'd worn no perfume last night, and he'd reveled in the essence of her arousal and the clean but subtle smell of sweet soap.

He'd gone from half hard to a raging erection in two seconds flat.

Now, he watched Gabrielle walk toward the front door, nervously fidgeting with her skirt and purse. Whatever thoughts or reservations had gone through her mind about last night had not kept her from his doorstep—a fact he was certainly grateful about. That nervousness reassured him more than any words could. If there wasn't a certain level of hesitation when embarking on this type of relationship, it likely wouldn't be worth the effort for either of them.

The hemline of Gabrielle's short skirt swished around her legs as she moved, drawing his attention to the swell of her hip and the rounded curves of her ass. From his perfect vantage point, he stared at her long and hard. Yes, she was beautiful. And yes, he certainly wanted her. Who wouldn't? It was the other that poked incessantly at the back of his mind that drove him crazy all day long. God, if he wasn't careful, she'd turn into an obsession.

She reached the front porch and hastily began straightening her skirt and checking her hair. Thomas smiled. Soon, it would be his touch skimming the sweet softness of her figure. His hands that would tangle in her long, golden hair as he claimed her mouth and so much more. He instantly made the decision that he'd do whatever it took to get her into his bed. There'd be no other choice for any of them if he had anything to say about it. Damn, this was going to be one hell of a night.

The doorbell chimed through the house, once again shaking him from the stupor that watching her created.

"Would you like me to get that for you, Sir?" one of the wait staff inquired.

"No." He waved her off and proceeded to the foyer. In an attempt to control his fucking hard on, Thomas focused on the boring facets of his job such as writing checks, placing orders, hiring new employees and so on. Anything to get his mind off what waited for him between Gabrielle's sweet thighs.

His cock jerked. Clearly, nothing was going to take his mind off of fucking her.

In the next moment, he took a deep breath and opened the door. "Gabrielle. You're early. I'm impressed." He stepped back and ushered her inside. "You can leave your purse and keys there on the table if you'd like." He pressed his hand to the small of her back and felt the slight stiffening of her spine. "Relax. You have nothing to be afraid of," he reassured her.

Her pink tongue darted across her lips as she hastily dropped her belongings before wringing her hands in front of her. Thomas didn't hesitate; he pulled her close. Her soft curves rubbed against the hard planes of his, nearly eliciting a groan from him. That simple touch ignited a firestorm raging through his blood, threatening to send him one step closer to the edge of his control. He barely restrained the urge to strip her where they stood in an urgent need to see her submit.

The urge to fuck her rode him hard but couldn't overtake the necessity of building trust. He had so many creative ways to draw her from behind the wall she kept peeking over. Last night had been a great first step in obliterating her reservations, but the obvious nerves displayed now reminded him they still had some work to do.

"I'm just not used to this."

"What? Coming to a dinner date?" He couldn't resist the tease. He knew exactly what she meant. Gabrielle relaxed. Now, he could delve a little deeper with her attention focused on their conversation not what he might do to her, although he had plenty of plans for her tonight— some of which included making her step pretty far outside of her comfort zone. He couldn't wait.

Chapter Six

"Is that what this is? A date?" Gabby tried to concentrate on asking an intelligent question and not blurting out how much she wanted more from him. All day long, she'd reveled in the residual feelings from the night before—lust, satisfaction, even a little embarrassment about how easily she'd acquiesced to his demands and thoroughly enjoyed them. Without any specific instructions regarding tonight's dinner, Gabrielle had tried on more outfits than any one woman should until she'd settled on what she hoped to be the ultimate sexy outfit.

At the last minute, she'd removed her thong and arrived on Thomas' doorstep with a bare and slightly sore ass. Now, with more and more moisture gathering between her legs the longer she stood in Thomas's embrace, she realized her decision might not have been the smartest move. Mortified, she ground her back teeth together and stared into his eyes, all the while doing the best she could to ignore the heat radiating from his body through her clothes. Or the stiff cock pressed against her thigh, entirely too close to her pussy for comfort.

His hold on her spoke volumes about the kind of control Thomas claimed. One word in particular came to mind. Possession.

"I take it since you're here that you did as I asked and thought long and hard about what it is you wanted." The firm lines around his mouth reminded her of how serious this would get. In fact, Angel had reminded her of how intense Thomas liked to get. As if Gabby could forget. You didn't get more serious than walking into a practical stranger's home and basically asking for a spanking.

"Kind of hard to think about anything else after last night." She tried to keep the breathless need out of her voice and failed. "Do you want me?" She drew in a shaking breath and held it, waiting for his response.

What was it about him that made her feel like this? Her stomach fluttered, her skin grew tight and her pulse beat a mile a minute in his presence. This wasn't how she reacted to other men she'd met. Only *him*.

"I've waited all day for you." He gripped her tighter. "I was willing to take no if I had to, but I'm sure glad I don't."

An electric zing swept through her. She couldn't picture this calm and collected man waiting for her. Surely, he had the pick of any of the women he met. How could he not? His voice alone held the controlled power to mesmerize and melt a woman from the inside out. She'd swear to it.

"Now's the time to discuss any second thoughts. Or any questions." He brushed the hair from the side of her face and rested his palm on her cheek. "Once you say yes, everything changes. Trust me when I say you'll never be the same. You'll never be able to go back to the way things were."

Gabby shivered. She didn't doubt him for a minute. Whether he knew it or not, he'd already ruined her the night before. The cravings that had resided in her heart now burned through her body and threatened to implode. She didn't think there was anything he could say at this point that would make her turn away. Still there were questions...

"Do you do this a lot? Offer to take on a woman who needs to learn?"

"Yes, some." He paused, probably gauging her reaction. Gabby carefully schooled her face into a neutral mask. She didn't really want to know how many women he'd had like her. If she did she'd probably run screaming for the door. "If you haven't already figured it out you need to know. I don't just dominate a woman as part of some sexual thrill. I am Dominant. That means it's who I am. The minute I meet a woman looking to learn about the lifestyle, it's damned hard to ignore her. The lifestyle is full of people with different needs, including those who want to just play. Most of the time, that's just fine. But sometimes... Let's just say I've seen too many women walk away scarred."

Gabby's heart ached for the sadness that had leeched into his eyes. This strong, seemingly in control every second man had a softness inside him that she'd momentarily glimpsed. "Does that make me a charity case?" The question slipped out before she could stop it.

The look in his eyes sharpened. "I don't fuck people for charity. But I'm not above taking over a submissive who could use my help when the simple sight of her makes my dick hard." The desire evident in his voice stroked over her senses, her nipples tightened and rasped against the fabric of her bra.

A few rough words from him and her need went from simple arousal to unbalanced craving in two few seconds to count. "Does that mean we—?"

Faster than she could blink, Thomas grabbed her head and tilted it back, forcing her gaze to lock on his. "Yes, it means that tonight I aim to do a hell of a lot more than spank your ass and finger-fuck your pussy," he growled. He caressed the side of her face with his thumb, that simple touch eliciting an electric reaction she felt clear to her clit. Silence stretched between them under his relentless glare until Gabby's brain screamed with the need to move.

"I gave you last night to be sure. Tonight, I intend to put you on your knees and keep you there." His lips

covered hers in a kiss that seared clear to her core. A blast
of heat filled her mouth as his tongue slid inside her. There
wasn't anything gentle about his touch. He demanded and
took, leaving a burning trail of intensity in his wake when
he finally pulled away.

"Tonight, you're mine to do with as I wish. If that
means fucking you all night long, I will. If it means
watching you scream and beg for the orgasm you've waited
hours for, I will. And if I decide to tie you to my spanking
bench and fuck that gorgeous ass of yours, I will."

Gabby gasped, desire overloading her system. A nag
in the back of her mind warned her to be offended,
something in the face of her need, she promptly ignored.
"Are you trying to scare me?"

Thomas sighed. "This isn't about trying to scare you
away. It's about facing your fears if and when you're
ready."

Gabby tried to pull from his embrace, but his grip held
firm. "If you don't want me here, I can go." Sudden tears
burned behind her eyes. Mortification seized her. She
wouldn't cry in front of him.

"That's my point. It's not all about what I want. At
least not directly. It's your desires I aim to get at. Even the
deep dark secret ones you've not told anyone about. When
we're done, there will be nothing I don't know about you.
Nothing I won't be willing to do to make sure you have
what you need."

Everything in the room began to spin. At the same
time her body melted under his sensual threats, her mind
fought the terror. He intended to turn her inside out and
upside down and for what? Sexual pleasure?

"You're going to fuck the truth out of me?"

Thomas laughed, a deep mellow sound that crept
through her blood like warm butter across a hot pancake.
"Does that sound like a bad thing to you? Because from my
vantage point, stripping you of control and pleasuring you

to the point of begging me to fuck you is pretty much a win-win for us both."

Another blast of heat exploded across her skin. Blood roared in her ears, and she swore her vision wavered under the onslaught of need overwhelming her. Her breath shortened and sweat popped out across her brow. The images flying through her brain threatened her ability to stand and hold a conversation. Not to mention the pressure now building behind her clit. To say she wanted him inside her became a massive understatement.

She craved his touch, oh God yes, his touch. Right between her legs where an orgasm threatened from the mere images he conjured in her mind. Gabby squirmed, seeking a modicum of relief.

"Don't."

She froze, embarrassment flooding her.

"Any orgasm you have from here on out belongs to me. If I want you to touch yourself, I'll let you know." His hand dug into her hip to the point of slight pain. The intense concentration on his face worried her. "Spread your legs, Gabrielle."

His demand struck her in the gut like a jolt of electricity, sending a wave of desire to crash over her. She hesitated only for a second, a testament to how close to the edge she already stood.

"Don't worry, I'm only going to touch you with my hands…for now. When you're ready for more, I trust you'll let me know."

Trust. The linchpin in all of this. He apparently trusted her to follow his directions. Now, it was her turn to decide if she trusted him or not. Although he made it damn hard to think beyond the moisture gathering in her sex. One thing Gabby did know was that if she didn't try she'd never know for sure. The intense but brief taste Thomas had given her the night before would never be enough. She had to know.

She moved her feet and took a deep breath watching his hand skim down her hip and underneath her skirt.

"There you go." In seconds, two fingers delved between the lips of her pussy and skimmed through the wetness. To keep from falling to the floor, she grabbed his biceps and found the steely strength of muscles hard as a rock.

Hard shudders racked her spine. She bit down on her lip and held her breath—waiting. One minute, she wanted to say no, and the next, she practically arched into his hand. Confusion swirled in her head.

Then he rubbed her clit with his finger. Sharp pleasure seized her, building higher than before. An orgasm began to build. Just a little more pressure... Her stomach clenched with a ferocious hunger she barely understood. If only he would do something more. He rimmed the sensitive opening to her channel teasing her to the brink of tolerance. Her breath came in pants.

Ready to succumb to the mind numbing pleasure, Gabby dug her nails into his skin and whimpered. One second, she was about to explode in pleasure; the next, Thomas withdrew his touch.

"Not yet, Gabrielle. Not yet," he murmured against her lips. The hitch in his voice grounded Gabrielle in reality like a dash of cold water on a hot day. She might have wanted to stomp her feet and demand he finish, but that one little sound stopped her. It was a heady feeling to know he'd been affected as much as her. Satisfied power surged through her. Now, if only the insistent ache would go away.

Thomas kissed her neck, a feather light glide across heated flesh that sent goose bumps racing across her skin. "You are going to be such a delight tonight. I'm glad you're here. Now, you just need to trust me that I know what I'm doing."

Gabby found it hard to do anything at the moment let along think straight. Thomas certainly had a knack for keeping her off balance. Still, leaving her like this seemed to mean. She needed. Wanted so much more.

"Thomas..." Before she could finish her stomach rumbled loud enough that anyone in the house probably heard. His eyes grew wide, and she covered her mouth to stifle a surprising giggle.

"I take it you're hungry."

Gabby nodded. He had no idea. "Well, you did invite me to dinner, didn't you?"

"Of course. In fact, I think dinner is about to be served so let's get you comfortable in the dining room before our guest arrives." He held her tight against him as he steered her to an open doorway in the far corner of the room where she spied the corner of a dining table.

"A-a guest?" She wasn't sure she was up to much conversation at this point. Hunger for food aside, he'd left her body strung tight with need, and she'd happily forgo dinner for something more.

"Don't worry, little one. This will be a very casual dinner, and I'll keep you right by my side in case you need me for anything." Fingers cupped her chin and turned her face to his. "I believe we're going to be very good together, and while full trust takes time, know this...I will have control of our surroundings and your safety will always be my priority."

Before she could say a word, his lips pressed softly to hers in a kiss that was chaste in comparison to the other and considering what had already transpired between them last night. Her bottom still smarted from the spanking he'd given. Although if pressed for the truth, she'd have to admit that after their time together last night she'd had the most restful night in a long time. In fact, with her muscles loose and warm, she'd slept like the dead. An amazing sense of calm had settled around her like a warm, fresh from the dryer blanket, giving her a sensation of peace she hadn't felt in a very long time, if ever.

When Thomas moved away from her, she got her first full glimpse of his dining room. A long, narrow rectangular mahogany table dominated the neutral colored area with ten matching chairs arranged around it. There were three formal place settings already arranged and candles flickered in shadows from every surface of the room.

"It's beautiful in here." Her fingers reached out and traced the hard wood surface as she followed Thomas around the table to the two place settings that were side by side. He pulled her chair out for her like a perfect gentleman answering her unspoken question of how she would be treated at the dinner table.

At least tonight.

She'd read various accounts of submissives and slaves being forced to sit on the floor at their Master's feet while being fed from their hands alone. And while those stories had piqued her curiosity as well as sparked her submissive desires in every way possible, she doubted she'd be ready to handle that tonight.

After getting her situated comfortably, Thomas took the seat next to hers. She fought the temptation to slide her chair closer although right now even that didn't seem like enough. She wanted to be sitting on his lap, his arms curled protectively around her. What the hell was wrong with her?

As if reading her mind, Thomas reached for her, his hand brushing the sensitive curve of her neck.

"You look at me with such needy eyes, my girl. Makes me want to do so many things to you—things I doubt you're ready for...but soon...soon, I think you will."

Gabby rubbed her cheek in his palm, savoring every velvet word he spoke. She could listen to him talk about anything all night and would be willing to bet this constant buzz of lust fueled adrenaline would continue as long as she was near him.

"Yes, Sir."

Chapter Seven

Damn, his dick was so hard it hurt. Gabrielle and her responses to his domination pushed at him to the point he wanted to break his own rules and take her to bed now. He doubted she would object and just the thought of sinking into that hot little pussy of hers made his erection press painfully against his pants. The way her moisture had coated his fingers when he touched her played over and over in his mind.

He hoped David got his ass in here quick so he wouldn't be so tempted to do something they both might regret in the morning. He worried about rushing things with Gabrielle, but he had made a commitment to David as a mentor and this was the ideal opportunity for them all. To engage from the beginning with the sweet submissive at his table would be more effective than any training session at Sanctuary would be.

Maybe he should explain to her in advance and give her some time to let it sink in...

"Good evening," a voice rumbled from the doorway.

Too late.

"Evening." He stood and shook David's hand when he approached, avoiding eye contact with Gabrielle. He admired David a lot and hoped that even when their training sessions were complete, they'd remain friends.

"Gabrielle, I'd like to introduce you to my houseguest, David." Thomas caught David's raised eyebrow from the corner of his eye while watching Gabrielle for her reactions. A pink flush traveled up her neck and face as the implications of houseguest sank in. He could imagine her mind moving a mile a minute as she debated whether he'd been here the night before and overheard. She shot Thomas a quick glance before settling her gaze on David and giving him a soft, sweet smile.

"It's nice to meet you, David." Both men had to strain to hear her response as she whispered and quickly cast her eyes downward.

"Don't be embarrassed, sweetheart. David did not watch your punishment last night, although he likely overheard you when you came."

Her head jerked toward him, and her face mottled bright red even while her eyes sparked at him with a hint of anger. It was the cutest thing he'd ever seen in his life. Her embarrassment added to the experience even now as she sat there fully clothed, hiding her body from both of them— something she'd learn soon enough was not acceptable during their training phase. While David settled in his seat across from Gabrielle, Thomas longed to confirm her heightened state of arousal. Along with her embarrassed blush, her nipples had pebbled against her shirt, and the energy had ratcheted a few levels higher in the room. But he wanted the evidence of it on his fingers.

Sitting next to her, it was easy enough to slide his hand under her skirt and rub her cream-coated slit.

"Don't." The one word slid from her lips, catching him off guard. His hand stilled, shocked by her refusal.

She hadn't turned to look at him or David but instead stared down at her plate.

"You would deny my touch, little one?"

"No, but he…"

"You think it matters to me that there is another man at the table? That my new submissive will only submit to me when it's comfortable for her? Look at me, Gabrielle."

Her head turned slowly until her hooded gaze settled on his.

"Stand and take off your clothes."

"But—"

He narrowed his eyes and pursed his mouth. Fortunately, she clamped her lips together.

"The proper response to that would be 'yes, Sir'."

"Yes, Sir," she managed on a shaky breath.

"Good, then do as I say—right now." He waited as precious seconds ticked by before she finally moved from her chair. He dared not take his gaze from her for a second. Even though David sat at the table watching, he wanted her to know that she was his total and complete focus.

Her hands shook as she worked the buttons of her shirt, one at a time. Without even realizing it, her slow and nervous movements made this strip down all the more erotic. At this rate, she'd be lucky if they made it through dinner without a thorough fucking. When the last button was finally undone she slipped the fabric from her shoulders to reveal plump breasts with nipples so hard they stood at attention practically begging to be plucked. No doubt he'd be having a bite of those before the night was over.

He returned his focus to her beautiful face where the lush lips and hooded eyes bespoke an inordinate amount of desire from one glance. With a small squeeze to her hand to reassure her, he nodded to her skirt. She unfastened her waistband, shimmied the fabric from her rounded hips and allowed the skirt to slide down her shapely legs. With her totally nude, he let her stand there and be observed because he wasn't quite ready for her to hide her spectacular pussy underneath the table when she sat. She had the kind of body he loved from the flushed full breasts topped with dark protruding nipples to the rounded belly and wide hips he ached to touch again. He easily imagined his own harder body wrapped around her lush softness as it cushioned him in sleep. He wanted to see her like this all of the time, and if he had his way, she would never be covered.

"What do you think, David?" He spoke the words while watching Gabrielle. He didn't want to miss a single reaction, especially since they told him more than her words ever could. That and the moisture between her legs.

"Absolutely beautiful."

Thomas smiled. "Yes, she is and aroused as well."

"I see that. She must be a natural at this."

A sudden urge to have her lie on the table and spread her legs for them while they ate overwhelmed him. Having her pink pussy exposed to them both for the rest of the evening would be divine and probably more than he could bear. Besides she wasn't quite ready for something like that. He'd pushed her about as far as he dared tonight. His goal was to draw out her desires for both their pleasures, not scare her away for good.

"Have a seat, Gabrielle, but from now on, whenever you enter this house you will immediately remove your clothing no matter what. Is that understood?"

"Yes, Sir." She spoke quickly as she moved into her chair at lightening speed. Thomas stifled a smile. His poor modest baby had a lot to learn, and he was going to love every minute of it.

Thomas picked up the dinner bell, and the caterer he had hired for the night walked in with their salads on a tray. Renewed alarm flashed across Gabrielle's face at the woman seeing her sitting there without a stitch of clothing. He grasped her hand and spoke softly. "Nothing to worry about, sweetheart. Becky here is a caterer from Sanctuary and well used to seeing people in various states of undress at all of our public or private get-togethers."

The tension didn't fully leave Gabrielle's body but her shoulders did relax a fraction. Good enough. He wanted her to be comfortable with what he asked of her but not too comfortable. Keeping her slightly off balance and aware that anything could happen next would feed both their needs. She seemed eager to submit, but her lack of actual experience meant there were natural barriers he had to break down. It annoyed him that society put pressure on people to act and conform to certain standards even if it went against a person's basic nature. A pity really.

She reached for her salad fork, freezing in midair when she realized what she'd done. For someone who'd had no formal training, she had more knowledge than he'd expected. They'd barely begun to discuss any rules or expectations for any situation, so he didn't expect her to know she should ask for permission, but her soft questioning gaze automatically turned to him and waited.

His cock jerked forcefully against his pants with renewed interest. *Damn.*

He nodded giving her the permission she sought and watched her spear a cherry tomato with her fork and bring it to her mouth. When her pretty red lips closed around the tines of the utensil, he had to bite back a moan at the picture she presented. It was time to get some conversation going about something—anything—that could take his mind from burying himself inside her.

Thomas glanced at David to see him watching with a smile perking at the corners of his mouth. It wouldn't do for him to lose control the first night of his friend's training.

"So Gabrielle, what kind of work do you do?" David broke the sexual tension with a benign question that Thomas mentally thanked him for.

"Please feel free to call me Gabby." She glanced at Thomas. "Although I know you prefer Gabrielle."

"I rather agree with Thomas. Gabrielle suits you better."

Both men began to eat as Gabrielle explained her job as a contract accountant. From her description, it sounded as if she had vast experience with a variety of clients.

"That reminds me about the job I wanted to discuss with you."

"Yes, I'm anxious to hear about it." She put down her fork and turned her full attention to him while Becky served their dinner of Chicken Marsala, Gabrielle's favorite he'd been told.

"It might not be as exciting as your thinking," Thomas laughed. "We've had a sudden influx of activities going on out at Sanctuary, and our resident accountant has been having a rough time of it. In fact, he's several months behind on balancing our books, and I'm a little concerned."

"So you need a temp to help him get caught up?"

"There's a little bit more to it than that."

"What do you mean?"

"I'd like for everything to get back on schedule, but I'd also like to get an audit on all the records for the past year."

Gabrielle's eyebrows drew together. He could practically see her mind calculating and contemplating the job. He was confident that with her references and obviously sharp mind, he'd made the right decision in choosing her. In more ways than one.

"Do you suspect something fishy?"

Yep, smart girl.

"I have no real reason to; I just think the being behind makes me uncomfortable." He wasn't prepared to get into the details of this with her. He'd rather she go in and double check without any preconceived notions.

"Sometimes, the first gut reaction is the most telling." Gabrielle twirled her wineglass, sliding it back and forth between her fingers. "I have a couple assignments that are ending in the next couple days so after that I could clear my schedule for you. It sounds like I'm going to need some time. Of course, I won't know how much until I see the status of the bookkeeping for myself."

"Of course." He had a hard time taking his eyes from the woman who watched him intently but with such caution. But the thing he did notice was the way she seemed to have forgotten the state of her undress. Talking about her work had animated her as well as distracted her, and now, she appeared comfortable.

"David, why don't you tell our beautiful guest how we met? I think she'll be interested in that story."

Gabrielle's head turned almost reluctantly back to David, not taking her gaze from his until the last possible second. A sense of attachment was beginning to form, which he took as a very positive sign.

"Well, about six months ago, I ended a long relationship with a sweet but very vanilla woman. I'd been having thoughts and desires for a more intense relationship, if you know what I mean, and when I finally confessed, she freaked. I left the next morning." Thomas knew his story well, but he wanted Gabrielle to hear it, to understand what they would be undertaking if she agreed to the co-training. "Once I got settled into a temporary apartment, I started to explore everything I'd learned through BDSM research."

Gabrielle shook her head and set her chin onto her hands, absorbed by what David had to say. "I know exactly what you mean; my experience was all too similar." Startled, Thomas schooled his face to not show his surprise as he settled in to watch them both.

"After a few visits with some local groups, I decided I needed a mentor. Someone with a lot of experience who could train me not to go to far, to learn to read the subtle signs a submissive gives when she needs something, that kind of thing. Long story short, through a few well-placed referrals, I landed on Sanctuary's doorsteps looking for Master Thomas."

Gabrielle's head swung sharply in Thomas' direction, her eyes wide and her mouth in the form of a small O. "You're his trainer?"

"As of last week." Thomas stroked the smooth skin of her cheek and glanced his fingers across her lips. "Gabrielle." His hand gripped her chin and tilted it up until she stared into his eyes with no option to look away. "I want to train you together."

Chapter Eight

Gabby's head jerked in his hand, but he held fast, not letting her get away. What did this mean? Did he not want her for himself?

"Please, Sir, let me go." Her voice trembled as she spoke.

"No running or hiding here, Gabrielle. Tell me what you're thinking." His hand tightened on her face and tears sprang to her eyes. She didn't think she could do this right now. Sitting here naked, with David watching every move they made, was now beyond humiliating.

"If you didn't want me for yourself, you shouldn't have brought me here...toyed with me like this."

His free hand gently wiped the tears from her cheeks. "Why would you think I don't want you?"

She saw the change in his expression the moment realization dawned.

"You think I brought you here just for David?" His voice seemed filled with disbelief, but she couldn't let that sway her. He had cleverly lured her into a sense of safety and compliance to hand her over to someone else.

"Please let go of me so I can cover myself and leave." She didn't know what else to do but salvage what was left of her pride, and the only way she could do that was to get the hell out of here—fast.

"You're in no condition to go home, Gabrielle. You're upset, and we need to clear the air."

"Please listen to what Thomas has to say. I think you've misunderstood his intentions."

Thomas shot David a quelling look, and he threw up his hands in mock surrender. After a few seconds of tension fueled silence, David and the caterer retreated from the room.

"I'm leaving." She despised the disrespect that now filled her voice, but anger fueled by humiliation had taken over.

"No, you're not. At least, not until I've said what needs to be said. Then we shall see." He let go of her face, and while she rubbed at her jaw, he hauled her from the chair and up against his body, her breasts squished against his chest.

"This was a bad idea. I knew I shouldn't have come." Tears burned behind her eyes. Whether he liked it or not, she was going home before she embarrassed herself further by crying.

"There is something you need to understand about me. I'm fervent in my commitment to training. If I tell you something, I mean it. There won't be hidden meanings or misdirection. So when I said that I wanted you, I meant it, probably more than you knew at the time." He jerked her hand between them and placed it over his hard erection.

Holy hell, he was big.

"That's what seeing you like this does to me. Your perfectly lush body is just to my liking, and I've thought of little else tonight except about when I could reasonably get inside you. I want to feel the heat and wetness of your pussy tightening around me, hear the breathless pants from your mouth. I want to fuck you mindless."

Gabby felt a fresh wave of desire unfurl inside her at his words. The picture he painted in her mind became crystal clear. His words made her wet. The betrayal of her body pushed at her mind to give him whatever the hell he wanted.

She whimpered.

"I-I—"

Thomas cut off her protest with a kiss she felt clear to her knees, weakening her stance. She buckled against him. His arm wrapped around her waist and pulled her in his direction until the table was directly behind her. He pushed her backward until her naked bottom hit the edge. Gabby struggled to breathe while Thomas consumed her. Her breasts ached for his touch. A fierce grip of need clenched in her belly and clit. He'd barely touched her, and already, the need to come consumed her.

With ease, he lifted her and plopped her on top of the dining table, away from the place settings. She desperately wanted to let go and give him control. Wasn't that exactly what she'd come for? Gabby wrenched her mouth free and gulped for much-needed air to clear her head. His kisses were so seductive, burning her from the inside out, she felt like an addict over them already.

"What are you—"

"What I should have done earlier. Taking what I want, and giving you what you need."

Mesmerized by every move he made, she watched him reach into his pocket and pull out a small foil packet. A condom. Her stomach jolted, and her clit pulsed as she realized what his intentions were. She tried to clench her thighs against the hot moisture building in her sex to no avail. It only made her yearn more.

He made quick work of removing his clothes and draping them across a nearby chair while Gabby sat captivated as he ripped open the packet with his teeth and rolled it over his hard cock. Despite the reservations still holding her mind hostage, her mouth watered at the sight. She longed to reach out and touch him, to explore the hard muscled planes of his body and the thick cock he now held in his fist.

Her ex had never welcomed her exploration. Their sexual encounters had been quick and efficient for him so that he could get back to whatever he had planned for his evening. It hadn't bothered her that much then. She'd grown accustomed to his disinterest. But this… Sitting here staring at Thomas' glorious naked form she desperately wanted to explore every inch of him and feel the texture of his skin under her tongue.

She reached for him, and Thomas took a step backward and out of her range.

"No touching." Her disappointment must have shown because the stern look on his face softened. "Not yet, sweetheart. I couldn't take it."

Her insides fluttered at the simple spoken endearment. He made her want to give him her submission way too fast. Really, would she ever be able to say no this man? More importantly, did she want to?

"Lie back and spread your legs for me." She did as he asked, a sharp gasp escaping her lips when her back hit the cold wood underneath her. Her attention was immediately drawn to the exquisite chandelier with its crystal teardrops until Thomas stepped between her legs and rubbed the head of his erection through her slick outer lips. Her breath stopped, and her heart raced as she waited for that first penetration. Need arrowed through her as he stood unmoving against her, watching her every movement.

"You're a beautiful woman, Gabrielle. You've honored me tonight with your willingness and open mind. But understand me clearly. I brought you here for me because I'm interested in training you to be the sub I think you can be. Do you understand?"

Gabby nodded her head frantically, so desperate with desire she expected her body to erupt from the heat she generated by straining to hold still and not move. When her legs began to tremble, Thomas's hands stroked them with slow, sure caresses.

"You're doing so good, being so obedient. Hold on for a little while longer. I know you can."

Why was he waiting? She couldn't stand it as the ache throbbed in her clit for him to move against her, even a little.

"Please...oh God...I can't stand it." Her words trembled along with the shaking of her body as the fire of need erupted inside her. She couldn't remember ever feeling like this with another man, this rush of sensation and intensity. Much longer and she might come before he made another move.

All of her worries fled her mind when he flexed forward, pushing himself inside her. The sensitive nerves of her swollen tissues sparked as he filled her inch by excruciatingly slow inch.

"Please, Sir..." she begged. " More."

The torture of her wait exploded around her when the instant friction rocketed her into orgasm. Her muscles clenched around him, eliciting a groan from him to accompany her cries. She arched from the table as a pleasure unlike anything she'd experienced before speared through her, stealing her breath.

"Remember this, Gabrielle. Next time you doubt my intentions and forget this feeling right now will likely be the day I tie you up and fuck you until you beg me to stop." His cock shuttled in and out of her, picking up the pace until his hips slammed into her groin over and over. Before she recovered from the first earth-shattering orgasm, the friction began building another as hard flesh slid against reawakened nerve endings.

She didn't doubt for a second this man could make her beg. With the pressure building and her mind reeling, the words for more lingered at the tip of her tongue. Their gazes connected, his dark with a look so unfamiliar to her she barely recognized it. Her stomach jerked in the face of reality. He wanted her.

With her body out of control and her mind reeling with implications, she couldn't refuse him. Her guards slammed down and wild sensation unfurled on each stroke. She reached for him, dying for a little more pressure. He grasped her wrists and pinned her arms to the table.

"You're going to have to learn to ask for what you want."

"Thomas," she whined.

"Not what I want to hear." He paused, stopping the delicious friction against her clit.

"Sir, please," she panted.

"No. I prefer you like this." He eased an inch inside her. "Tell me what you want. Say it."

Gabby writhed and struggled against his hold. "Fuck me. Please!"

With her answer, he thrust to the hilt, striking her clit in a precision move. Her pants turned to screams, and her body spasmed, thrashing against him as another release tore through her.

A throaty growl sounded from Thomas at the same time she felt him swell inside her. "Mine, Gabrielle. Remember it."

She barely heard his uttered words before the darkest pleasure pulled her down in a violent swirl of intensity. Light and color flashed in her head. Blanketed by a bliss so pure and painful, Gabby heard nothing beyond the ringing in her ears and the guttural sounds coming from her own mouth.

Minutes later, Thomas collapsed against her, his full weight pushing down on her, and she loved every minute of it. With her hands free, she tentatively reached for his shoulders. A soft groan vibrated from his chest when her skin rubbed against the tight muscles of his shoulders and neck.

She mulled over the possessive words he'd uttered in the throes of passion, and those butterflies in her belly took frantic flight all over again. More than anything, she'd wanted to find someone to need her as much as she needed them, someone who didn't look at her like a freak just because she had a dark side or a need to belong. The realization that Thomas understood brought a fresh burn behind her tired eyes.

Thomas shifted off of her, and she whimpered in protest. "I'm not leaving you, sweetheart, but we are going to get more comfortable. That was just the appetizer, a taste of what's to come."

Gabrielle's eyes widened at his meaning. Was he saying what she thought he was? She followed his every move as he grabbed a cloth napkin to clean up and discarded the condom. What drew her gaze more than anything was his still half hard state. *Guess he wasn't kidding.*

He returned to her side and scooped her into his arms. "You belong in my bed. Can you stay here tonight?"

She nodded, afraid her voice would fail her if she tried to talk yet. Her body hadn't recovered from their tabletop sex and already he wanted to carry her to bed for more. When they passed through the living room, she found herself grateful David had turned down the lights until she noticed him sitting on the couch. Embarrassment flooded her as she realized he'd heard every second of Thomas taking her. If the sudden heat she felt was any indication, she'd bet her face had turned beet red. Yet...when she imagined him sitting here listening, maybe even stroking himself, a twinge pulsed through her lower body igniting a new and unfamiliar arousal.

"We're done for the night. I'm taking our new little sub to bed to finish this lesson. We'll start something a little more official tomorrow if you both agree."

David nodded. "Sounds good to me. I'm ready."

Thomas chuckled and looked down at her. "And you? Will you allow him to participate in your training?"

Oh God, she couldn't do that, could she? Spend her nights and weekends in close intimate encounters with both men? As scandalous as it sounded, deep down inside she'd grown intrigued. She'd taken an instant liking to David, and it honestly didn't take much of her imagination to see herself being touched by both men. Gabby tamped down the sudden rush of guilt those feelings created.

She didn't know the details of what Thomas had planned, but she'd researched enough to know many of the options. He wanted this, and truth be told, if she opened her mind to her darker desires, she did too.

"Yes, Sir," she whispered before she could change her mind.

Chapter Nine

With the sun peeking over the horizon and into the windows of Thomas's bedroom, Gabby tiptoed from the room, hoping not to wake him. He'd spent hours teaching her the most delicious lesson of her life, and she'd been thoroughly made love to through most of the night.

Her body ached in every place imaginable as she remembered the spanking, the table and the unbelievable night before. She'd been amazed by Thomas's stamina when he'd exercised incredible control and fucked her for hours. A fleeting thought of her giant tub with its heated jets at home had a quiet moan slipping from her mouth. First things first, she needed to pee and get coffee and not necessarily in that order.

She wandered from room to room in the oversized house until she finally located the grand kitchen. And yes, grand was the only word she could think of to describe it. Half of her townhome would fit in this room, and the oversized appliances and granite countertops blew away her small kitchenette with its standard Formica and apartment-sized appliances. It was the one thing she hated about her house, but being able to call it all her own had won out over her desire for a larger kitchen.

Gabby paused and took a moment to gaze over every surface, imagining having free rein to cook in here. Maybe sometime, if things progressed, Thomas would allow her to cook for him here. After all, they said the way to a man's heart was through his stomach.

Don't go there, Gabby. It wouldn't do her heart well to get to attached to any of this. Thomas was looking for a sub not a wife, and she didn't need that kind of attachment, either. She'd had enough of that with her ex.

"Penny for your thoughts."

Gabby jerked and clutched her heart at the sudden voice from the other side of the room. She turned and found David sitting in the breakfast nook with a cup of coffee and a newspaper spread out in front of him.

"Sorry, I didn't mean to scare you, but the look on your face seemed so intense and you were frowning. I'm curious what that was about. Did you not enjoy your night with Master Thomas?"

Gabby stood transfixed at the sight of him in jeans and bare chest. His disheveled blond hair and smooth skin made him impossibly beautiful; it was hard not to stare. She averted her eyes to the floor, trying to think of something else before she melted in front of him in a puddle of arousal. She could well imagine the effect he would have on women at Sanctuary. He would be a very popular Dom indeed. A brief flash of jealousy surged through her.

"I'm sorry, I didn't know anyone was in here." She crossed her arms over her breasts to hide the fact that her nipples had hardened and it dawned on her she was still naked. Panic filled her as she frantically sought to hide or cover herself.

"I'm an early riser. I like to get a swim in first thing in the morning before breakfast, especially today."

"Why especially today?" Gabby scurried around the kitchen island so that her lower half would no longer be in view. God, next to his perfection, he must find her body repulsive.

He flashed her a huge grin. "While beautiful, listening to your screams of ecstasy through the night tends to leave a man restless with some aggression to burn."

Gabby's face burned hot. "I'm sorry if we kept you from sleep."

David set his paper aside and stood from the table. "Don't be sorry, sugar. I'm certainly not. In fact, I can't wait to get started in our training so I can make you scream like that for me." As he walked toward her, Gabby couldn't help but notice the look of arousal in his eyes as well as the bulge in his jeans. And he wasn't alone. His words gave her a jolt of lust, and already, moisture pooled between her thighs. The desire to be on her knees with his hands in her hair as his cock slid between her lips whipped through her. She screwed he eyes shut trying to block that particular image from her mind.

After last night, only Thomas should be dominating her wants and desires. She definitely shouldn't have cravings for the man standing in front of her.

Easier said than done. David was a good-looking man with a nice personality to match. A woman would have to be dead not to feel anything for him, right?

He stopped on the other side of the counter, observing her with knowing eyes. "Why are you hiding behind there? Are you uncomfortable with your nudity?"

She nodded, wishing now she would have just stayed in bed. What if Thomas walked in and saw them like this? Would he toss her out if he found out she was attracted to David? Or worse give her to him like she'd originally feared.

David reached for her hand and attempted to tug her arms from around her chest. She held on for dear life, reluctant to reveal herself anymore than she already had.

"Why be embarrassed now? I saw everything last night, and I liked what I saw very much. A woman should be round and soft, not skinny with bones showing through their skin."

Gabby snorted in disbelief.

Whatever.

How could he prefer her over the gorgeous thin women crawling all over town?

"Bare your breasts to him now, Gabrielle." Thomas's stern voice startled her from her indulgent thoughts.

She turned her head to see him standing in the entryway looking freshly showered and dressed impeccably. With his gaze on her, and David in the corner of her eye, she reluctantly lowered her arms to her side.

"Good girl." He moved into the room, grabbing a mug from the shelf and poured himself a cup of coffee. She stood stock still while he took a few sips and waited for what would come next.

"Why are you trying to hide? Did I not make myself clear last night?"

"Yes, Sir you did." Even in a mild state of irritation, Thomas's voice made her shiver in delight.

"Then move around and stand in front of David. He shouldn't have to ask you twice. Unless you have a problem. Do you have a problem we need to discuss, Gabrielle?"

Yes. No. Fuck! She shook her head.

"Good, then do as I asked. We're going to start with a basic lesson now and see if we can get you past wanting to hide from either of us."

Gabby followed Thomas' instruction and walked around the counter, stopping a couple of feet in front of the other man.

"I think we're going to need some rules. The first rule I want you to understand is this. Whenever I'm not around, you will obey David and any request he makes of you as if it were me making the request. Do you understand and agree with this?"

"Yes, Sir." Gabby's stomach clenched at the thought of two men commanding her at their will. She'd never dreamed things would go this far, but more than a little part of her was excited. That excitement warred with her fear of the unknown as she stood and waited to see what Thomas had in mind for her this morning.

"First thing we'll do is inspect you Gabrielle. It's a little more formal than I had intended to start off with, but you seem to still have an issue with showing your naked body. So we'll work on that since it's the perfect opportunity for David to join in. Do you know what a full inspection entails?"

She shook her head, fear paralyzing her voice. She could only imagine what all he had in mind. He'd already taken a close look at her the other day when he'd spanked her. What more did he want? For the first time in a long time, her research felt inadequate, leaving her unbalanced and vulnerable. Without the comfort of knowledge, she would have no control of the situation.

"No...Not really." She tried to control the shaking of her voice but miserably failed.

"Try to relax, Gabrielle. We're going to take this nice and slow."

A light touch at the small of her back soothed her as he spoke. Her mind took the show of strength he gave her and used it to calm her nerves one slow breath at a time.

"First, I want you to put your hands behind your head and spread your legs shoulder width apart."

Gabby moved her arms and legs as instructed, opening her body to both David in front of her and Thomas behind her. In this position, her breasts were pushed up and outward, giving either man access to her pussy and ass. Her automatic response screamed at her to run for cover now before it was too late, but the hunger in David's gaze as he swept from her head to her hips brought a rush of heat to her sex that kept her rooted to the spot.

"Don't think about it, Gabrielle. Don't wonder whether anything is right or wrong. Don't try to control the situation even in your mind. Give yourself to us and trust that we will do what is best for us all." Thomas had moved in closer, his breath caressing her neck and ear while he spoke. "Spread your legs wider." His foot touched the inside of her leg nudging her to where he wanted it to go.

"David will examine your breasts first, so hold very still and don't move unless either one of us instructs you to."

"Yes, Sir." She watched David take a sure step forward and reach for her without hesitation or reserve. Gabby held her breath.

His long fingers traced the outside curve from the top to the bottom of each one before lifting and pushing them slightly together. The gentle caresses were steady and comforting until his thumbs flicked across her nipples. A small gasp slipped from her mouth, and David smiled at her.

"Sensitive nipples I see."

She nodded.

"Does nipple play get you wet? Can you come from it?" He pulled and twisted the hardened tips until her breath panted from between her lips.

"I-I've never come from just someone touching my nipples before."

With a tight squeeze and pull on both tips, pain and pleasure streaked through her like a blazing fire straight to her clit. Gabby's mouth opened on a shriek of shock as a fresh wave of moisture pooled between her legs. When his fingers released her as suddenly as they had grabbed her, she whimpered from relief and loss.

"You'd like to have more now, wouldn't you?" Thomas whispered. "I don't think it will take much training to have her coming on demand without either of us ever touching her little clit. But to be sure, you need to examine just how aroused that got her."

David's hands gave her breasts one last squeeze before he traced a path down her torso and into the small patch of curls that hid her pussy from full view. "Don't most submissives keep their pussy shaved bare?" David looked over her shoulder as he asked his question so she knew he was talking to Thomas not her. She hadn't actually thought of that before now although it should have dawned on her. She'd heard the very same thing.

"Yes, they do, especially if their Doms are the kind into exhibitionism like myself who like to show off their girls."

A fresh jolt of fear sliced through her at the thought of being engaged in exhibitionist play.

"I think you scared her on that one, Thomas."

"I'll bet I did." His hands tightened at her waist.

Before she could voice her questions about what he meant, David's fingers slid through her slick folds to find her more turned on than she'd thought possible.

"Fuck. She is soaked." His fingers swirled and stroked, even glancing across her clit a few times. When her legs began to tremble with the need he'd created, Thomas told him to stop.

"I don't want her coming yet."

Regret lanced through her as she fought for the control not to ruin the whole thing. A few slow breaths in and out, and she felt the crazy urge to orgasm begin to recede. Thank God.

"Now, you want to check with your fingers to see if her tightness is to your liking."

Oh no.

David didn't waste any time as he quickly pushed two fingers inside of her. He fucked them methodically in and out with an occasional pause to stretch his fingers or curl them against her G-spot. Her hard fought control dissipated to nothingness as an impending orgasm had her bucking her hips against his hand, hoping he would rub her clit and give her the sweet relief so desperately needed. Later, when she could think straight again, she'd contemplate how they got to her so fast.

A hard swat landed on her ass. "Did I tell you it was okay to move?"

"No, Sir," she breathed heavily.

"Did anyone give you permission to come?"

"No, Sir."

"Then I suggest you hold still as instructed." Thomas wrapped his fingers gently around her neck and held her still. "You need a collar and leash for what all I have planned for you, but for now, at the very least, a collar."

Gabby whined. The image that popped in her head was too much to bear. The pressure behind her clit bordered on the edge of pain.

"David are you satisfied with her pussy?"

"Very much so."

"Good then remove your fingers, and let's move on." David pulled from her body and Gabby fought not to let the tears fall that sprang into her eyes. Thomas withdrew his touch as well, leaving her cold without their combined heat warming her.

"Gabrielle, turn and face me please."

She swiveled, looking up at Thomas to await further instruction.

His fingers cupped her chin. "You're doing very well, sweetheart. I'm quite proud of you. Do you believe yet that I will take care of you?"

Gabby hesitated unsure of what he wanted to hear.

A frown crossed his face, and he shook his head. "That's okay, it takes time. Let's continue. Spread your legs wide and bend down, touching your fingers to the floor." Gabby stared at him, not even bothering to disguise her disbelief. The position he'd asked her to take would open both her ass and pussy to David in such an intimate way...

A shiver worked down her spine. She should be humiliated. Any normal woman would be. Instead, her skin heated for an entirely different reason.

"Do you want to stop?"

She shook her head.

Thomas raised an eyebrow.

"I mean no, Sir." She couldn't stop now. They'd come so far, and the need clawing at her insides had priority over a twinge of discomfort. Gabby moved her legs a little wider and bent at the waist, placing her palms flat on the floor. When Thomas began explaining to David the need to check every inch of a submissive's body, she tuned out their voices. She didn't want to hear them discussing her asshole and vagina in clinical terms. She wanted someone to fuck her, and at the moment she didn't really care which one did.

How had that happened? And what did it mean that she no longer worried about two men she didn't know all that well touching and fondling her in any manner they chose. With both men standing behind her she had no idea which man owned the hand that rubbed the smooth skin of her bottom or which one traced the seam all the way to her heated sex. Her pussy squeezed.

"Gabrielle. Are you listening?" Thomas's voice broke through her arousal-fogged brain, although she had no idea what he'd been saying.

"Um...yes, Sir."

The hand resting on the crack of her ass trailed along the seam, through the slick folds and gave her labia a quick hard pinch. She gasped.

"You should be listening, considering the importance of what's being done here. Would a spanking get your attention?"

"I'm...I'm sorry, Sir." *Fuck. Please don't pinch me there again.* She knew better than to say that out loud but still...

"Then reach your hands back here and pull apart your cheeks like I asked the first time. David wants to get a closer look."

Her body jolted at his words. She pressed her hands to her knees to regain her balance, giving herself a chance to dig deep for the resolve to get this done.

"Gabrielle..."

She sensed his displeasure at her hesitation.

You can do this Gabby.

Maybe once this was over they would allow her to come. It was a little disconcerting how easily she succumbed in the face of her need. Despite that, she grasped her cheeks and pulled them apart, exposing herself like she'd never before, reminding herself that pleasing them pleased her and would likely lead to the reward her body screamed for.

Both men complimented her on her obedience as well as her beautiful body. Not that she totally believed them on the second part. Most men did not find women her size especially attractive. Passable maybe, nice even, but beautiful? Hardly. Although a few men who had a thing for big asses had given her many a compliment. That always made her smile. She did have an hourglass shape with a round bubble butt.

A finger tapped against the tight hole of her bottom and roused Gabby from her runaway thoughts as sensation roiled through her, leaving her clit to pulse and ache even more than before.

"Have you ever been fucked in the ass?"

Gabby frequently fantasized about anal play, despite her one bad experience with her ex, and had used her vibrator there several times. It wasn't easy to admit that she wanted to be taken there as much as she feared it.

"Only once, but I experimented a little on my own." Her voice shook as the tapping increased to a steady rhythm that kept a constant stream of tremors racing across her skin. Goose bumps exploded.

"You will be and likely often. Are you okay with that?"

Muscles clenched at the unknown while more moisture coated her sex. Did he really expect her to answer that?

"Gabrielle, relax. You're safe here. No desire is too dark or too deep. The only bad in all of this is if you aren't honest." He paused long enough to move closer and lowered his voice. "Will you let us take what we want and in return give you everything you need?"

The steady tone of his voice calmed through her. He soothed her with his reassurances.

"Yes, Sir," she answered.

Immediately, fingers dipped into her pussy and spread ample moisture to her behind, lubricating her just enough for a finger to push inside and past the tight ring of muscle. Her body stiffened at the invasion.

"Relax, babe. We're just getting a feel for it," David said.

She did her best to follow David's instructions while he pushed his finger all the way inside.

"So very tight. I certainly hope Thomas will share this with me some day."

She moaned at his words. She longed to experience so much, even some things she didn't comprehend. David continued to work, rubbing his fingers against sensitive tissues. Fresh heat clawed at her insides, demanding more. She pushed back hoping to show him her eagerness to serve that desire right now.

"Such an eager little girl, aren't you?" David teased her with words as well as his finger until she wanted to cry with frustration.

"I think that's enough for her inspection."

David's touch slipped away and an arm wrapped around her waist.

"You can stand now, sweetheart." Thomas's voice softened as he helped her to an upright position on weak and shaky legs.

"I-I need…"

"I know, Gabrielle, and you deserve it." He turned her into his arms and held her tight against his warmth. That simple show of pride increased her need tenfold until finally his lips took hers in a slow, luxurious kiss. His thigh lifted and rubbed against her swollen clit, the fabric of his pants adding to the already red-hot friction. Completely focused on his arms holding her and the constant ache in her pussy, she rode his leg, whimpering mindlessly into his mouth. She was too damned aroused to be embarrassed by the fact she stood in his kitchen, being watched by another man as she humped Thomas without shame.

Her body shook. *Please. Help me!*

Pulling back, he broke the kiss. "Do it, sweetheart. Come for me now."

She'd waited so long for that permission she almost cried when he gave it. Her hips bucked and rolled against him over and over until the world around her exploded. She thrashed and twisted in his arms, the orgasm penetrating every cell in her body. Fast and rough, she moved on him beyond the point of exhaustion.

When she would have collapsed into a puddle on the floor, Thomas gripped her waist with a firm grip and held her upright. Gabby buried her face into his shoulder as her heart rate returned to normal, the realization of her actions pounding into her on every beat. Despite her eager obedience, a sense of embarrassment washed over her. She struggled in Thomas' arms for freedom. Her only thought to flee and hide in the bedroom.

"Stop fighting it, beautiful. You have nothing to be ashamed of. Your desires are a fucking turn on. You should remember that." As if to prove his point, Thomas pressed the hard length of his cock into the soft skin of her belly. Despite the fabric between them, his heat seeped into her flesh. A new ache formed low and deep. "You want and you fear. I can see it across your face. You have to completely submit. Until then, we teach, you listen, we fuck."

Gabby's brain melted. She glanced furtively at the doorway and sighed. Hiding was simply out of the question. Neither Thomas nor David would ever allow it again.

"So what were your plans for this morning?"

As the sexual haze slowly faded away she remembered the coffee she'd been after. Some caffeine would do wonders right about now.

"I...uh...just wanted to get some coffee." She mumbled against his shirt. Both men chuckled, and even she couldn't hold in a grin.

"I'll get it for her." When David walked away to get her cup, Thomas carried her to the table and tucked her into a chair.

"Be sure to drink some water and eat something as well. It's critical to stay hydrated and healthy when your body has been taxed repeatedly." He winked at her. "As for me, I've got to go and change my clothes and then we'll see about making our future arrangements."

She blushed furiously as she tried not to look down at his pant leg where she'd certainly left a wet spot. The man had a way of making her come so damn hard.

She eagerly accepted the steaming mug from David who settled in the seat across from her. He watched her as she took her first gulp, closing her eyes at the warm sensation sliding down her throat, refreshing her. There was something magical about that first cup of java early in the morning. She normally drank two to three cups a day, but nothing was as precious as the first.

When her throat cooled and she was ready for more, she opened her eyes to find David still staring at her.

"What?"

"You even make drinking a cup of coffee sensuous. I think my dick got even harder watching that little look of pure ecstasy while you drank that. You're an amazing woman, Gabrielle. Thank you."

She swallowed hard, her emotions still raw from their scene. "Shouldn't you thank Thomas instead of me?"

"Oh I will, rest assured, but more importantly is the way you acquiesced to the entire thing, allowing me to share in your submission. I know some of that wasn't easy for you."

"How could you tell?" She had gone to great lengths to hide her discomfort.

"Every time you were asked to do something you didn't like, a little muscle ticked in your shoulder. It wasn't very noticeable, but in my line of work, I have to notice even the tiniest of details. Your willingness to continue, to submit well, it truly was the most beautiful thing I've ever seen in my life."

Gabby sat down her cup and stared back at David. His handsome features still dazzled her, but his kindness and honesty were the real treasure. She hoped when he left her and Thomas that he'd find the woman who deserved him. She also secretly hoped in that deep, dark place of hers that his leaving would be a long time from today. His gentle kindness was a wonderful contrast to Thomas's more formal ways. Not that David would make less of a Dom than Thomas, he would just have a different approach.

"So, what do you do for a living then?" She sipped more of the warm coffee and settled into the conversation, amazed that it didn't make her uncomfortable to sit next to him without a stitch of clothing on. His pleasure in her behavior and kind words seemed to give her a sense of peace about the whole thing. For some amazing reason, these two men weren't offended by her plump form, and instead, they both rather enjoyed it. A girl could definitely get used to their kind of attention—or spoiled by it.

"I'm a security consultant. Corporate work mostly. But there are occasions when a private individual or family hires me to test and or update their security staff."

"That sounds exciting."

A rich deep laugh rumbled from his chest and his vivid blue eyes sparkled with a humor she wanted to see more of. If she'd thought him handsome before, it was nothing compared to how he looked now. Of course, it made her wonder how his face would change in the throes of passion. From the sparkle of humor to the dark and intense nature of sexual heat, she believed he'd be utterly irresistible. A quick shot of arousal arrowed through her at the thought, and her pussy began its journey to readiness once again. She crossed her legs to staunch the sensation, which ended up being her first mistake. That movement created a rasp along her clit that had moisture gathering that would have dampened her panties had she been wearing any.

"I don't think I'd necessarily choose the word exciting to describe my work, although there have been a few moments here and there that might have raised the heart rate enough to qualify. But most of the time, it's tedious and requires a keen sense of concentration and patience." David maintained constant eye contact while he spoke, and Gabby couldn't tear herself away if she'd wanted to. He possessed a commanding presence she couldn't turn away from.

"I definitely identify with that. My work as an accountant can be tedious as well, but sometimes when things are not working out like they are supposed to, it can be like solving a difficult puzzle. Then I can really dig in and get to work. It's a heady feeling."

"Like taking on the work Thomas has offered you? You find that intriguing?"

The heat of a blush crept up her neck. He had no idea. While she'd been excited to receive another client, if she had to be honest with herself, she was more excited about working at Sanctuary. She'd heard very little over the years about what went on there, and she couldn't wait to learn. She had an insatiable curiosity that she was certain would one day get her into a lot of trouble. Or at least that's what her mother kept telling her anyway.

"Yes, I would say so. Sanctuary has always been a bit of a mystery to me. What better way to get the lay of the land than from within doing what I do best."

"I don't know about what you do best." He winked, a not so subtle smile across his face. "But I get it. It's kind of like a security blanket." She could have been offended at his statement, but the smile with which he said it wasn't mean or malicious. He was teasing her. Maybe even flirting a little.

She laughed, unable to help herself. It had been a long time since she'd had this much attention.

"What's so funny in here?" Her head swiveled around to find Thomas changed and leaning against the doorframe, watching them with his own sedate smile curling at the edges of his mouth. He had a way with business casual that made her mouth water. He wore snug black slacks that caressed his solid thighs and a starched white shirt that said smart business to everyone else and barely leashed power to her. Gabby swallowed thickly.

Apparently, her perusal didn't go unnoticed if the heat in his gaze was any indication.

"I've managed to embarrass you're girl again. She's blushing," David drawled.

"Don't you mean our girl?" Thomas pushed himself from the wall and sauntered over to stand next to her. Neither she nor David made any kind of response. "Yes, that's what you mean." Thomas traced his finger from her cheek to chin where he tilted her head up until their gazes locked. "At least for now. As long as we're training her together, she serves both of us. That is if that's what you want?"

"Of course," they answered in unison.

Gabby bowed her head and added "Sir" at the last second.

Thomas bent down to her level and whispered in her ear. "Does David turn you on my sweet?"

She didn't know how to answer. He did, oh God, he did, and now, she felt guilty all over again. Would Thomas be angry with her? It was too hard to accept he wouldn't. Before she could answer, Thomas's hand traveled down the front of her body, leaving a streak of fire in their wake— bone deep wild heat. Her body tingled. God, no matter what he did her body responded. Ached for more. To her delight, he continued his quest and dipped a finger between her wet flesh. Her breath held on a quiet gasp as she waited for his outrage.

"You've been quite busy, David."

"Have I?"

"Oh yes, she's warm and slick just the way I like her. I'd say she's had quite a reaction to you."

"It's not the first time I've had that affect, and considering the hard-on I'm sitting here with, it's good to know I'm not the only one." David shifted from side to side in his seat his arm under the table arranging himself.

Thomas swirled his finger, spreading her moisture in slow methodical strokes. She thrust her hips for more of his touch. A small chuckle greeted her in response. "You're so eager. I love that you know."

He removed his finger and brought it to her lips. Without a word, she knew exactly what he wanted. Gabby opened obediently and licked her own juice from his finger, watching his eyes darken as she did.

"It doesn't seem fair to get David all worked up and leave him hanging like that, does it?"

"No, Sir."

"Do you want him to fuck you?"

A punch of arousal hit Gabby in the gut. Something fierce. Never mind her brain insisted her desires were all wrong. The near constant struggle between want and need waged on. If she chose David over Thomas, he'd send her away. If he wanted David to use her then he would just tell him to. This wasn't supposed to be her decision.

Thomas's smile disappeared at her hesitation. He pulled her to her feet. "I'm afraid she isn't ready, David. If she can't ask for it then she can't have it." He steered her toward the doorway but paused there. "If you'd like to go to Sanctuary this morning, I could have Linda meet you there."

Gabby bit at her lip, holding back a cry of protest. Tears pooled in her eyes. Confusion swirled through her.

She didn't want David going to another submissive for his release.

Her job.

The newspaper rustled behind her, and a chair scraped across the tiled floors. "That won't be necessary. I need to get to work."

"If you change your mind, just let me know." Thomas nudged her forward. They strode together to the bedroom, his fingers curled around her arm in a firm grip the entire time. Gabby imagined the fury and disappointment she would meet once they were in private and steeled herself for the harsh words to come.

Chapter Ten

Thomas stared down at the numbers on the balance sheet in front of him once again, but the figures still weren't right. With the increase in outside groups renting rooms at Sanctuary and the implementation of his new cost cutting efforts, there should be more of an impact by now. His gut burned every time he considered the shit his accountant was trying to pull.

He needed that audit done as soon as possible. There was only two ways out of his contract with the little fucker, and he didn't expect the other man to quit anytime soon unless he got caught red-handed. With any luck, Gabrielle would be able to start work on it in the next day or two, and Thomas would be able to put it rest once and for all.

He shifted in his seat as the semi erection he'd been sporting all day swelled into a full blown hard-on just from thinking of the sweet little submissive he'd watched pull out of his driveway before he'd left for work. In a perfect world, where he didn't have to worry about her job or his, he would have kept her at his side all day.

Gabrielle in his office and on the edge of arousal all day long sounded like the perfect plan. Add in a lunchtime training session with both David and her, and he'd be in his own version of heaven. Her reaction to David this morning had lit a fire in his blood that no amount of work could extinguish. But her hesitation bothered him. He'd felt the proof of her desire, but she'd been unable to put that into words like he'd requested.

Did she fear choosing one over the other?

That thought slammed into Thomas with startling clarity. That made sense actually. They'd not spent enough time going over the fact that her desires were his. He made a mental note to discuss this subject later. Right now, his mind wasn't on training but instead simply on her hot little mouth and, specifically, how delicious it would look wrapped around his cock—something he planned to experience as soon as possible. Thomas pressed against the front of his pants. With as turned on as he'd been all day just thinking of her, it wouldn't take much to have him coming in her mouth.

Mmm.

If he'd had a lick of sense this morning, he'd have pushed her to her knees and demanded her to suck him. Instead, he'd ordered her to dress and sent her home—something he planned to rectify as soon as possible. He turned to his computer and fired off a quick email to his little vixen.

Oh yeah, he couldn't wait. He'd keep her on edge with some fun tasks for the day and by tonight, she'd be ready for whatever he threw her way.

A knock at the door startled Thomas from his thoughts as he tucked his chair behind his desk. "Yeah?"

The door opened, and David's familiar blond head poked in. He grinned. "Is it safe to enter?"

Thomas glanced at his desktop clock, surprised to see it was indeed already noon and time for lunch with his friend. "If the door's not locked then it's okay to come in no matter what's going on in here."

"Well, there might be a few things I don't want to accidentally see."

Thomas cocked his brow and watched David saunter across the room and take a seat in one of the leather chairs in front of his desk. He was dressed in his security firm's uniform of black pants, black button down shirt and black tie. He must have left the black blazer out in his car. Thomas enjoyed teasing David about his firm's "men in black" policy.

"I've yet to see you turn down an opportunity to watch a scene, so I can't imagine what I could be doing in here that you wouldn't want to check out for yourself." Thomas shut down the email program on his computer and locked his machine so he and David could scoot on down to the dining room where lunch should be waiting. His friend usually didn't stay more than hour for their lunches.

David was completely devoted to his work and often put in long hours to complete a job—something Thomas was all too familiar with. It was one of the many things they had in common and had begun to build a solid friendship on.

"Yeah, I guess you have a point. But still…"

Thomas clapped David on the back as they stepped from his office and headed down the hall to the dining room. He loved this old house and even more so what it stood for. A place of freedom for all those interested in an alternative lifestyle. It wasn't just about BDSM here at Sanctuary. They catered to any group that found themselves on the fringe of what society considered normal. There were a variety of clubs in the city and throughout the state who rented out rooms and on special occasions the whole house for their gatherings.

So while on the night he'd met Gabrielle it had been a local BDSM group renting the first floor for their get together, on any given day it could be swingers, fetishists or a simple event like a high tea for submissives. They were open to anything, and he loved nothing more than being a safe haven for these groups.

The house was decorated in an opulence befitting a royal palace and could fit into a number of themed parties.

He and David strolled into the near-empty formal dining room and took a seat. One of the perks he offered to the staff here were the catered lunches.

"Good afternoon, Thomas. David." The resident kitchen manager smiled at them as they took their seats. "The usual today?"

"Yes, Linda, thanks."

She poured two tall glasses of sweet tea and set them down on the table along with silverware and napkins. "I'll have your club sandwiches out momentarily."

After Linda walked out the silence in the room grew. Thomas sat back in his chair to observe David. On the outside, he appeared calm and cool, but there were tiny telltale signs of something bothering him.

"What's wrong? Are you uncomfortable with our plan?"

To Thomas's surprise and admiration, David didn't hesitate before looking at him.

"About what? Gabrielle?"

Thomas nodded and steepled his fingers in front of him.

"I wouldn't say uncomfortable. Cautious maybe. Wondering where this is going to lead."

"You don't like her?"

"On the contrary, I like her very much. Maybe too much."

Thomas grinned at his friend and shook his head.

"I know exactly what you mean. There's nothing to worry about though. I want you to like her. It'll be more enjoyable for us all that way."

"Are you sure you want to do this? She seems different from the others, more serious. It doesn't seem to be about just the sex."

"You noticed that already?" Thomas hesitated while Linda delivered their food.

"Will there be anything else, Sir?" The hint in her voice caught his attention, and he looked up and examined her lovely face. If anyone he'd ever met was a perfect human specimen, it would be Linda. She was perfectly proportioned with a gracious sense of obedience. In fact, he'd enjoyed flogging her many times since he'd known her, yet she didn't affect him like his Gabrielle did.

His.

That one word was almost enough to stop his heart from beating. Sure, he'd taken submissives before and even claimed ownership for an agreed upon timeframe, but already this seemed something more. Something dangerous. While he could provide exactly what Gabrielle needed, it wouldn't be him that could give it to her. For that he needed David. He would be the buffer that kept things from going where they weren't supposed to.

"No, Linda that will be all. Thanks, doll." He winked at her and dug into his food until she'd closed the door to the kitchen behind her.

"Gabrielle is a rare breed, David. A natural submissive with intense needs and an unfailing desire to please. It's a beautiful thing. It's also a big responsibility."

"Well, if anyone is capable, I'm sure it's you. You have the experience and the knowledge to take on anything you set your mind to." David hesitated before he took another bite. "Don't you want her? Is that what this is about?"

Damn. Thomas needed to be more careful about what he said to his friend. He'd underestimated him today. "Not at all. I'm enamored with everything about her. Probably too much but hell, at my age, I've gotten pretty set in my ways."

"At your age? Give me a break. It's not as if you're an old man. What are you forty?"

"Forty-five."

"Like I said."

Thomas shook his head and finished eating his lunch. He'd said more than enough for one day. The burden to carry the delicate balance of this relationship lay at his feet not David's. He only wanted to gauge David's commitment to Gabrielle's training.

"What was you impression this morning in the kitchen? Did you enjoy the inspection?"

"It was exciting to watch her overcome her fears at each turn of expectations. I thought she handled herself quite well considering her nerves. Sure made my dick hard."

A deep chuckle rumbled through Thomas's chest at the look on his friend's face. Instead of the smile, he expected, David's face was drawn and pinched, his lips set in a grim line. "I offered you Linda. You didn't have to walk around with blue balls today, you know."

"As generous as that offer is, I don't think anyone could substitute for Gabrielle."

"Now, you're breaking my heart. Holding out for our girl is just so… sweet." Thomas found it impossible to hide his grin. "I don't think it will take long for her to ask for it. She was so fucking wet this morning."

David groaned around his sandwich. "You need to quit telling me that."

"Soon, David, soon. In fact, she has invited us for dinner tonight at her place. Are you interested?"

"Hell, yeah, I am. Home-cooked meal and a hot little sub? Sounds perfect."

"I intend to push her again tonight. I can't resist that blush of hers."

"I'm glad I don't have to miss it."

Thomas mulled over the possibilities. He remembered—to well—how tight she'd been around him. The words that had fallen from her lush lips each time he'd fucked her to oblivion. Hell, he liked everything about her. Her beautiful curves, her skin, her smell, her bravery. What he didn't understand was her ability to knock him off course. It was obvious a few sessions with his beauty would never be enough. She'd take time to figure out, and he definitely wanted to access that deep, dark center that needed him.

He hadn't figured out exactly what he wanted to do tonight; it would depend on their surroundings. But either way, he was certain it would be very, very interesting.

Chapter Eleven

Gabrielle ran through her house, trying to double check every little detail. She wanted everything to be perfect tonight for Thomas and David when they arrived. Earlier in the evening she'd pulled out all the stops and baked a delicious chicken manicotti meal with a few gourmet flourishes she hoped would impress them. Now, her obsession with perfection kicked in as she double-checked every last detail.

She'd reread the emails that had come from Thomas this afternoon probably half a dozen times. He'd given her explicit instructions for what he wanted her to wear as well as what time they would be arriving. A glance at the clock on the wall showed she had less than two minutes. She untied her apron and shoved it into the pantry then slipped into the guest bathroom to give her appearance one last look-see.

After hours of debating what to wear, she'd finally settled on the deep purple short dress she'd bought a few years ago in an impulsive moment of weakness. In the store, she'd felt ultra sexy as she twirled in the dressing room mirror. Then she'd tried it on for her ex who'd quickly informed her it was a slut's dress. She'd never put it on again. Until now...

The plunging neckline offered a generous amount of cleavage, and the stretchy material could easily be pushed aside to bare a breast if they were so inclined, and she hoped Thomas or David would be. Heat suffused her lower body at her wicked thoughts. She'd fantasized for years about having two men but had easily categorized it as a silly fantasy.

Gabby popped open her lip gloss and applied a fresh layer, smacking her lips together when she was done. Now, that fantasy seemed one step closer to reality, and she still couldn't believe it.

How far did Thomas really want to go with this? Did she want to serve two men? The images that popped into her mind were positively naughty, and Gabby could feel the moisture gathering on her cotton panties. Her clit ached. She shook her head. This kind of reaction shocked her. She'd never been so obsessed with sex before. Now, it's all she thought about. Time to pull herself together.

She smoothed down the skirt of the dress and forced herself to concentrate on a few slow, deep breaths. The doorbell rang, pulling Gabby's attention back to the mirror.

Showtime.

* * * *

Gabby opened her front door to the most breathtaking sight she'd ever seen. Two gorgeous men with smiles on their faces that would bring any woman to her knees from the sheer power of their gazes. Thomas's brown slacks and cream-colored silk shirt skimmed the hard planes his body just enough to show off his impressive physique. She didn't know how he had the time to take such good care of himself, but she sure appreciated it. She'd discovered first hand the night before just how delicious it was to grab onto those muscles and the sensation of raw power she got from them when they rippled beneath her hands.

She stepped back and ushered them in with a small smile on her face. Each man kissed her cheek and complimented her on her clothing choices. She knew from the heat creeping up her neck that she blushed furiously. Thankfully, neither seemed to notice or mind.

In a contrast to Thomas, David had worn black pants and a pale blue shirt that was left unbuttoned enough to give her a glimpse of the light blond hairs she knew were sprinkled across his chest before they narrowed down into a seductive trail at the waistband of his pants. Her mouth watered just imagining touching him there. His flat, sleek abs would be so firm underneath her fingertips.

Jeez, Gabby, get a grip already. The night is just getting started.

"Cute place you have here, Gabrielle." David's comment drew her attention.

"It's not fancy, but it's mine and I love it. How about a quick tour?"

Thomas grabbed her hand and kissed it, even pressing the tip of his tongue to her skin. "We would love that, beautiful."

She moved aside so she could motion to the kitchen and the living room and even point out where the downstairs bathroom was.

"You have lovely taste, sweetheart."

"It's taken me a long time to get this place to where it is now. I got a great deal on it because the tenants before the sale had trashed the place."

"It looks like all of your hard work has paid off then. You have a beautiful home."

"I haven't even showed you my favorite part." She led the way to the French doors tucked underneath the stairs that led to her backyard. "This is where I poured my heart out, the one place where I did every bit of the work all on my own, my pride and joy." She stepped aside and motioned to the landscape in front of her.

She had turned the patio into an outdoor living room and tonight the dining table took front and center with its fine linens and china. There were pots of blooming colorful flowers everywhere that lent to the lovely fragrance and beauty of all of her hard work. Beyond the patio were paths of flowers, herbs and even a small Koi pond in the corner. No detail had been spared.

"Wow!" Both men looked around then back at her. "You did all of this by yourself?" David's voice sounded incredulous, but she could understand. It had been a giant undertaking, one well worth it in the long run. Not only because of the gorgeous results but the form of self-therapy it had taken. It had helped her heal from her failed marriage, keeping her too busy to feel sorry for herself.

She nodded unable to keep the proud grin from her face.

"Have you ever considered you're in the wrong line of work? I'm sure there are many in this town who would be impressed with your landscape skills."

"Oh no, I love my job. This is strictly my stress relief. My escape. I would never want to turn that into work and lose the joy of it."

Thomas grabbed her around the waist and pulled her to him, pressing her softer body against his hard planes. The contrast sent shivers down her spine especially when she spied David watching carefully.

"You're an amazing woman. Very talented. Exactly how many other hidden talents do you have?"

Gabby laughed—a bubbling sound that caught her by surprise. All from the attention and compliments of her men. Her stomach clenched. Maybe they weren't technically her men, but tonight, here in her garden, she believed.

"I noticed this area is very private. Where exactly were you when you masturbated for me on the phone?"

Gabby sputtered in surprise, embarrassed all over again.

"Show me."

She led both Thomas and David down the short path to the lounge area she had set up next to the Koi pond. "Here." She pointed to the lone lounge chair.

"While no one can see you out here, I did notice your neighbors are close so they can probably hear quite well if they were listening."

She nodded.

"Do you think they were listening that day, Gabrielle? When you cried out with your orgasm?"

Oh dear God, had she? She'd been so caught up in his words, his voice, she hadn't even noticed. "I—uh—I don't know."

Thomas chuckled softly. "I like the idea of you being overheard almost as much as the fact that you were so focused on me that you forgot your surroundings. I'm impressed again."

His pride brought on a fresh wave of arousal. Her pussy practically wept at the memories of what she'd done for him. She really hadn't cared. It had been all about him and her pleasure—nothing else had mattered.

"Are you wet now?"

Desire slammed into her. "Yes, Sir." Her breath shortened. Thomas stepped so close she felt the heat radiating from his body.

"From that moment on the phone, I've thought of nothing but ways to make you submit. And I have a pretty vivid imagination."

His unabashed way of saying whatever the hell he wanted drove her wild. Bold. Forceful. Thomas took what he wanted. Logic said she should hate it. She fucking loved it.

"Will your masturbate for us now? While we watch?"

"Yes." She didn't need to consider or hesitate. Seeing the arousal in both their eyes and the hungry way they kept looking at her body had flames licking across her skin. Her nipples had tightened to painful little points that nearly made her cry out every time she moved, making the fabric of her dress rasp against them. She longed to touch, to taste, to feel...

"Such a good little girl you are." Thomas moved his lips against hers when he spoke, and his warm breath stroked over her like a lover's hand. "But first, poor David needs some relief. You've left him in need, and I want to watch you suck his cock until he comes down your pretty little throat." He twisted her body around until she faced David a foot away from her. "On your knees," Thomas demanded.

Surprise glittered in David's eyes as she sank to her knees in front of him. Tonight, there was no hesitation. She'd thought about it all day and had decided she would go with what her body said, not her head. Nothing would give her more pleasure than to see both Thomas and David pleased with her.

"Much better this time. I take it you gave my words some consideration today like I suggested." Thomas's smooth and deep voice behind her calmed and soothed her shaking insides. He didn't sound at all like a jealous man. He seemed to genuinely want her to follow her instincts. On her knees in the grass before David, she found her head at eye level with his bulging cock. She reached for his waistband and made quick work of his belt and button, smiling when a groan sounded from him. She faltered a few seconds with the zipper before tugging it down with a noisy rasp.

When smooth flesh instead of fabric came into view, she nearly moaned herself. Without briefs, his erection bounced in her direction. Eager to please, she wrapped her hands around the thickened flesh. Her clit pulsed with its own torturous need as she guided the smooth and swollen tip of his cock into her mouth. He was huge.

Gabby lapped at the fluid already leaking, enjoying the burst of salty spice of the man across her tongue.

"Holy fuck." David's exclamation at her touch fueled her to keep going. She pushed forward taking more and more of him one inch at a time until she had him at the back of her throat. His cock pulsed, forcing her to fight the impulse to gag. It had been a long time since she'd done anything this bold.

Fingers threaded through her hair, tugging her head back and stretching her mouth further to accommodate him. She couldn't tell for sure whose hand held her head, but if she had to guess, she'd say Thomas controlled this scene.

Gabby relaxed her muscles so David could slide inside an inch more. "She has the hottest mouth I've had the pleasure of in a long—"

David's words cut off abruptly on a gasp when she swallowed, tightening around him. Her juices flowed between her thighs, soaking her panties.

Caught by surprise, she was pulled back from David's cock until just the tip remained between her teeth. Her tongue swiped the slit, lapping at him while her teeth gently grazed the sensitive skin.

"Open wider." Thomas' harsh demand lit a fire inside her. She eagerly complied with his wishes just in time for David to surge forward, burying himself in her mouth once again. This time, he didn't linger there as he pulled away and pushed back in. David controlled the movements of his cock, and Thomas moved her head when he wanted while David fucked her mouth. Saliva pooled in her mouth giving David all the lubrication and heat he needed as his movements grew urgent. His orgasm seemed imminent as she found herself trapped in place for him to do what he wished. A flash of panic quickly subsided when she glanced again at his face.

Pride and more infused her when she saw the evidence of the pleasure he took from her body. She reached for his balls and cradled them in her hands.

"God, woman, you're killing me. I have to come."

Her body jerked at his response. She moaned against his thick flesh. Getting this man to come in her mouth became her single-minded focus. With a little more pressure, she squeezed his scrotum. She was rewarded with an almost violent thrust of his hips.

"Yes baby, yes." Two short thrusts and his tangy release burst across her tongue, flooding her mouth. "Ahhhh."

His moans suffused her with enormous pride as the power of the pleasure she was able to give became clear. The fact she was on her knees, locked onto him by the hand holding her head, did little to diminish the feeling of control she felt. To her surprise, a submissive held a lot of power whether they realized it or not, and that seemed evident here.

His cock pulsed a few more times as the last of his semen flowed from the tip. With her final swallow, she tightened her mouth around him and laved his shaft with her tongue, making sure she didn't miss a single drop.

The hand in Gabby's hair pulled her off of David and tilted her head at an upward angle so she could see both men's faces.

"Thank you, Sir." The words slipped out of her mouth before she'd even thought about them.

"What are you thanking me for, my beauty?" Thomas let go of her hair and grasped her shoulders to pull her to her feet. Both men stepped close and supported each side of her while she steadied herself.

"For...for letting me..." She trailed off. With both men looking at her curiously, she didn't know how to explain how much she'd needed that. And the fact Thomas had wanted her to do it meant the world to her.

"You're not upset with me?" The question trembled from her lips. A tear slid down her cheek, and David wiped it away.

"Upset? Are you kidding me? That was so damned incredible." Thomas' statement shocked her.

"Did I hurt you, sweetheart?"

She shook her head furiously.

"Then what is it?"

She bowed her head embarrassed to look at them. "I-I don't know... I'm just not used to anyone understanding my needs. I've lived a long time convinced that the darker side of me had to be ignored...that it was bad. That I'm bad."

Thomas cupped her cheek and drew her head up, forcing her to look at him. "Whoever made you feel that way is a damned idiot. In our relationship, I fully expect you to tell us your deepest, darkest needs so that we can determine what's best for you. That's our duty as well as our promise. You are not bad."

David nodded his head at Thomas's words, and Gabby wanted to fall into their arms and never leave the safety of them. Could it really be this easy? Just tell the truth?

David fastened his pants then wrapped his arm around her waist. "Did we mention how beautiful you look tonight?"

A smile formed unbidden—how could she not. "Yes, you may have mentioned that, but I don't mind hearing it again," she teased.

"I bet you don't. But first things first. What is it that smells so good and is making me hungry?"

Gabby nipped at David's arm and squirmed from his grasp. "Such a man to be thinking of food at a time like this." she said with a grin.

"Oh a little minx now, huh? Maybe you need a good spanking to remind you of your place with us." David swatted her ass.

Her face heated as a blush crept up her neck.

"Or maybe not since you seemed to enjoy the last one far too much. When it comes to punishment I think we are going to have to get creative." David winked at her, and she huffed and turned toward the house. She did need to get dinner out of the oven and on the table before it got ruined so she left them standing there in the garden and disappeared into the house.

David watched her skirt swish across her ass as she moved inside. He swore his dick stirred again despite the mind-blowing blowjob he'd just received.

"She's a handful, isn't she?" he mused.

"She is, but I think we're both up to the challenge. Not to mention the rewards when you get her going. You seemed to enjoy her mouth."

"Enjoy? Fuck that was so hot I'm already plotting when I can do it again."

"She's eager to serve. I imagine you could have it any time you wanted."

This time his cock did thicken, and he pressed the base, easing the strain against his slacks.

"What do you know about her past?" David turned and faced Thomas in order to lower his voice in case she came back onto the terrace.

"Not much, but enough. Her friend Angel told me she went through a tough divorce last year after her ex found out that she was interested in kink. Told her she was warped."

"Damn, that's fucked up. Explains a lot though. I get the impression that on some level she's still ashamed by what she needs."

"She is. It's not an easy transition. I'm damn proud of how hard she tries..."

Thomas' attention was elsewhere. David followed his line of sight and found him watching Gabrielle through the window. Her curvy figure taunted him. He'd always had a thing for a real woman. Her intelligence and fierce determination to improve her life commanded his respect. Add to that her sweet willingness to yield to both men, and he might have found the perfect submissive.

There were still issues that could trip them up though. Her past had to be dealt with. It wasn't enough that she responded to their touch. They needed her to accept the needs they all shared without reservations. In time, he reminded himself. There was also the hunger etched across Thomas' face. No amount of sex or submission sated something like that. If this was going to work, they'd all have to think outside the box.

Gabrielle turned and smiled at them through the window. Her nipples were hard and straining against the fabric of her blouse. Forget dinner, David only wanted more of her. "What kind of man wouldn't want an eager and adventurous woman like that?" he mused.

"The straight-laced vanilla kind."

"I guess...but even my vanilla friends want dirty girls in bed."

"What Gabrielle needs is far beyond just kinky sex; surely you know that by now. She craves the freedom that occurs when she's given permission to be as dark as her body yearns for without feeling bad about it. But she's still struggling with feeling guilty."

David shook his head. "How can you be so certain about what she needs? Did she tell you this?"

"No, but her body did. By pushing past her fears with every new scene, she's begun to flower like a rose in the morning sun. It'll take a while to learn all that we need to, but the journey will be exquisite and well worth it."

David listened to everything Thomas had to say, soaking in his knowledge like a dry sponge. But in the end, what he wondered the most was if Thomas knew that he was already falling for Gabrielle.

A feeling he knew all too well.

If he wasn't careful, he'd end up too attached to a woman that really belonged to someone else. For now, the three of them were together, but Thomas had some pretty unorthodox methods. How long would this last? Until Thomas said so? He certainly had primary status in this relationship, and the decision would ultimately lie with him. But would his friend be able to simply walk away when that time came?

"How do you keep your emotions out of a situation like this?" David hadn't wanted to reveal his doubts, but as a close friend, he valued and needed Thomas's opinion.

"With someone like her? The woman who tugs at every protective streak you possess?"

David nodded.

"You don't."

Chapter Twelve

The private rear entrance to Sanctuary loomed directly ahead, and Gabby grew nervous about facing her first day of work. She hadn't seen Thomas or David since the night they'd come for dinner, and she was anxious for them both. She'd received countless emails and instant messages as both men checked up on her periodically, but they'd wanted to leave her alone long enough for her to focus on wrapping up her prior obligations so she could start work at Sanctuary free and clear.

Butterflies took flight in her stomach as she pulled her car into a parking spot next to Thomas's Jag. After dinner, the three of them had snuggled up on her couch and watched movies for most of the night. They had surprised and impressed her all in one night. She'd been expecting them both to want more from her sexually and instead, they'd spent hours just talking as they got to know each other. She'd discovered that they had many interests in common as well as a few she shared individually with each man.

Curled between them on her couch, she'd found an amazing sense of comfort and calm that she'd craved as long as she could remember. They'd set her so at ease it hadn't taken her long to drift off to sleep. Late in the night, Thomas had woken her long enough to carry her upstairs to her room where they'd gently removed her clothing and tucked her into bed. Not once had anyone taken care of her like that.

She loved the feel of their hands on her even when it wasn't sexual. It still carried a possessive touch that made her feel wanted like never before. What would it be like to go to bed every night tucked in between them? A flash of warmth heated her blood. Selfish thoughts like that would get her nowhere. Not that a girl couldn't dream.

Once her vehicle had been secured, she took the few strides to the door and rang the buzzer as instructed. Gabby licked her lips and checked to make sure her blouse and skirt were straight. Despite her relationship with Thomas, she had no intention of letting down her professional guard while working for him in a business capacity. Every job was as important as the last. She took immense pride in her work.

The door opened, and a lovely, petite woman with a beautiful smile greeted her warmly. "Gabrielle?"

She nodded.

"Please come in. I've been expecting you. I'm Deidre, the office manager for Sanctuary. You're the accounting consultant, right?"

"Yes, that's correct."

"Wonderful, Thomas has been anxious for your arrival so you can get started. Let me show you around our business office real quick. We can save the rest for later. Have you ever been here before?"

Gabby blushed furiously at the question. How could she maintain her professionalism if she admitted to being a guest here? What would the woman think?

"Yes, once for a brief visit." She wasn't about to lie and have the truth come out later so she opted to stick to as little information as possible.

"Great, so you're familiar with the kind of clientele we entertain here. That's a relief."

Gabby looked at her curiously. "Not entirely. I was only here as a guest for a brief demonstration and then left afterward."

"No problem. With full access to our accounting records, you'll become quite familiar with our clientele, and I'm positive Thomas would not have hired you if he doubted your discretion or acceptance."

Deidre's vague response left Gabby more intrigued than ever. Activities at Sanctuary were kept very private, and Angel had only described one of the BDSM groups that held functions here.

The woman ushered her into a suite of offices with an organized desk and reception area out front. "This is my desk and each of those offices holds accounting, security and, of course, Thomas' office there." Deidre pointed to a closed door to the right of her desk. "He's in a meeting at the moment and asked if I could get you settled in until he finished."

"Oh, okay." Of course, Thomas had to be a busy man, but she couldn't help a knot of disappointment from forming anyway. At this point, two days of not seeing Thomas or David had become an eternity. After the big build up of showing up for the job, her nerves were a little frayed.

Deidre led Gabby through the office door marked Accounting. Two desks sat on opposite walls. One of them was a complete nightmare covered in papers at least a couple of feet high, along with discarded food trash.

Deidre frowned. "Our current accountant is a slob. He's been putting in long hours trying to get caught up and won't allow the cleaning staff to touch a thing."

Gabby nodded and turned her attention to the other desk. It looked brand new, and except for the basic supplies like lamp, calculator and a stapler, it stood naked in comparison.

Naked.

She wanted to be naked right now. Preferably on her knees in front of either David or Thomas or both. Her sex squeezed. This whole sex obsession thing was going to drive her mad.

Gabby jerked when a soft, chilled hand touched her arm.

"Gabrielle, are you okay?"

"What? Oh yes, yes, I'm fine. And please call me Gabby. I prefer it." She refocused her attention on the assistant and the job at hand. Thomas was counting on her to complete this job quickly and efficiently. In fact, every time they'd discussed it, she'd sensed a great sense of urgency. She wanted to discuss that with him today once she'd had a chance to get a lay of the land so to speak. See what she was up against.

"Okay, Gabby it is. Where would you like to get started? I'm here to help you in any way that I can." Deidre moved over to the file cabinet. "Most of the historical stuff should be found in here, but I'm afraid most of the current paper records will be in that mess over there." She motioned to the cluttered desk that hurt Gabby's sensibilities and sense of organization just to look at.

"How about access to the electronic records? These days, I'd expect to find most of the current data there." Deidre gave her a blank look and walked quickly from the room.

Gabby took a seat and started pulling things from her briefcase. First things first, she had to be organized. Before she got even a notepad removed, Deidre returned with a Macbook in hand along with its power cord. She silently plugged it in and booted it up, setting it on the desk in front of Gabby.

"This computer is already set up on the company network, and Thomas made sure it included all of the access you'll need. He kept it under lock and key until this morning to ensure it remained clean."

Gabby watched and listened closely. This process—this caution being taken—seemed to indicate there was more to the story than Thomas had explained. Did he suspect foul play with his accounting books? She glanced at the messy desk.

"Why is he not here this morning?" Gabby tipped her head toward the empty chair.

"He works a second shift schedule and will be here after lunch. He and his wife used to work different shifts to save on daycare, but now, that he's divorced I assume he just keeps the schedule because it's what he's used to. That and he usually plays here at Sanctuary late into the night."

Gabby raised her eyebrows at the tone in Deidre's voice. She got the distinct impression that the office manager did not like the accountant at all. A low burn of anger began to simmer. She and Thomas were going to have a talk about this. His letting her walk into a hornet's nest unaware was unacceptable. Submission to him in her personal life was one thing. Not taking her seriously as a consultant...

"So anyway, you'll find all of the current accounting records on the hard drive in the folders labeled by year. If you don't have any questions, I'll just get back to work and let you get settled in. If you need anything, please don't hesitate to ask. I'm here to assist you in any manner that I can."

"Thank you, I'll let you know if I think of anything."

Deidre nodded and strode from the room, closing the door behind her.

Gabby let out the breath she hadn't even realized she'd been holding and got to work. She removed her notepad, pencils and her beloved and well-worn calculator she never worked without from her bag. Happy to have a private space to work in, she removed the jacket she'd worn over a sheer blouse and kicked off her shoes. She'd grown accustomed to working at home so much lately that being in an office and wearing a suit seemed foreign to her.

She'd have to ask Thomas how he felt about casual clothes. Gabby smiled. Knowing him, he'd likely have her working in the nude if she wasn't careful.

Once she was comfortable, her fingers hit the touchpad of the computer a few times until she located the folders she sought. She grabbed a pencil and began taking notes as she worked her way through every subfolder. Before long, she quickly forgot everything around her as she went into sleuth mode. If there was even the slightest anomaly, she'd find it.

* * * *

Sexy strands of golden hair curled around Gabrielle's face as she worked, giving her an alluring aura that pulled at Thomas. From his vantage point, he could just make out the sweet dark nipples poking at the sheer fabric of her blouse, enticing him to touch and nibble. He'd instructed her to wear no undergarments while at Sanctuary. So far so good. Not that he'd expected anything less.

Thomas had heard her arrive and regretted being unable to greet her. He had ached to see her this morning and pretty much every waking hour since he'd seen her last. Watching her now, he wanted to command her to spread her sweet thighs for him. He already knew what paradise awaited him. That worried him.

Instead, he'd forced himself to make a sales call that he knew would take hours, anything to take his mind from the woman who had him by the balls—something no other woman had accomplished.

But no amount of time away from her seemed to make a difference. In fact, the situation had worsened. He had half a mind to grab her, push her face first onto the desk and plow into the tight heat that beckoned. Images of her soft body pliant underneath him threatened his sanity. The urge to take, claim and simply rut like an animal rode him with every second he'd been away from her. He'd finally come to the conclusion that there was no reason to deny himself another second.

She belonged to him. At least for now.

Ten minutes had passed since he'd stopped in her doorway, and she'd neither noticed nor moved other than to scribble something on the notebook beside her. Whatever she'd found on the computer screen enthralled her completely. While he was curious to see what she'd been up to so far today, his needs were priority. Time to find out what she'd worn underneath that skirt.

"Hello, beautiful."

She jumped when he spoke, scrambling to pull herself together. Her pencil fell to the floor, and she dropped from the chair to retrieve it. When she bent over her skirt rode up, practically revealing her ass. Thomas took advantage of the situation and moved quickly behind her. He slid his hands up her legs and over her bare, smooth bottom. Gabrielle froze at his touch; her breath hitched while his fingers wound their way to the lips of her now exposed pussy.

"Spread your legs," he ordered.

She panted, a cross between a sigh and moan, but she did as he asked and moved her knees, willingly giving him total access to her body.

"Such a good girl." His fingers traced along the soft folds before spreading her wide. "A nice pretty pink pussy that's getting wetter by the second. God, I've missed touching you." With this free hand, he speared her cunt with two fingers, closing his eyes as her heat surrounded him.

"Oh." Her moan incited him to push deeper. He rubbed gently against the tender walls inside, back and forth until her hips moved in tandem with his hand. To his delight, her moans grew loud with little thought to her surroundings.

"Oh Sir, I've missed you *so* much." The words were drawn and harsh as she moved her hips, encouraging him to finger fuck her nice and deep.

"And I've missed you, my beauty. So much so that my dick aches for you every minute." He needed to share his need with her. Her sweet words to him, the ones of desire and longing had not gone unheard, and she deserved to know that. Gabrielle's juices flowed around his fingers now as she pushed harder against him. He understood that urgent need to fuck all too well, which was all the more reason to draw this out. He smacked his hand hard against the creamy white expanse of her bottom, the resulting quiver rippling over his hand.

"You haven't forgotten that you can't come without permission, have you?"

Gabrielle whimpered. "No, Sir."

"Good, then later when you've proven how much you need it, we'll see about allowing for that." His fingers slid from her then, and he brought them to his mouth to taste. Amidst her whimpers of protest, her sweet and tart taste exploded across his senses.

"Aw, don't fret, sweetheart. We aren't finished." He gripped her waist and helped her to her feet. "But I don't quite think you're ready to put on a show here, and since your new coworker will be here any minute, I think we should take this somewhere a little more private, wouldn't you agree."

"Yes, Sir." Her voice quivered in response.

Thomas smoothed down her skirt, giving her clit a little pinch as he did and watched her mouth form a little O in surprise. "Oh baby, you have no idea what I have in store for you. I intend to take advantage of you at every opportunity I can until we're both worn out from it." He watched the red color of her blush creep up her face as she sucked in her lower lip. That shy, beautiful look made anything and everything about her worthwhile. It would be the look that got him through his days after he was forced to say goodbye to her. Which fortunately was not today.

With a few quick keystrokes, Thomas saved the data on Gabrielle's computer and powered it down. He paused while Gabby scooped up her notebook and dumped it in her purse, leaving her desk clear of her work. His thick fingers intertwined with her slim, dainty ones as he led her toward his office. Luckily, Deidre hadn't yet returned from lunch so they made it into his office without being seen. Not that he cared, but he didn't want that worry to interfere with Gabrielle's ability to enjoy her service this afternoon.

"Have you had lunch yet?"

"No, Sir, I've been wrapped up in going over the accounting figures for this year so far."

"Lucky for you, I ordered something to be brought to my private terrace." He pushed aside the heavy curtains in his office and revealed the French doors that lead out to his private patio. He pushed open the doors and ushered her outside.

"Wow, this is gorgeous. Good thing, I don't have something like this in my office or I'd never get anything done."

He laughed. "You have your personal oasis at home, I've seen it remember."

She turned and smiled, her eyes sparkling. "Yes, I remember well."

"But you might be right, because I don't think you have this." He led her into the covered alcove tucked around the corner and waved at the sumptuous bed before them.

"Oh. My. God. You have a bed out here." She leapt onto it landing on her bottom with a laugh. "This is positively decadent."

"Not as decadent as you lying there on top of it, teasing me with flashes of pussy and nipples." Automatically, her arms went to cross her breasts, and he grabbed her hands to stop her. "No, you never cover yourself from me. Do it again, and I'll paddle you."

With a look of barely controlled challenge, Gabrielle loosened her limbs and let them fall to her sides. Thomas leaned into her, pushing her back into a lying position where he quickly pinned her arms above her head. Without a word, he grabbed the cuff that was attached to the middle of the headboard, wrapped it around her wrists and quickly buckled it together before she could utter a protest.

When he glanced at her face, he was surprised to find her smiling shyly at him. "You're not afraid of being bound?"

"Nervous? Yes. Afraid? No."

"You don't have to be nervous. You're always safe with me. You only need to do as you're told and feel. Experience the pleasure without focusing on anything else. I intend to take good care of you this afternoon."

She nodded and sucked on that damn bottom lip again. Sitting next to her, he undid the buttons of her blouse one at a time, revealing more of her porcelain skin an inch at a time. With her top spread wide, her breasts beckoned to him with their dark nipples that had hardened to extended little points just begging to be touched.

Mine.

The incessant nagging in his head wasn't about to leave him alone until he claimed her. This close to giving in, an instinct inside him yelled at Thomas to back off. To not get emotional about this woman. For a second, the war going on inside him made him feel as if he'd lost his mind. Either way he went, things were bound to get messy. He'd have to save that issue for later. Right now, he had a woman bound to his bed, watching him with equal parts lust and hesitation. The second part he was damned determined to get rid of.

"Relax, my beauty. I've got you."

Leaning forward, Thomas captured an erect nipple between his teeth. Gabrielle gasped and arched underneath, a silent plea to continue. His girl was very eager for his touch, and he fucking loved it. He released her nipple and laved it generously with his tongue, soothing the erotic pain with pleasure. Her legs and hips twisted and bucked as he moved to the opposite breast to repeat the procedure.

"Lay still, Gabrielle, or I'll bind your legs as well."

She immediately stilled next to him, but the image of her legs spread wide and tied to the corners of the bed made his dick twitch. He loved nothing more than to see a willing submissive bound open in front of him, begging for more.

"Does that excite you? Being helpless in front me?"

"Yes!" she answered breathlessly.

His brow furrowed. With a quick pinch to an already sensitive nipple, he reminded her of her lapse.

"I mean, yes, Sir!"

"Better. I'll definitely keep that in mind." Thomas roamed his hands from her soft breasts to the edge of her skirt. For now, he had something else in mind. He abruptly stood from the bed and pulled on her skirt. He took his time, sliding the silk fabric down her smooth legs. When he glanced at her face, the pure unspoken lust shining there pulled at him to hurry.

With her clothes removed, he pressed her thighs apart and stroked the inside of her leg from her ankle to the sprinkling of hair that covered her sweet pussy. As pretty as her sex was now, tonight, he'd see that the hair was removed so when he fucked her it would be skin to skin without a single barrier to impede any of the exquisite sensations he planned to torture her with. A smile quirked at his lips as he moved his hands from her body to his pants, eager to remove his own confining clothes.

Gabby swallowed hard when Thomas peeled his shirt over his head. The dark hair spattered across his muscles beckoned to her. If she wasn't bound, she'd be pleading to touch him. To feel the sleek muscles of his chest and arms flex underneath her fingers. God, he drove her crazy just looking at his male perfection. His abs were flat and hard with a thin trail of curly hair that led into the waistband of his pants. Tanned muscular fingers deftly undid the button and zipper to whisk the fabric from his hips, leaving him naked with his gorgeous cock protruding from more of that soft dark hair she longed to touch.

Uncontrollable need rode up her body with a sudden desire to taste him, to wrap her lips around that hard steel and swallow as much of him as she could. On a bold move, she decided to ask.

"May I please suck your cock, Sir?"

Thomas's head jerked at her question, as did his erection. The look of surprise in his eyes secretly pleased her, but she schooled her face not to show it.

His right hand wrapped around the base of his cock and stroked up and down a few times until a pearly bead of pre-cum glistened from the small slit at the tip. "You want a taste of this, sweetheart?"

She nodded frantically. "Oh yes, Sir. More than anything."

He had no idea how her body ached and her pussy wept for him. Two days wasn't a long time, but to her, it had been an eternity that shifted something inside her. She'd never ached for something or someone so bad. At this point, begging wasn't out of the question. Whatever it took to connect them.

"Then that is what you shall have." He moved to the head of the bed and settled his body across her chest, one knee on each side of her shoulders until his dick hovered a mere few inches from her eager mouth. "Open wider."

Gabby did as asked and spread her lips as far as she could as he nudged the tip against them. Her tongue peeked out and swiped around the crown, gathering the moisture in a rather greedy and bold move. She groaned at the salty taste. There was something so wild and inherently male about him.

With only a few inches worked inside, he halted, giving her a chance to close around him and suck. "Damn woman."

His hips bucked against her, and he inched inside a little bit more. His cock pushed farther inside until he slowly pulled it back out to the tip. As she dragged her tongue across the crown, he hissed and plunged deep. His movements continued like that until he fucked her mouth in a nice and steady rhythm. Her eyes slid closed as she focused on pleasuring him and not the arousal flooding her pussy as she got more and more excited from each moan and groan he gave her when her tongue swiped against the sensitive underside.

Rough fingers caressed her cheek, and in the midst of all that lust and heat her heart cracked, letting Thomas in closer than she thought possible. His touch electrified her, spurring her to suckle harder. She was so wrapped up in pleasing Thomas that when a pair of hands touched her thighs, it took her several seconds to realize it wasn't Thomas.

Shocked, Gabby eyes flew open, and she tried to pull away from the cock filling her. Thomas must have sensed her unease, and to prevent her withdrawal, his hand tightened on the back of her neck and forced her to remain in place.

"Easy, Gabrielle," he answered softly. "Do you trust me?"

His movements had stilled, and she looked at him questioningly. It was hard for her to think when her heart beat painfully against her chest, and lust still sizzled through her veins. She didn't know who was touching her behind Thomas, but her pussy ached to be filled. Gabby fought with her head and her incessant need to know every move being made. Thomas expected her trust, and she couldn't bear the thought of disappointing him.

She moaned around him, letting the vibration ripple against his skin.

Thomas gasped. "You little witch. Guess I'll take that as an indication you don't want to stop."

Gabby shook her head slightly and let loose with her tongue again, stroking as much of his length she could manage. She had to trust him. They were in Thomas' private space where he had complete and total control. The time to take a chance was now or never.

When Thomas started moving again so did the hands on her thighs. They crept up her legs until they tickled the hair of her pussy. Wet hair she imagined. When those sneaky fingers curled into the hair and tugged, Gabby gasped at the intensity of it. For a fleeting moment, she thought of David and wondered if it could be him between her legs. *Yes, it had to be.* She focused on that thought and relaxed.

Until a warm tongue stroked fleetingly over her clit... Gabby bucked at the shot of lust that rushed between her thighs. Fiery flames licked over her skin, need and hunger overwhelming her with sensations. Her brain was unable to keep up with the task of sucking Thomas while someone ate her pussy. God, it had to be David. Only he and Thomas knew where her weaknesses lay and were guaranteed to push every button she had.

More pre-cum pulsed over her tongue as Thomas's movements quickened. His strokes were now short, fast thrusts giving her barely enough time to graze her teeth over the tip before he plunged again. When she cast a glance at Thomas, the need staring back at her pinned in place. The unspoken demand for her to continue settled in the taut lines of his face.

Two fingers breached her aching sex and pushed their way inside of her, stretching and filling her with one swift stroke. His tongue pushed and swiped against her tight bundle of nerves clit relentlessly. Sweat broke out across her skin as she fought against the pressure building inside her. She couldn't withstand much more.

As if reading her mind, Thomas warned her. "No coming. Not until he says so. Do you understand?"

Gabby stared back at him, an unwavering devotion welling inside her. Thomas understood the side of her that often frightened her, and he had no trouble making her face it at his command. Tears of relief burned at the back of her eyes.

She could do this; she was sure of it. Unable to answer or move her head she simply opened wider and took more of him inside her as he plundered her mouth completely.

"Oh fuck yes," Thomas groaned and thrust, tightening his fingers in her hair until the edge of erotic pain sent her once again racing to the edge. Forcing her focus on him, she thrashed her tongue across every ridge on the underside of his cock. His shaft pulsed and swelled in response.

Desperation blasted through her. She had to make him come before she lost control and broke the rules. Painful pleasure stretched through her as images of Thomas and David taunted her need. Thomas had to come. Now. Gabby scraped her teeth along his thick length. A long guttural groan sounded seconds before jets of semen blasted into her mouth, where she swallowed every drop.

Thomas eased his spent cock from her and fell forward catching himself on his hands. David had slowed his movements, allowing her to concentrate, and now with Thomas's flat brown nipples hovering above her, she reached up and bit him.

"Ow, you are a little witch today."

She didn't get a chance to respond before teeth grabbed onto her clit and a sharp stab of pain shot through her giving way to intensified pleasure all the way to her toes. A third finger slipped inside her nice and slow, more sensation than she could bear streaked across her body. Once again, her release began to build, and she struggled to move away from the mouth latched onto her pussy, determined to obey and fight her orgasm.

The edge was too close. "I...I can't stop it. Please...please, Sir, may I come?" she begged breathlessly.

"Yes, my beauty, you may." It was David who answered, giving her the permission she desperately sought. Tension spiraled through her torso as his fingers fucked in and out of her, creating a soft sucking sound.

Fingers grasped her nipples as Thomas returned to her side. "Come on, baby. Come for us. Let go and trust us to catch you."

She did trust them—she did. One final swipe across her clit and she lost it. Her hips bucked, splintering the tension and pleasure holding her taut. Fiery explosions went off in her body, and Thomas grasped her head.

"Look at me, Gabrielle. See me while you fill David's mouth with your sweet cum."

Her eyes fluttered open as wave after wave of pleasure washed over her.

"You belong to us. Do you agree?"

The intensity of his gaze overwhelmed her as she rode out the orgasm.

"Yes!"

David lashed across her clit with teeth and tongue until she whimpered at the sensitivity. Finally, he released her, sliding up her body as Thomas moved to give him room. In a split second, David sheathed his erection with a condom and hooked his arms under her knees, angling her hips upward for the perfect entry. With no hesitation, he plunged into her, filling and stretching her with every sweet inch of his erection.

Gabby pulled on her bindings, unaccustomed to not being free to grab and touch when she wanted. The two men together had unleashed something feral inside of her, and she bucked and fought like a wild animal. "Yes. Yes! Fuck me, David, please. Fuck me hard!"

His lips peeled back from his teeth, giving him a look that probably mirrored her own. His hips pistoned faster, thrusting his dick in and out of her. Rough. Intense.

"You're so goddamned tight and hot. Fuck!" David's head dipped and latched onto a nipple where he bit and tugged adding sweet pain to the ecstasy building between them.

"Yes. Yes," she screamed as she fucked him back. Pleasure engulfed her as her pussy squeezed around him, convulsing in a second even bigger release than the first. When she thought she would splinter in two, David moaned and came, filling her with more pleasure than any one woman had a right to.

Long minutes later, David released her legs and slid from her body just as Thomas approached her cuffed hands. Gabby watched David ease around to her side as Thomas made quick work of releasing her before settling against her opposite hip. Her arms ached from her struggles and each man took the time to massage her sore limbs and kiss the abraded skin at her wrists. She'd not even noticed how abused her skin had gotten during her struggles.

Gabby pressed her face to David's chest and slowly came back down to the here and now. Her entire body throbbed from the attention and pleasure they had given her. She wanted nothing more than sleep.

"You look drowsy. Guess you won't be up to any more accounting work today."

A few cylinders in Gabby's mind fired at Thomas's words. "Sure, if you just give me some more time to recover. Maybe even a nap?" That sounded like pure heaven at the moment.

"Take all the time you need. I won't be a slave driver…today."

Gabby smiled and relaxed into the surrounding heat of her two men. She'd happily submitted to them both, and they'd loved her well. What more could a girl ask for?

Chapter Thirteen

"Wake up, pretty girl. I have a present for you." Hands nudged her shoulder as Thomas's voice floated over her. She'd been having a wonderful dream about a bed on a terrace with her starring as the pleasure slave to two hard and handsome men. A dream from which she wasn't quite ready to wake up.

"We might have to start calling you lazy if you sleep all day, you know." David's mocking words seeped into her fuzzy brain as she struggled towards consciousness. Her eyes cracked open to the bright sunshine across the room, and her hand flew up to cover them.

"Can you close the blinds? That sun is too bright," she mumbled.

Rich laughter rumbled next to her as David laughed. "Kind of hard to block out the sun when you're outside my dear."

Gabby parted her fingers and looked upward to see that, yes indeed, they were lying outside. Memories flooded back as she realized she'd only been reliving a memory not a dream. She was in fact in a bed on a terrace, and both Thomas and David were lying next to her.

"How long did I sleep?" She struggled to sit, and thankfully, David helped her up. Her body felt leaden.

"You've been asleep for about three hours now."

"Really? Wow, I'm so sorry. You should have woken me up. I still have a lot of work to do." She scrambled to her knees so she could find her clothes and get dressed.

"That's not why we woke you. We have something more important to give you," Thomas murmured.

She remembered then. "You said something about a present."

"That's right."

She turned to face Thomas.

"Gabrielle, have you ever been collared before?" he asked.

Her stomach jolted and equal parts fear and joy leapt into her heart. They didn't mean what she thought they did, did they? *No way.*

"Um...no...I haven't," she stammered. She tried to hide the sudden fear from her voice and failed miserably.

Thomas grinned. "Don't be scared. And don't leap to any conclusions here. Let us explain."

Heat flooded her face as she blushed furiously at her assumptions. She'd thought for a fleeting second they wanted to collar her, something she knew better than to ever hope for.

"Tell me what you know about collaring. I'd like to know," Thomas prodded.

Gabby licked her lips before pulling the bottom one between her teeth. She didn't know all that much, but she'd envied submissives she'd seen wearing them. "I know that they're given as a commitment when a Dominant has chosen submissive to be his permanently."

"Yes, that's true. What else?"

"I'm...I'm not sure."

"Relax, Gabrielle. We aren't testing you." David rubbed her shoulders, loosening the muscles she'd drawn taut. "We're just looking to see how much you know."

"Have you ever heard of a training collar?" Thomas asked.

Gabby shook her head.

"A training collar is sometimes given to a submissive as a token of consideration. In a public setting, such as Sanctuary, it provides notice to other Dominants that you're taken, at least for now, and for some submissives, it's taken as a symbol that enhances their desire to serve while wearing a collar." Thomas brought his hands from behind his back and showed her a thin white collar he'd been hiding.

Gabby's eyes widened at the beauty and symbolism of that seemingly simple strip of leather that would mean so much to her. Tears welled in her eyes as David and Thomas moved to stand in front of her.

"Would you wear our training collar? Not only as a display to others that you're under our training, but as an acceptance and desire to serve us?" Thomas asked quietly.

A sob tore from her throat as she struggled to breathe. They'd caught her completely off guard. Not in her wildest dreams has she expected this.

"I-I don't know what to say."

"I know it's fast, Gabrielle, but we're both of the mind to take what we want and you're her." David grabbed her hand and pressed a quick kiss to her open palm.

She looked from one to the other as they waited for her answer. She didn't have the words to express the joy they'd given her or the fact that this gesture meant the world to her. She'd still been struggling with the fact of wanting two men the way she did. Did this mean they accepted that? That it really was okay for her to need them both?

"Yes, I would be happy to wear your collar." Tears slipped from her eyes, wetness tracking down her cheeks.

While Thomas maintained his firm expression, she saw David bite back a smile. Did they have any idea how David's playfulness and Thomas' intensity were the perfect combination?

"We need you on your knees, Gabrielle." While not exactly phrased as a demand, it carried the familiar tone that made her insides melt. Thomas' instructions always did that to her. Her obedience was never questioned, only assumed.

Gabby pushed from the bed while David grabbed a pillow and placed it on the ground in front of them. She'd have gladly knelt on the tiled floor of the terrace, but his extra attention to her well being only buoyed her decision.

She sank down at their feet and placed her trembling hands on her thighs. A few deep breaths later, she inclined her head to look at them.

Thomas held the collar closer. "The three crystals on the front were chosen to signify the three of us. With the pink stone in the middle and the two white standing by its side. While you wear this collar, you are ours to command and no one else's."

With that, his hands wrapped around her neck and snapped the collar in place. She now was theirs in training. More tears flowed as they each grabbed an arm and pulled her to feet.

"Don't cry, baby." David wiped the tears from her cheeks.

"I can't help it. This means so much to me." The leather band felt snug around her neck, and she couldn't wait to see how it looked.

Thomas took her mouth then in a hard and hungry kiss. His tongue delved inside, and she met him with her own. They tangled and dueled like that until she whimpered in pleasure. He certainly knew how to kiss her senseless.

Pulling back, he made room for David to seal the deal in his own way. But instead of kissing her mouth like she expected, he went for her neck. He kissed the collar and bit at the skin just below it. Her breath hitched in her throat when his mouth traveled lower to nip at her breast.

"You have the most beautiful breasts, Gabrielle. Rich, dark nipples that stand up and beg to be plucked and pinched. I think I'll get you some nice clamps today."

Her clit throbbed at his words as she leaned into his mouth, eager for him to continue.

"No, not right now. Thomas is expecting some members to stop by shortly so unless you want to spend your first collared night on exhibition, I suggest we stop now and get you dressed.

Gabby squeaked and darted around the terrace searching for her clothes as both Thomas and David laughed at her. Both her skirt and blouse had been tossed onto the chair at the foot of the bed and were now a wrinkled mess. Anyone who saw her would know exactly what she'd been doing this afternoon.

"There's a bathroom in my office if you want to freshen up." Thomas pointed to the open doors at the far end of the terrace, and she took off in a huff to get through them. The last thing she heard before closing the bathroom door was their laughter. Even though it was slightly at her expense, their happiness made her heart bloom.

* * * *

"She's quite a woman."

Thomas turned to his friend, catching the glint in his eye and innuendo in his voice. "Yes, she is." He walked into his office slowly, reluctant to leave their afternoon behind. She'd been everything he expected and more.

"So, I know why I wanted to see her collared. What's your excuse?" David poked at him when Thomas didn't want to be poked. He was afraid to look too closely at his decision before it bit him in the ass.

"She's going to be spending time here at Sanctuary. It's only a matter of time before other Dom's get a whiff of her, and they'll be interested. This way they know she's not available."

"So it was just all about marking your training territory and nothing else?" David moved to one of the leather chairs in front of Thomas' desk and took a seat.

He didn't look as if he was going anywhere.

"Don't you have work to get back to? We've managed to kill most of the day." Thomas clicked a few buttons on his computer and booted up his email account.

"Nope. Told everyone I would be out of commission for the rest of the day and that I'd see them tomorrow. So I'm free until then."

Thomas looked at the smirk on his friend's face and shook his head. "Why are you pushing me on this right now?"

"Just curious is all. I've never seen you get this serious about a sub, and I can't help but wonder how far you're willing to take this."

"Are you asking me if I plan to collar her permanently?" Might as well get David to the point.

"Maybe."

"Worried?"

"Smart ass."

"Well, if you don't really want to know then you shouldn't ask the question." When Thomas' email popped up he focused his attention there, letting the conversation between him and David wither. He quickly scanned the unread messages until one caught his eye.

"Fuck." Thomas's fist landed on the desk next to the computer.

"What is it?"

"More proof." He rubbed his forehead and contemplated his next move.

"Proof of what?" David sat up his tone sharp. The security specialist had kicked in.

"The guy you loaned me for that private matter ..."

"Yeah?"

"He just sent me a message to tell me that the man I had him watching is about to skip town."

David stood and paced around the desk. "Who was it?"

"My accountant." His fingers pushed through his hair, tugging on the strands.

"Shit." David paused, a look of concentration on his face. "You want me to send someone to stop him?"

Thomas considered the offer. He didn't yet have the proof he needed. Although he knew. "I was going to wait and see if Gabrielle confirmed my theory."

"Gabrielle did." Her voice startled them both as she walked into the room from the bathroom. For a second, he'd been so distracted he'd forgotten she was still in there.

"What are you talking about?" Thomas noticed Gabrielle had managed to put herself together and looked even sexier than before if that was possible. Her silk blouse had covered her tits but the nipples still pressed against the fabric, straining the see through material.

"I was working on some notes when you came in earlier and wanted to tell you sooner, but we got a little sidetracked."

"I'd say," David agreed.

Unconsciously her hand went to her neck to touch the collar wrapped there.

Thomas' cock thickened and pushed against his zipper at the image she presented. It had been so long since he'd put a collar on a submissive he'd forgotten how good it felt. Now, he just needed to figure out how to get the blood back to his head so he could think straight around her. Out of the corner of his eye, he saw David staring between them, a mocking curiosity written all over his face.

"So tell me now. You've got my full attention." Thomas clicked off the computer and eased back in his chair. Might as well get comfortable since something told him he wasn't going to like what she had to say.

"Well, about three hours into my review I started noticing anomalies. Entries that seemed off and eventually began to unbalance themselves. Honestly, it was the sloppiest sort of bookkeeping that I've seen in a long time. Whatever he's been doing around here, he wasn't even trying to hide it very well. The deposits and the records of cash intake on your busy nights never match up."

A red haze of rage began to cloud Thomas's mind as his worst fears were confirmed. He'd given his trust to his accountant despite the instincts telling him not to. Hell, the man had been a friend for more than two decades. Thomas wanted to lash out and punish someone for letting this happen. But the only two people sitting here had nothing to do with the crime.

"How much?"

Gabrielle hesitated, a look of reluctance on her face. "I haven't finished even the first twelve months of review yet."

Thomas pushed his fingers through his hair and blew out a harsh breath. "Fine, fine. How much so far?"

"In the neighborhood of two hundred and fifty thousand dollars."

David whistled from across the desk, and Thomas tamped down his anger before he started taking it out of the hides around him. A Dominant was expected to have control of himself at all times, especially when around a submissive. But this kind of betrayal tested his limits.

"On that note. With your permission, I'd like to put in a couple more hours this afternoon on the financials."

"Certainly."

She turned toward the door and headed out.

"But Gabrielle…"

She stopped.

"I want you at my house tonight and every night after that. So after work, let David take you home to get what you need for the next couple of days then I'll meet the two of you at home for a late dinner. Don't worry about your car. Leave your keys with Deidre, and we'll make sure someone delivers it to my house."

Her back went ramrod straight, and her face clouded. Thomas definitely got the impression she wanted to say something. Fortunately for them all, after a few long seconds, she murmured, "Yes, Sir."

He watched her until she'd sashayed her curvy butt out of his sight before turning back to David. His hand raised.. "I don't want to hear it."

"Relax, Thomas. I know when to hold my tongue. I was only going to offer to help in any way that I can. I'm sure my guy can track him down. If he was that sloppy with his paperwork here, then I doubt he bothered to do a great job in covering his trail in the real world."

Thomas nodded. "You're probably right, and I do want the little bastard picked up. It's not even the money that's the issue as much as him pulling this kind of shit against me."

"Little shit must be crazy, or maybe, he has a death wish."

Thomas sharpened his gaze on David. He didn't want to discuss it anymore.

"Just find him." He turned his back to David at the wet bar and poured two fingers of scotch. He deserved them. "I'll see you tonight with Gabrielle."

Thankfully, David got the message and slipped quietly from the office, closing the door behind him. There were calls to be made and work that wouldn't wait. He would have a naked submissive waiting for him at home, and he couldn't wait.

* * * *

Two and half hours later, David pulled open the employee entrance to Sanctuary. Frustration boiled through him as he sucked in a breath of the chilled air inside. His security team had lost track of the accountant, and so far, no leads had been found. Now, he had to give Thomas a status update, and he didn't relish telling him they had no new information. When he made his way back to the offices, he found the outer room empty and quiet. Deidre's desk looked clean and organized as if she'd already left for the day and Thomas' door was closed, a foreboding barrier.

One door stood open though, the accounting office. He moved past Thomas' office to go and check on Gabrielle first. Their afternoon had been intense as well as meaningful, and he wanted to see how she was doing. Not to mention seeing her might improve his foul mood—at least, he hoped so.

"Hey, pretty lady." David propped his shoulder on the doorframe and drank in the sight of her. A huge grin formed on her face when she spied him. His dick stood up and took notice of it, not to mention the sight of the collar around her neck. What a difference a little white strip of leather made.

"Hey, yourself." She jumped from her chair, running over to him. "Your timing is perfect. I've had about all the numbers I can take for one day. After a while, they all start running together." Her arms wrapped around his neck, and her breasts rubbed against his chest. The thin silk shirt did little to cover the hard points of her nipples as they poked against him.

David bit back a groan as he wrapped his arms around her waist. He loved the way she fit against him, and right now, in his mood, if she had been naked, they would be fucking.

"I need to talk to Thomas before we can leave."

Gabrielle shook her head. "You can't. He left strict instructions with Deidre that he did not want to be disturbed at all under any circumstances. She said if you got here before Thomas came out then we're supposed to go on home and he would be along later."

He didn't really want to leave before speaking to Thomas. But damn if that's what the man wished then he might as well let it go and spend some quality time with a submissive that he couldn't get off of his mind.

"Well, all right then, darling. How about you and I grab some of your things and see if we can't find something to do to keep us occupied until he makes it home?" David winked at her before throwing his arm over her shoulder and ushering her from the room.

"So tell me, my sweet new submissive, what kind of takeout food is your favorite? I think tonight calls for a little celebration, wouldn't you say?"

"A celebration?"

David reached up and tapped on the slim leather collar she still wore even as they were headed out.

"Of course. I'm sorry. In the excitement of the accounting issues I wasn't focusing." She fiddled with the edges of the leather.

David pushed open the door leading to the parking lot and ushered Gabrielle outside. "You know you don't have to wear that in public if you aren't comfortable. It's important at home and especially important while you're in Sanctuary, but not everyone is so accepting of our lifestyle out here."

"I don't want to take it off," she uttered quietly.

"You don't have to. I just wanted you to know that neither Thomas nor I want to interfere with your vanilla life."

"You don't know how long I've wanted this. For a collar to be placed around my neck. I never expected... It's almost indescribable the feeling of security and connection I feel from it."

He nodded. "Not altogether different from the feeling I get seeing it around your neck and knowing that while officially you don't belong to us yet, you're ours and ours alone. It's a heady feeling and new for me as well."

They had stopped next to the car mere inches apart, and David swore he felt the heat radiating from her body. When her fingers reached up and traced down his cheek, his stomach muscles tightened at the swift river of need that swept through him. The feather light touch seemed simple enough, but the liquid look of lust in her eyes was more than enough to set his body on fire. His dick swelled and strained for freedom.

Her upturned nose and lush mouth begged for the taking. Something he couldn't resist. Besides, why should he? With her height, he had to bend down a few inches, but it was worth the look in her eyes when he nipped at her lower lip with his teeth.

Her mouth opened on a sigh as he wrapped himself around her and pulled her close. He loved the sensation of her sweet body pressed against him as his tongue delved between her lips, seeking the heat he knew he would find there. For a moment, time stood still and the worries of his day fell from his shoulders as he sought comfort in her submission, in her willingness to serve and his need to protect and care her. This is exactly what is was all about. He understood so much more now. It was easy enough for Thomas to tell him, but learning from a woman like her— so different. The need between went both ways and melded perfectly.

When his tongue rubbed against hers, she parried back with her own fervent desire, taking control of her response. He threaded his hand through her hair and pulled her head back and off his mouth. "Damn, woman. Do you have any idea what you do to me?"

She whimpered in response, her eyes soft with lust. David crushed against her lips, harder more urgent this time. The way his dick pulsed and throbbed in his slacks, he had half a mind to bend her over the hood of his car and fuck her right here, with little thought as to who might be watching. The image of her belly down on the shiny metal with her skirt lifted above that fine spankable ass nearly undid his tightly held control.

He released her suddenly and growled, "Get in the car."

His words came out harsher than he'd intended, but he was doing the best he could to maintain some semblance of control on himself.

Her breath caught. "I'm sorry, I didn't mean to—"

"No Gabrielle, don't go there. You did nothing wrong. But if we don't leave now, you'll find yourself face down on the car with a dick inside you."

Her mouth formed a surprised O, and her eyes went wide.

"That's right babe, you've got me rock hard and aching for a fast fuck, so let's go before you get a new lesson in humiliation."

A wicked smile flashed across her face before she hustled around the car. She grabbed the handle and waited for him to unlock the car. "I'm aching for you, too, Sir."

Chapter Fourteen

Thomas watched David and Gabrielle from the security screen on his computer. He'd heard them leave, and his curiosity had gotten the better of him. His afternoon had been tied up in conference calls and thoughts of his friend's betrayal. It didn't negate the experience of the lunchtime scene he'd indulged in, but it did mess with his head. It had been his idea to give Gabrielle the collar to protect her from other Dominants while in Sanctuary, but somehow, the actual giving it to her had morphed into something more.

How quickly things got complicated. When David had kissed her in the parking lot, Thomas' dick had leapt to life. The urgency in his friend and Gabrielle's obvious sweet, sweet compliance got to him every time. From the first moment he'd met her, he'd recognized that something special in her, a sort of jaded innocence that called to him. He'd had no power to resist her then, and now that his plan to push them together was going as smoothly as he'd expected, he was feeling a pang of regret.

Maybe, he needed to slow down his plan and take some time to savor the relationship the three of them were building. It would end sooner or later, but either way, it would suck. Thomas shook his head. No, this wasn't a relationship. It was three people finding their way through a lifestyle that set them apart. An exploration of their sexuality that delved deeper than it probably should. He couldn't help it. The need to peel the layers back from Gabrielle and see to the heart of her mental and physical needs drove him. Instead of wanting more, he should be pleased with the connection between David and Gabrielle and working to exploit it.

He stared closer at the screen, watching Gabrielle's body language. There was no doubt submission suited her. But something was still missing. He studied her hooded eyes. Recognized the heat, loved the aching arousal. Now, he needed to discover what waited beneath the obvious. Patience and perseverance always won out. He'd discover it soon enough then he'd earn her complete and total surrender once and for all.

Thomas turned off the security monitor and flipped open his email. He had to get his mind off his new submissive and back on the work at hand. He had a missing accountant with a substantial amount of his money and some new groups clamoring to move into Sanctuary. By the time he made it home tonight, he would need some stress relief, and he had a pretty good idea of who would serve that need.

Wicked thoughts of Gabrielle on her back, spread eagle with her wrists and ankles bound, having her pain threshold tested gave him just the boost he needed to hurry up and get this work done and his ass home.

* * * *

After a quick stop at her place for some of her things, they'd arrived at Thomas's house in time to meet the Chinese food deliveryman. While they ate, David received a call on his cell phone and disappeared into the other room. Gabby settled into the kitchen and savored her favorite meal of beef lo mein and springrolls. In the peace and quiet, her thoughts wandered to Thomas. She looked forward to his arrival and the mysterious plans he and David had for her tonight.

She shivered in anticipation. How they would top this afternoon she had no idea, but she trusted Thomas to take them all where they needed to go. Just being in his kitchen again reminded her of the last time she'd been here and the delicious things they'd done.

She set down her food as her appetite for food disappeared, quickly replaced with renewed desire. After this afternoon, she wanted more of them. It still seemed a little wrong to want two men in bed with her, but she wanted to work through that hang up. If she cared for both men and everyone was on the same page, it shouldn't be a bad thing at all.

"Sorry about that. Thomas needed some information from me, and he had a few instructions to pass on." David entered the kitchen and took a seat across from her.

Gabby noticed the amusement in his voice as he spoke the last part, and that same shiver snaked down her back again. They were definitely up to something.

"It's not a problem. I'm finished here anyway so I'll just get everything cleaned up while you eat."

David grabbed her hand. "I'm not hungry for food anymore, either." He pulled her up from the chair and into his arms, holding her. "Let's hurry up and take care of this mess, and I'll show you exactly what I'm thinking about."

Gabby grinned. "Yes, Sir."

She moved quickly around the kitchen, disposing of the trash and washing the few dishes they'd dirtied. In less than ten minutes, she'd finished and turned to find David propped against the island, watching her.

"What's wrong?"

"Nothing at all. Just wondering if you have any idea how much I love your body." He shifted then, moved toward her. "You forgot something."

Gabby turned and searched the room for anything she'd left behind in her cleanup efforts.

"No, Gabrielle, not in the kitchen. I'm talking about you. Something you were supposed to do. One of the first instructions you were given."

She had no idea what the hell he was talking about as she racked her brain for the answer.

"The house rule, Gabrielle."

Oh my God. Thomas had established only one rule for her anytime she was in residence here. No clothes.

"I forgot all about it." Her hands flew to her blouse and quickly stripped it off, followed by the skirt covering her ample hips. Cool air brushed against her skin, and her nipples puckered tightly. "I guess since Thomas isn't here, I just didn't think about it."

"I see. So if Thomas isn't around, you don't want to follow rules or obey?"

Gabby saw a storm brewing in his eyes.

"No, Sir. Of course not. I truly wasn't thinking." She stood there naked as the day she'd been born under his hard gaze as he looked her up and down. Despite the slight tremble of her legs, her sex heated, readying her for anything he desired.

"I'm not sure I believe you. You might have to show me instead of just telling me." The words sounded harsh, but his eyes had softened.

"For you, Sir, anything." She just hoped whatever he had in mind she could actually handle.

"First things first. Thomas called with explicit instructions for you tonight. He wants our pussy clean and smooth and free of hair before he gets home, and I'm here to make sure that gets done."

Her clit pulsed at his words. It had been a while since she'd bothered, and she'd be more than happy to do it again. It was a lovely feeling. A smooth pussy made her so slick and masturbation even more fun than usual.

"I'll go and take care of that right now, Sir." She moved toward the door and David's arm swung out hooking her around the waist. He dragged her against his body and ground his erection against her backside. Rational thought cleared her mind as the soft fabric of his pants rubbed against her skin, ratcheting her desire to a dangerous level, the level where she'd do just about anything to get him to fuck her.

"No way, young lady. Not that easy." He dug his cock between her cheeks one more time then hoisted her into his arms. "You are going to shave, but we're doing this my way. Understood?"

God, that gruff demanding voice would definitely be her undoing. She suspected long before the night was over, she'd be begging for relief. "Yes...yes, Sir," she stammered.

He carried her to the master bathroom and set her down on the edge of the giant whirlpool tub that was more than big enough for two.

"Go ahead and do what you have to do to get ready, and I'll be back in a few minutes. Do not touch that pussy until I tell you to."

Gabby shivered. "Yes, Sir."

After he left the room, she fidgeted with the water and searched through Thomas's cabinets for shaving supplies. In the medicine cabinet, she hit pay dirt with not only some shaving oil but several different kinds of razors. She'd never done this in front of someone, and just the thought of it sent another chill down her spine. She grabbed the handheld mirror as well and got back into place on the edge of the tub.

Jitters fluttered through her stomach as she anticipated what would happen. It seemed unusual for a man to want to watch her take care of such a basic need, this was definitely new territory for her.

First, she'd forgotten Thomas's house rule, and now, she found herself in his bathroom about to shave herself while another man watched. In any other situation, this would have been surreal. For her, this represented everything she'd dreamed and longed about for years. As a submissive, there would be hard times and good, fun and not so fun, none of that changed her need to serve and her need to belong. She had to trust in her men to make the right decisions, to know how to take care of her and allow her to fulfill their needs as well.

Tears welled in her eyes, and her fingers brushed them away as quickly as they formed. She didn't want David to get the wrong idea about how she felt right now. Her emotions were too close to the surface. How long could she hide them? What did they mean? After years in a stifling marriage, she'd just wanted her freedom. Developing feelings for two men had never been part of her plan.

Gabby dipped her toes into the water, splashing some of the heated water onto her legs.

"Are you ready?" David's voice startled her from her thoughts, reminding her why she was here.

"Yes, Sir." She eased her lower body into the water long enough to moisten her skin, the first step in preparation for the removal of her pubic hair. She thought to reach down and touch but remembered David's warning not to touch herself without his permission.

"Hop up here and get comfortable. I want to watch, and I need a good view." He indicated the back end of the tub where there was a ledge more than large enough for her to sit and dangle her legs. Gabby moved in position keeping her legs pressed together until the last possible moment.

David's brow cocked as he looked pointedly at the tops of her thighs. Without another word, she knew what to do. Gabby spread her legs, revealing her pussy one inch at a time. The intensity of his gaze while he watched every movement made her tremble with nerves.

"Relax, Gabrielle. You don't need to be nervous with me. I love your body." His words soothed her, comforting her until she found herself open and relaxed under his observation. "There you go, baby. There's nothing to be afraid of with me. You're safe, and we have plenty of time."

Did that mean Thomas wouldn't be joining them tonight? She hoped not. It would mean the world to her to have both of them with her. David didn't take his gaze away from her for a minute, and in no time, her pussy became slick with desire. Her two Doms had a habit of making her wet in a New York minute.

The more time passed, the more comfortable she became. It was about as ready as she was going to get. She scooped up the shaving oil from the tub ledge and squeezed a generous amount into her hand. If he wanted a show then she would give him one. She placed her left foot on the rim of one side of the tub then slowly repeated with her right foot to the opposite side, stretching her legs wide, bringing the glistening lips of her pussy into David's view.

"I'd like to begin now, Sir, if I have your permission."

David licked his lips and nodded his consent.

Gabby touched the cool oil to her skin, lubricating the area she would shave. Once or twice her fingers strayed to her clit, glancing across it before David could tell her to stop. Each touch sent a shiver of thrill down her spine, enough pleasure to get her juices flowing and her muscles clenching.

She had a job at hand, but she couldn't deny her body ached to be filled, and his deep blue gaze watching her every move fed into that need.

When every spot slicked up she swished her hand back and forth in the tub a few times to wash away the remnants of the oil. Gabby stared at David as she reached for her razor, not wanting to lose eye contact. Her body hummed with a forceful need that begged for his touch. For a few seconds, her hand hovered over the curly hairs covering her sex until David swallowed and spoke.

"What are you waiting for, Gabrielle? Do you not want to shave it?"

"That's not it at all. I love the look and feel of a bare pussy. I-I'm just…"

"Just what? Nervous? Scared? Needy?"

"Yes," she breathed. *All of the above.* It blew her mind how far she'd come so fast.

"Do it now." His demand did not come out harsh but, instead, firm and throaty, almost like a growl. She suspected that he, too, had desires that needed to be fulfilled. She swiped the first path on the right side then the next, watching him as she rinsed. His eyes darkened, and a few times his tongue swiped at his lips. Cool air brushed across her skin as the hair disappeared and smooth, baby soft skin appeared.

Every time she caught his gaze, her muscles quivered and blood rushed to her clit until every accidental touch made her gasp or cry out. When the last of the hair had been removed, she returned the razor to the edge of the tub and sat waiting for David's instruction. Her body whined and throbbed for a touch on all her sensitive spots until she screamed in release, but David had yet to give her permission. She waited.

With her legs trembling and tears threatening, he finally moved, reaching into the bag at his feet and moving toward her.

"Your pretty little pussy is wet and aching, isn't it?"

Gabby nodded. She was afraid that if she tried to speak the only sound that would come out would be a sob. Her body betrayed her with every passing second as she sat motionless, waiting.

"Show me."

Gabby used her fingers to spread her lips wide, opening herself even farther to his intense perusal. She should be embarrassed to be watched this closely, but she felt nothing but gut deep arousal.

"And what is it that you need?"

"I need you." Her lip trembled.

"You need me to do what?"

"To...to fuck me," she managed on a harsh whisper before casting her eyes downward.

"Details, Gabrielle. I want details from you. If you tell me exactly what you need, I might consider giving it to you." He moved closer until he stood almost parallel to her body with his crotch merely a foot from her face.

She licked at her lips as she stared at the erection tenting his loose slacks. He did need her as much as she needed him. That information gave her the courage to say what he wanted to hear.

"I need you inside me, Sir. My cunt aches because it's empty. Please fill me."

He smiled. "That's more like it." His hand eased from his duffel, and her eyes widened when she saw the vibrator he held. Not exactly what she had in mind, but anything that would ease the ache driving her mad would work at this point.

"Open your mouth."

She opened, and he placed the vibrator inside.

"Hold it there for me please."

She wrapped her lips around it as he let go and stood back, peeling the clothes from his body. God, she loved watching him do that. Sinewy muscle, flat abs and thighs that would make any woman writhe. When his cock sprang free, she moaned around the toy as more of her juices trickled across her fingers. Her arms trembled with the want to pull him to her—something strictly forbidden without permission.

David climbed into the bath and stood between her legs, his cock mere inches from her weeping pussy. His hand grabbed the end of the toy. "Suck it, baby. Show me how you good you would suck my cock. Convince me you want it."

He pushed the penis-shaped vibrator farther into her mouth until her gag reflex kicked in. Her cheeks hollowed as she sucked on it as hard as she could, even swirling her tongue around the tip until he pulled it back a few inches.

His hand thrust forward and the majority of its length pushed into her mouth. "Come on, sweetheart. I'm not feeling convinced." He pushed and pulled, fucking her mouth until she whimpered around it. Unthinking, her fingers reached for her clit to be smacked away by his hand.

"Do that again, and you'll get a whipping and no cock tonight." He pulled the vibrator away, and she gasped for breath.

"I'm...I'm so sorry, Sir. I wasn't thinking. Please, Sir. Please forgive me."

David stood back and studied her carefully. Tears welled in her eyes as she fought them from falling. Gabby wasn't sure how she could bear it if he sent her to bed like this. Or if he disciplined—

Lips descended on hers in a crushing kiss. Teeth bit at her lips until she opened for him, and his tongue plundered inside. Definitely not the sweet slow kiss she was accustomed to. Oh no, this was a claiming through and through.

Unable to control her reaction, Gabby moaned into his mouth wanting so much more. A sharp gasp sounded from her throat when the cool touch of the vibrator rubbed against her soaking wet slit, parting her folds, rubbing against sensitive nerve endings as he rimmed her hole before pushing it inside.

The breath whooshed from her lungs as pleasure arrowed through her. Gabby's head lolled, and her eyes rolled back in her head. The heady sensation of fingers stroking her newly shaven skin was almost too much to bear.

"You feel incredible. So soft and soaking wet."

Gabby stared into David's eyes as he continued to fill her, splitting her wide, stretching her. The length was more than she was accustomed to and even a little uncomfortable, but the pleasure streaking through her was undeniable. David's eyes never wavered from her face. The sensations were so intense she was forced to take short, shallow breaths as she struggled to get air into her lungs.

"That's it, baby. Such a good girl." David pushed the last of it inside and paused, letting her adjust around the toy. Her muscles clenched and ached, and she needed him to move. Gabby attempted to roll her hips forward, but her position prevented that. David watched her struggles, giving her no instructions or permissions until she thought she couldn't take it anymore.

His hand twisted the knob at the end, and a humming vibration erupted inside her. Shards of sensation splintered through her as an unbidden orgasm broke free and she had no hope of stopping it. A strangled scream tore from her throat as her body shook with the force. The whole time David never stopped watching her face, taking in every gasp and move she made.

"I'm so sorry." She tried to speak through her release but found it hard to talk when she couldn't breathe. Especially not with the vibrations drawing out the pleasure.

"Eyes on me," he demanded. "Just go with it, sweetheart. Stop trying to fight it, and just go with it."

With his spoken permission, she relaxed and the next orgasm crashed onto the heels of the first. This time, David moved the toy in and out of her sucking pussy.

When the second release faded into aftershocks, Gabby slumped forward, her head crashing against the taut muscles of David's chest as he continued to pump the pleasure from her. Every nerve ending she possessed had become over sensitized to the point she found herself torn between pleasure and pain, unable to go on.

"Please, please, David. It's too much," she whimpered.

"Good, then you're just about ready for what comes next."

Gabby eyed him warily as he pulled the dildo from her sex. What the hell did that mean?

David watched Gabrielle's eyes grow wide with great satisfaction. She had the most responsive body, so much so that he couldn't wait to do more. He wanted to push her farther, test her limits. Damn, she was beautiful. Not just physically, although there was plenty of that. No, it was her inner emotional response that made her perfect for him. His submissive beauty.

Her ability to let go and trust him to keep her safe and give her pleasure stole his breath. He wanted to yell from the rooftop. Something he didn't quite understand stirred in his chest, changing their relationship. She'd accepted their training collar and shown her desire to submit to both men, but neither he nor Thomas had pushed her as hard as they needed to. The full force of their need was still to come.

Gabrielle's nails bit into his arm as her body began its slow descent back to normal. Her gasping shallow breaths took on a more even cadence. David tossed the toy to the side and focused on the woman in front of him. He had to get inside her.

David grabbed at the bag on the floor and fished a condom from within, quickly tearing at the foil and rolling it along his swollen shaft. With a quick twist of her waist, he had Gabby flipped and facing away from him. The ledge behind the tub gave her plenty of leverage as she stood eager, wet and ready for his pleasure.

David spread the cheeks of her ass, admiring the tight puckered hole. His dick ached to squeeze into that tiny, sensitive channel, but he wasn't sure either of them was ready for that. His patience had worn too thin at the moment to prepare her for that. Instead, he prodded at the slick, swollen flesh of her labia, dipping two fingers inside. Her heated walls clutched at his fingers, eliciting a groan from his throat.

Gabrielle's loud moan filled the room as she pushed back against him in an obvious attempt for more and broke the last tendrils of his control. With a decided lack of finesse, David withdrew his fingers and grasped tightly to the flesh of her hips, pushing his cock into her in one rough thrust. Fuck. Her heated pussy was so damn wet and juicy he wanted to come then. She pushed back again, attempting to move, but he held her tight against him, letting his balls rest snug against her sopping flesh.

"Dammit, babe!" He'd wanted to regain control and fuck her nice and slow, but the familiar tingling crept up his spine and pushed past his resistance. David quickly withdrew to the tip, pausing for a brief moment before tunneling back inside.

"Oh god yes, David, please. Harder!" Gabrielle's body convulsed against him as she too had no control over her own orgasm. It was his and his alone.

"Come, Gabrielle. Come all over me, baby. Fuck me."

She screamed into the room, guttural sounds, as he thrust faster and deep inside, his fingers digging into her hips. Each stroke heated the sensitive nerve endings between them, searing until the blistering friction exploded from his cock. She was killing him with the pleasure. It hit him then. Beyond the pleasure, beyond the submission and dominance, this woman was his. He didn't want to wake up tomorrow or any day after that and not have her in his bed.

In what could have been seconds or minutes later, he couldn't remember, his body quit convulsing and he collapsed against her. Careful not to hurt her, he braced his weight on his arms and listened to her harsh breathing as he laid his cheek against the sweet curve of her back.

David closed his eyes and breathed in her scent. The smell of their sex mingled with her lighter, sweet fragrance. It would forever be seared into his memory along with this moment. He wouldn't let her go, and he would have to tell Thomas as soon as he could. Underneath him lay the perfect woman.

Back under a semblance of control, David eased from her body and stepped from the tub then quickly disposed of the condom. Not wanting to leave her for long, he rushed back to the tub to finally notice they'd dislodged the plug and the water had drained. He opened the faucets and let the tub refill before gently lowering her into the warm water. David grabbed for the soap and cloth.

The dazed look on her face fed into his need to take care of her, to cherish not only her body but her loving nature. God, he loved the way she responded when either he or Thomas pushed her limits. Amazingly, he felt his cock stir again. Thinking about what Thomas had up his sleeve for the rest of the night would have him rock hard and ready again if he wasn't careful. He needed to pace himself.

Not to mention the discipline she had coming for her earlier transgression. That round ass would look perfect when she was tied down and a flogger or a whip pinkened the flesh. Damn. So much for trying to keep his erection under control. Thomas would see him coming a mile away.

Gabrielle's eyes had slid shut, but when David stroked the soapy cloth from her ankle to the freshly shaven skin of her pussy, little mewls of pleasure whimpered from her lips. David gentled his touch not wanting the cloth to abrade her creamy skin; he'd save that for later when she was primed and begging for it.

His fingers toyed with her plump folds until he pressed her clit, and her eyes flew open and her gaze locked with his. Color flushed the skin traveling from her neck to her face.

"Why are you blushing, baby. Isn't it a little late for that now?"

Her shoulders lifted a fraction as her teeth grabbed onto her bottom lips and sucked it inside of her mouth. It was the perfect combination of innocence and sexy kitten.

"Are you embarrassed over what we did?"

"No. Just feeling a little shy now, I guess."

David laughed at the incongruity of that statement. One minute, she had been the perfect slut, and now as he bathed her, she reminded him of a sweet little girl. His girl. David sighed and finished quickly with his task. Thomas would be home soon, and he wanted her primed and ready. Which meant David needed to quit thinking about how she made him feel inside. It should have been easier than this to keep his feelings out of it. David dried them both with warm bath sheets, admiring every inch of Gabby's body as he did. From the rosy red nipples atop fantastic tits to the swell of her hips and generous ass. God, she really did have the perfect behind.

When he lifted her, she wrapped her arms around his neck and buried her face in his shoulder. More of those protective instincts he carried with him roared forward as he carried her into the master bedroom.

"Thomas is going to be here any minute, and I'm going to have to tell him everything. Not only how good you were but also how easily you forgot his rule."

Her mouth drew into a tight line. "I know, David. I expected nothing less."

"You've earned a punishment. Are you ready for that?"

She didn't smile, but her eyes sparkled with anticipation.

He laughed and swatted at her bottom as he tossed her onto the bed. "You are a very bad girl, and one who probably shouldn't be excited about discipline. I doubt very much it will be all fun and games for you, my dear."

"Yes, David, I know, but I can't help it. You've got me feeling really good and I'm happy here. Knowing and trusting the two of you to take care of me means more than you could know."

"We aren't done you know."

She looked at him quizzically.

"Thomas left me explicit instructions about what he wanted and removing the hair on your pussy was just the first step." Hell, he couldn't wait for what came next. She had the perfect body to bind and he couldn't wait to see the lovely shades of pink and red her body would produce. "Lie on the bed."

Gabrielle scrambled on top of the covers, stretched out flat on her back with her hair fanned across her pillow. With her lush and naked form, she reminded him of a Greek goddess offering herself up for pleasure and the most incredible sight he'd seen in a long damn time.

David grabbed the first wrist cuff attached to the headboard. "Give me your arm." Without a second of hesitation, she complied, lying still as he wrapped the leather band around her slim wrist, buckling it closed. "Do you enjoy being restrained?"

"Yes." Her whispered answer tickled his senses.

"It doesn't frighten you?"

"A little."

"Good, I'd be more worried if you weren't at least a little nervous tonight. It is all about trust after all. Trusting in us to give you what you need, not just what you want." Once he got the second wrist bound, he moved on to her ankles. "Spread your legs nice and wide for me, baby." When she complied, he had to bite back a groan. The graceful way she moved and opened herself up made him want to dive right in. The second he saw the pink flesh of that bare pussy he could practically taste her on his tongue. Damn, he had it bad.

"Like this?" The seductive tone of her voice made his dick twitch as he wrapped her ankles in the leather straps.

"Your turning into quite the little slut, aren't you?"

Her body visibly stiffened at his words and he winced at his thoughtlessness.

"You don't like the term slut?"

"Not particularly." Gone was the sultry kitten he'd just had. She suddenly sounded reserved and uptight. He was going to change that.

"Why is that?"

"It's not a nice word."

"Really? It's one of my favorite words." David stood at the end of the bed in between her open legs and let his fingers travel the inside of each leg. "In fact, I love all the dirty words."

"But a slut is someone bad."

"Oh no, baby, a slut, especially if she's mine is a very, very good thing. A slut to me is a woman who not only does all the things I want her to, but she does them because she likes them too. Because she trusts me, and in this case my partner, so much that she's able to access the deepest, darkest and most depraved side of her sexual needs." His fingers swiped at the moisture forming on her labia, gathering it, before he brought his hand to his mouth and licked at the sweet juice of his woman.

David watched the rapid rise and fall of her breasts as her breathing increased at his touch, while her gaze remained locked on his mouth and the fingers he licked clean. "When a woman stops being afraid of saying or doing the wrong thing based on what society has told her and instead accepts every inner desire as a normal thing to express and becomes the wanton slut for her Master, she achieves a level of freedom like nothing else she has experienced before."

"But I don't have a Master."

"Not yet. But you have two Dominants who plan to push you beyond even more barriers than you can imagine. Your pleasure is our pleasure, and your freedom is our freedom. You just have to trust."

David leaned forward and closed his mouth over her mound, plunging his tongue into the heated depths of her entrance. He'd watched her squirm at his words until he couldn't take not tasting her for another second. He had needed the warm flesh against his tongue more than he'd needed his next breath.

"What do we have here?" Thomas' voice sounded from behind him, and Gabrielle gasped her surprise. David continued to plunge his tongue inside, fucking her like he did with his dick. She wriggled and fought against her restraints, trying to move away from him, and he would have nothing of it. Just because Thomas was in the room, didn't mean she controlled him. Fuck no.

He increased the pressure of his tongue against the smooth, slick inner walls until her legs trembled and her whimpering turned to screaming.

"I'm going to come. I can't help it," she cried.

"No!" Thomas roared. "If you come before he tells you to, there will be hell to pay. Control it, Gabrielle."

David looked up to see her head thrashing from side to side and considered pulling away to give her the chance to get herself back under control, but if truth be told, the need to push her to her limit over and over rode him hard. He wanted her to become his slut, and if it took a little creative pain to get her there, then so be it.

He heard the distinct sound of Thomas wrestling with his clothes, and his dick pulsed at the thought. Tonight, it would be the two of them together taking everything Gabrielle had to give, and if his suspicions were right, the three of them would never be the same again.

David grabbed at Gabrielle's clit with his teeth and sucked it into his mouth. She screamed and shuddered as he worked it over and over, loving the reaction. If she could just hold out for another thirty seconds, he would give her a minute or two to relax and let the rising orgasm pass. He applied more pressure adding a touch more pain to the process, but instead of halting her progress, a fresh scream tore from her throat and her body arced in an explosion that rocked the bed and flooded his mouth.

"Shit, David, what did you do to her?" Thomas crawled next to Gabrielle and wiped the tears from her cheeks, soothing her with words David couldn't hear.

He released her clit and slowly lapped at her cream, drawing out the last of her orgasm until finally her body rested and he pushed himself up to his feet.

"I bit her."

"Interesting." Thomas brushed the hair from her sweat-soaked skin. "Our girl must be more into pain than we thought."

"Or maybe I just have more power with my tongue than I thought." He smiled at Thomas who shot him a smirk.

Thomas turned back to Gabrielle and spoke quietly to her, urging her to relax and close her eyes, that the both of them would be here to take care of her no matter what happened.

He eased from the bed and stood facing David. The hard muscles of his body stretched over every plane, and even from the corner of his eye, he could see that Thomas was ramrod stiff.

"She's going to need to rest after that. Whatever you did sure set her off like a Fourth of July rocket. Turned me on so bad I may have to jack off just to relieve the pressure."

"I need something to drink. My mouth is so dry," Gabrielle interrupted.

David rushed to her side and unfastened her wrists from her bonds. He moved to do the same with her ankles. He rubbed at the light marks on her skin, remembering the mind-blowing reaction she'd had to his bite.

"I'll get it for you. Just rest. You're going to need it." He winked at Gabrielle and hurried from the room. Saved by the needy submissive.

Chapter Fifteen

Gabby watched David slip from the room before snuggling up against Thomas. Her limbs were stiff, and she needed to stretch them out, but right now, she only wanted to touch Thomas and let the heat of his skin soak deep inside her. With her body coming down from the scariest and most exciting orgasm she'd ever experienced, the only thing to make this moment better would for David to hurry back to bed and snuggle up to her backside.

"I'm sorry about not obeying." She spoke quietly, unsure of Thomas's response.

"Don't worry about that right now. I don't think David or I could have foreseen that response. After you've recovered, we'll work on that control of yours." His head dipped down and kissed the side of her face, his soft lips trailing down her cheek and chin to her neck and the slim collar around her neck.

"How's the collar working out for you?"

Her hand flew up and brushed against the leather. Nothing made her prouder than to wear this collar. So much so that she'd refused to take it off to go in public. It could be mistaken for a necklace, but honestly, she didn't care anymore. She was done hiding her lifestyle choice.

"I love it." And she loved the men who had given it to her. A lump formed in her throat at the truth in her mind, something that would not be welcomed out loud. She'd worry about her feelings and her future tomorrow. For tonight, she belonged wholly to Thomas and David and relished the idea that they had made some plans for the three of them to be together.

Her stomach clutched on that image. Two men. She'd read stories, seen the porn but had never imagined herself with two men at one time. A twinge of guilt pierced through her until she remembered David's words. Freedom lie in her ability to let go of her preconceived notions and follow the desire to wherever it was she needed to go. It wasn't her job to worry about the details, only to feel.

"Here you go, baby. Can you sit up and drink some of this?"

She hadn't even heard David return until he'd spoken, and now, he stood next to her with a water bottle in his hand. Sitting up, she took the offered water and gulped down several large swallows. The chilled liquid cooled her parched throat, easing the tension she'd been focusing on as well. When she opened her eyes and looked forward, she found herself eye level with David's thick cock and even in its semi-erect state it looked big.

She swallowed past the lump in her throat and licked her lips. She felt the bed shift behind her, and Thomas move against her back. His breath tickled her ear seconds before that commanding voice spoke.

"It's beautiful, isn't it?"

She swallowed hard and nodded her head.

"Take him in your mouth; suck him. Show me how much you like his dick."

Gabby quickly shifted to her knees and moved closer to David. She shot him a quick look and felt the pressure build in her pussy at the lust she saw blazing from his eyes. She licked slowly at the tip, running her tongue around the edge of the crown, lapping up the pre-cum that had formed.

"Spread you legs wide for me, Gabrielle."

Her stomach clenched in excitement as she realized Thomas intended to take her from behind. There was just something about that position, the very primal feeling of being taken, that did her in. She adjusted her legs so that her knees were as far apart as she could get them, forcing her bottom to tilt upward. The perfect position for Thomas. Her pussy creamed in anticipation.

"Such an eager girl. I like that." Thomas's hand smoothed along her ass before a smack landed across her flesh. She sucked in the crown of David's cock and wiggled her bottom for Thomas. It was a heady feeling to pleasure David at the same time Thomas took what he wanted.

"Damn woman, you have the hottest mouth." Thomas grabbed at her hair and pushed her down. "Take more. I know you can."

She was more than happy to as she swallowed David to the root, rubbing the underside with her tongue as she went. Satisfaction warmed her when David jerked his hips and groaned his approval.

Gabby whimpered her own pleasure when Thomas's fingers circled her opening and dove inside, rubbing against nerve endings that made her greedy. She wanted so much more. She wanted him to fuck her not tease her, but he would do things his way, and the man loved to torture her. His fingers curled inward as he dragged them from her body one slow inch at a time. He would drive her insane before he was finished.

The hot need Thomas built inside her spun her into a frenzy on David's dick as she swallowed and sucked for all she was worth. His hands tangled in her hair, tightening to the point of erotic pain that drove them both closer to the edge. Thomas needed to hurry up and fuck her already. Instead, his wet from her juices fingers trailed through the crack of her ass to the tight opening he favored so much.

"Damn, Thomas. What the hell are you doing to her? She's going to make me blow in record time."

Thomas responded by burrowing those fingers into her ass, nice and deep, probing, stretching and pushing her perilously close to her own release. Her skin tingled with the lust whipping through her as she pushed back, hoping for more.

"Don't worry, Gabrielle. I know what you need. Focus on David swelling in your mouth. Make him come."

Gabby whimpered and cupped David's balls with one hand as she allowed her teeth to graze against the soft skin and hardened steel.

"Ahhh," David groaned, and the pulse against her tongue was the only warning she got before his tangy release shot into her mouth. Gabby swallowed it all as fingers worked her ass, driving her response as she moaned for more.

Trapped between the two men driving her wild, she couldn't speak or think, only feel and ache. With no need to prepare her, Thomas slammed his cock into her cunt as the last of David's release slid down her throat.

"Yes, that's it, beauty. Squeeze me with that tight pussy of yours. I've been looking forward to this all day."

Breathing heavily, she thrust against the cock and fingers invading her body. She cried out when David slid from her mouth and moved around to her side. His fingers plucked at her nipples with tight steady pressure that had her screaming out.

"More like this?" David pulled harder, not releasing the tension for a second.

"Come now, Gabrielle!" Thomas angled the tilt of his hips and slammed deeper still.

Fingers rubbed at her clit, and it all became too much. The pain in her nipples, the fingers burning her ass and Thomas pounding into her. Sensation spiked through her until, unable to stop, she splintered.

"Oh. God," she howled as her pussy rippled around him. David released her nipples, and the painful flow of blood returning sent shudders wracking through her body.

Thomas's fingers continued to fuck her ass as he tunneled in and out of her so hard she was surprised her teeth didn't rattle. When she thought she might collapse, he powered into her one last time as his own climax engulfed him.

She dropped onto her face, and Thomas fell down with her, turning them both on their sides as the little aftershocks rumbled through her body and his.

"Hot damn, that was unbelievable." David moved in front of her sandwiching her between her two Doms. Two Doms... Would she ever get used to saying that?

Grateful tears sprang to her eyes, which she fought to hide before anyone noticed. When David wiped the first away with his thumb, she braced herself for questions. They didn't come. He remained silent only watching her face and wiping away any wetness that escaped her eyes.

Fingers danced across her skin as Thomas blazed a trail with his hand up and down her limbs. Heated flames licked at her body with each pass, reminding her that he controlled her responses. But what would he think of her if he guessed the depth of her feelings. She closed her eyes against David's careful scrutiny and focused on the sensations Thomas continued to create. Moisture once again flooded her sex and the top of her thighs as need and desire built to crescendo.

"Is my beauty ready for more?" Thomas' whispered words pulsed across her heated skin until her pussy and nipples tingled. Damn, the man barely had to touch her for her to react. It was the ever-present commanding tone of his voice. She suspected he could get her wet with a simple word if he so wished it.

His hand slid between her legs to the slick opening of her slit. "Mmm, just what I suspected. Wet and ready. Such a good little submissive girl." His teeth grazed against her shoulder, and an involuntary shudder of pleasure shuttled down her body. "And smooth, too. Without the hair, there is no barrier between your silken pussy and my cock. I can sink into the sweet caressing flesh of your cunt and feel nothing but skin and arousal as I do so."

He tilted his hips forward so that the steel ridge of his cock pressed against her lower back.

"This is what having my fingers buried in your heat does to me. I've always considered myself a man with a voracious appetite, but since meeting you, that has increased threefold. I want more."

He lifted her top leg and shifted his body slightly over hers until the plump head of his cock pressed into her opening, stretching and foraging its way inside. A sharp gasp fell from her lips as he filled her completely. She opened her eyes to find David studying her, a small smile on his face.

"I could watch you like this all night. Watching you get fucked by Thomas is more of a turn on than I ever dreamed." He leaned forward and nibbled her lips with his teeth.

Thomas settled into a nice and steady pace that created a slow build up with the occasional spark when he'd twist and hit the bottom of her clit or the more hidden g-spot. His hands continued to rub her skin with an occasional slap on her ass cheek to give her that zing of erotic pain that brought her one step closer to release. With each deep thrust, her pelvis rubbed against David's hard as steel cock hovering at the top of her most sensitive nub.

Between the two of them, they were torturing her with heavy desire and pleasure beyond her wildest dreams. Everything ached. Nipples, clit, even the tight bud of her anus that Thomas had warmed with his fingers. The images raced her to the edge of arousal, pressure building out of control behind her clit. She had to come.

"Don't come yet," Thomas warned with a firm smack to her ass.

"I have to," she cried, the sweet agony burning her alive.

Thomas withdrew from her body. Tears of frustration filled her eyes. "No. Please."

"Hush and follow directions." Thomas shuffled behind her, and David moved to lay across the bed. Firm hands at her waist lifted her in position, straddling David's legs. He fisted his rock hard cock and pointed it between her thighs. When he rubbed the crown across her clit, Gabby jerked in surprise.

Thomas laughed and pressed a hand between her shoulder blades, easing her forward across David's chest. She wanted to cuss and rail at them for moving so slow. Didn't they know she was dying?

"Brace yourself, baby." Thomas warning came only seconds before he breached her ass with his lubricated fingers. A new ache of desire throbbed through her. She'd had no idea how exciting this forbidden act could be before Thomas and David. Already images of them taking her at the same time filled her head. God, she craved it so much. Right or wrong really didn't matter. Only sensation and pleasure. She was drowning in it.

With each drag against ultra-sensitive tissue, Gabby jumped. She screamed for more. In the back of her brain, she heard the rip of paper seconds before Thomas' fingers slid away. Empty and aching, she could hardly stand the anticipation. Her clit swelled. Her skin grew hot and tight.

David pushed the head of his cock a fraction inside her and paused. Gabby held her breath. Thomas grabbed her hips and pressed against the tight ring.

A flash of fear rolled through. "Thomas…"

"Take it. Take us. Push back."

With a precision move, he passed the tight muscle and slid in. Gabby bore down and blew out a breath until he'd buried inside her balls deep. Thankfully, Thomas paused and allowed her body to adjust. Amazingly, it wasn't enough. She wiggled and cried for more.

Then David thrust inside…

Holy Fuck.

He drove his way through her impossibly tight channel, stretching her wide and forcing her to accept him. Inch after inch, he filled her beyond capacity. The burn sizzled her brain, ratcheting her arousal to an impossible to breathe level. She cried out. First David then Thomas. Begging them to make her come.

Their alternate thrusts detonated along nerve endings never touched, sending her hurtling to the edge of the abyss.

"God damn, she's tight," David groaned.

"I know I can feel everything. Fuck!"

The image of their dicks practically rubbing together sent her careening. Gabby lost all control. There was no stopping.

"Thomas! Help!" She begged for relief before it was too late.

"Yes, come. Come now, baby," Thomas growled at her ear.

Before the last word was out of his mouth, she exploded. Wave after wave of pleasure burst through her. The mixture of heaven and hell consumed her. Her muscles clenched in a powerful grip, holding both cocks inside her during the storm. Inside the eruption, Gabby found a new peace. A place where no one or anything mattered except the three of them. A perfect peace for a perfect pleasure.

Thomas and David slid into the abyss with her, loud grunts and groans mixing with her screams. The wall around her heart cracked and fractured into tiny pieces. These were her Doms. *Hers*.

Chapter Sixteen

Gabby turned her car onto her quiet street for the first time in several days. With a brighter outlook, she examined everything from the landscaping of her neighbors' yards to the design and structures of the row of townhouses. She really did love this neighborhood. What would happen if her relationship with Thomas and David became more permanent? Would she have to sell her beloved home?

She shook the thoughts from her head. She was getting way ahead of their relationship. Yes, they'd given her a training collar, but they were far from anything that permanent. They hadn't been together very long, and she had a lot of learning to get through before Thomas would decide if he wanted to keep her for the long-term.

Her gut twisted painfully at the thought of him letting her go at the end of the training period. Sure it hadn't been that long since that fateful night Angel had stood her up, but already her emotions had moved across the board, and she'd begun to face the pull she experienced toward both Thomas and David. A strange phenomenon in itself. She'd never thought belonging to two men would be her thing. She'd experienced jealousy from and toward her ex husband when either of them let their eyes wander. It still seemed so odd to her that neither Thomas nor David would eventually experience the same.

Still...she was a lucky woman to have this opportunity. She pulled into her driveway and turned off the car. Glancing out the window, she thought everything looked the same. Other than her lawn and garden needing her attention, that is. She'd always spent at least an hour a day outdoors, not only for the good it did her body and health, but for the satisfaction of keeping everything meticulous.

She'd have to spend more than an hour today making up for that. She glanced at the sky and reveled in the fact that it was one of those perfect, sunny Carolina days. Not too hot nor too cold. She rushed to the mailbox and gathered the large stack of envelopes awaiting her. She'd have to remember to go to the post office for a post office box or a forward on her mail if she started staying at Thomas's house much longer.

She pushed the key into her lock and opened the door into the foyer. It felt damn good to be in her own space, but crossing the threshold alone sent a pang of something through her chest. Loneliness maybe. That seemed silly considering she'd only left their bed an hour ago. Between the two of them, they wanted to fuck almost nonstop. She'd secretly suffered with an overactive sex drive for years, which had gone unfulfilled and driven her slowly mad. Other outlets worked for a while, but eventually, it had been one of the reasons her marriage had ended.

She didn't want to think about Scott now, not when her body was flushed and red from the flogger Thomas had used on her this morning. God, that had been incredibly erotic. The man knew his way around a woman's body, that's for sure.

She dropped the mail on her desk and noticed the blinking light on her answering machine. The number read twenty-seven messages. How the hell was that possible? It had only been a few days and her only active client at the moment was Sanctuary. Gabby pressed the play button and wandered into the kitchen to fix some fresh sweet tea. It would be perfect to enjoy out on the back deck before she got started on all the yard work.

She paused at the familiar sound of Scott's voice on the first message.

"Hey, babe. Are you there? Pick up the phone. I've got something I'd like to talk to you about. Okay, guess you're not there. Call me back. We really need to talk."

Surprised but not worried, she turned on the water and filled the teapot.

Then the next message came on, and it was Scott again.

"Gabby, babe. Did you get my message? I haven't heard back from you, and I'm wondering why. Is this machine working? Where are you? Probably out in the garden doing your thing. Hurry up and call me back. We need to talk."

What in the world could be up with him? She hadn't heard from him in months and hadn't expected to after the last words he'd said to her. She shuddered at the memory.

She arrived home from a day-long shopping trip to find Scott in her bedroom waiting for her. Strewn across her bed were all of the private belongings she'd begun to collect after Scott had left. Books about submission.

"Where did you get this garbage?" he demanded.

Frozen in fear, she didn't respond. The look on his face and the hatred in his voice pretty much said it all.

"Is this why you want a divorce? Because I don't tie you up and beat you." He moved into her personal space, and it took everything she had not to withdraw. Her skin crawled. "No one wants a slut wife, you know? That's what whore's are paid for."

"Stop it, Scott."

"What? Isn't this what you want?" He grabbed her by the hair and yanked her to the floor.

"Stop," she whispered.

"Don't worry, slut. You disgust me."

The next message started. Scott again. Gabby's eyes rolled upward as she placed the pot on a burner of the stove.

"Gabby, why are you not taking my calls? What's wrong babe?"

Duh. Was he kidding? Even if she'd been here, she wouldn't have wanted to talk to him.

"I know I wasn't very nice the last time we spoke, but I was just upset. You understand that, don't you?" He paused for several seconds, and Gabby found herself holding her breath.

Finally, he spoke again. "Call me. It's urgent."

She jumped at the clanging noise before the call disconnected with the answering machine. He'd slammed the phone down. Gabby sighed. This was not good. The last thing she needed right now was Scott giving her a hard time and interfering in her life.

The next message started.

"Goddamn it, Gabby! Stop acting like a fucking child and pick up the phone. There is no reason we can't both be adults and work through this."

A chill snaked down Gabby's spine. Now, that tone she recognized all too well and according to the machine that had come in yesterday morning. If the rest of the messages were from him, she wasn't sure she wanted to hear them. Something akin to fear settled into the pit of her belly as she walked to the front door and locked the dead bolt. She shouldn't be afraid in her own home, but the anger in his voice made her nervous just the same. She looked at the machine and hovered her finger over the erase button.

Listen to them. Maybe at some point, he'd finally said what it was that he wanted. Surely, he didn't think after all this time they were going to reconcile. Hell, from what she'd heard, he'd been out screwing every woman he could get his hands on since before she'd moved out.

"You frigid bitch, I should have never married you. I put up with your bullshit for too many years to now be treated like this. You owe me so pick up the fucking phone, or I'm coming over there to haul you out of your shitty garden myself."

Another deafening clang as he pounded the phone against something several times before disconnecting the call. Goose bumps erupted across her flesh, and she wrapped her arms around her waist. Maybe she should call David or Thomas, let them know. They'd expect it.

No, she couldn't do that. She couldn't bring them into this mess if Scott decided to get nasty. He had a foul temper that would only get worse if he found out she was dating again. God forbid if he found out she was serving two men as a submissive. He'd probably have a heart attack. An unbidden giggle tumbled from her mouth. It wasn't right to think that funny, but damn if the image wasn't.

She moved away from her desk, opting to let the messages run as she waited for her tea to brew. She flung open the curtains to the bright streaming sunshine as the next message started to play.

"I drove by your new place tonight, Gabby, and see that your car isn't in the driveway. So where the hell are you? Out cheating on me with another man? Who is he? Doesn't he know you already have a husband? You better hope I don't find out who he is babe. It won't be pretty."

Her head swiveled in the direction of the recorder. The new chill in his tone really worried her. It was calm, very unlike the explosive anger he usually reacted with.

The messages continued one right after another, all Scott and each one more frightening than the next. She plopped down on the sofa and laid her head in her hands. Why now? What had she done to deserve this?

"Gabby, my darling wife, it's 3:00 a.m., and I'm standing outside your front door. Are you really not there? No car again. Surely, you aren't staying the night somewhere else whoring yourself. Pick up the phone. I need you, Gabby. In fact, I've decided that I can't let you go, and I certainly won't lose you to some asshole who likes the sick shit you said you crave. *Pick. Up. The. Goddamn. Phone.*"

She'd had enough, her head throbbed in her hands and her stomach threatened to revolt.

"Hey babe, it's me again. I came by again at five this morning. Thought maybe we could watch the sunrise together. Did you get my present?" He laughed, a particularly wicked sound. That did not bode well.

A gift? She hadn't seen anything outside. She jumped up to the bay window and look out in the front yard. She scanned every inch, looking for anything out of place. Nothing. She rushed to the door but skidded to a stop before she opened it. She had to know what he'd been doing, but the knot in her stomach made her afraid to look. This was Scott they were talking about. He'd never done anything crazier than yell and threaten and punch a few walls. But the man on the answering machine sounded different. Calm and reasonable at times and crazy and out of his mind with jealousy others.

Fuck it.

She twisted the knob and stepped out into the sunshine. She wasn't about to let her ex-husband hold her hostage in her own home too afraid to go outside in her yard. He knew how much she loved her garden. Still, she left the door open and took only a few tentative steps, searching the ground of her small, covered entry for any sign of something that had been left for her.

"Oh and Gabby, I forgot to tell you. You really need to invest in a better security system."

She froze in place when her blood chilled at his final words. The security system was only on the actual house. To know about that, he would have had to gone inside. She took three steps back, nearly tumbling down her front steps before catching herself on the railing. What had he done?

Broken in? She had yet to wander into all of the rooms, and now, she wasn't sure she wanted to. Who could she call? She still didn't want to involve Thomas or David in this nor did she want to call the police. This town wasn't big enough to keep a domestic situation a very good secret, and one secret always led to another. She wasn't sure her clients would want to know all the sordid details about her new life.

No, she had to do this without that kind of help. So who did that leave?

Angel! She reached into her pocket and pulled out her cell phone. She hit the shortcut to Angel's number. She thankfully answered on the second ring.

"Where the hell have you been, missy? I've been worried sick about you. You go and disappear for days and don't even call your best friend?"

"Angel, I need your help. Can you come over?"

Angel must have heard the fear in Gabby's voice.

"Are you at home?"

"Yes."

"I'm on my way. Give me five minutes."

The call disconnected, and Gabby returned the phone to her pocket. She knew Angel would support her and understand what was going on. She always did. She was always there whenever she needed someone, and she was damn lucky for it. What would she do without her?

Unable to sit still, Gabby walked around to the side of the house and used her key to get into the backyard. She took a few cautious steps forward, searching the ground and gardens for anything unusual. The last thing she needed right now was a new surprise. Seeing nothing she walked toward the fountain and her lounge chair. She needed to get herself under control and this was her special place, the one place she could always find her calm no matter how bad things got.

She sank down into the soft cushion of the chair and ran her fingers through her hair. This wasn't happening.

Not now, not when things were finally turning themselves around. Resting her head back, she listened to the water tumbling over the stone steps of the pond she'd created with her own two hands. This really was the perfect place of solitude. The tinkling sound of fluid water falling into the pool below soothed her frazzled nerves until she closed her eyes and willed herself to relax. Surely, Scott had been pulling her leg. Why would he have broken into her house, and how could she have not noticed?

Birds chirped in the trees surrounding her oasis, and she glanced over at the climbing roses that hid the fence separating her property from the neighbor behind her. The riotous color of orange, red and pinks that her Joseph's Coat gave her brought a smile to her lips. If she stayed much longer at Thomas', she might have to convince him to give her a little space in his backyard. His yard was nice, obviously done by a professional landscaper, but nice nonetheless. There weren't any water features or an overabundance over color, but the beds were filled with green perennials and trimmed neatly—perfect for a wealthy bachelor who had little time for that kind of thing. She had noticed, however, that he had a large back deck with a built-in fire pit and barbeque so he either enjoyed spending some time out there or he liked to throw outdoor parties in the summer time. She loved that kind of thing and with free rein she'd have his backyard blooming before he knew it. The idea of a blank slate excited her beyond belief as she mentally prepared a checklist of what she'd need to get started.

Maybe in a week or two, she could bring it up and see what he thought. Even if she didn't stay there beyond her training, it would be a gift she would love to leave him with. His own special oasis that, when he went out there or even glanced out the back windows, would maybe make him think of her. She sighed wistfully. Here she was scared to go in her house because her ex had scared the shit out of her, and she was still making plans to play house with Thomas and David.

"Gabby, I'm here. Are you out here?" Angel had arrived, and she didn't wait for a response before she pushed through the gate and headed her way.

"I'm over here." She waved her arm above her head so her friend could see her.

"So, what the hell happened? Are you okay? You sounded scared to death on the phone." Angel sat at her spot near Gabby's feet, an imploring look in her eyes.

"I'm sorry, Angel. I didn't mean to scare you it's just—" she choked up. With her friend looking at her with such worry and compassion, she lost her composure and burst into tears.

Angel jumped up and wrapped her arms around her. "Tell me. I'm here for you, you know that, right?"

She nodded. The huge lump now sitting in her throat prevented her from talking. No way were words getting choked by that.

"Did something happen between you and Thomas? I knew he would contact you and figured he'd want to train you until you found your own Dom. Was I wrong in that? Did he hurt you?"

Gabby shook her head. "No, no, it's nothing like that at all. He has been beyond wonderful, and hopefully soon, we can get into the details of it. You would not believe what has happened in the last week."

"Then what sweetheart? What has you in tears?"

"It's Scott," she whispered, afraid to even say his name out loud. Talking about him always had a way of making things worse. At least, sometimes it did. Dwelling on his ability to tear her down always gave him too much power over her. Something he'd abused for a very long time.

"Oh hell no. What has that bastard done this time? I'll gladly tear him limb from limb if he's hurt you again."

"I've not been home for a few days."

"Yeah, I noticed. I came by a couple of times, and you weren't here which was kind of freaky considering you're attached to this place. But I figured you and Thomas had hooked up, and well, Master told me not to worry or bother you."

"Oh Angel, I came home about an hour ago to check on things and get some more clothes, but when I got here, I found dozens of messages on the answering machine. All from him."

"What did he say? Please tell me he hasn't gone back to berating you for the life choices you wanted to make. Isn't he past that now?" Her hands rubbed absently up and down Gabby's arm, and instantly, Gabby calmed, an ability Angel always had with her. She could comfort anyone in any crisis. It was a gift.

"I don't think I could even paraphrase all that he had to say. Maybe you should listen to them yourself. Then maybe you can tell me if I'm blowing things out of proportion because, right now, he's scared the hell out of me, and I don't know what to do."

"Yeah, maybe you're right. You sit here and relax. I know how great this garden makes you feel, and I'll go in the house and listen."

"Angel, be careful. He said he left me a gift and that my security sucked. I don't know what that means, but I was afraid to go back in the house."

"Son of a bitch, he's gone too far this time." Angel jumped to her feet and headed toward the house. "Are the French doors here in the back open?"

"No, but the front door is still open."

"Sit tight, sweetie. I'll be back in a jiffy, and I'll even make us some margaritas. You've still got all the fixin's right?"

She turned and arched her brow.

"Yeah, that's what I thought. No self respecting southern woman would be without the ingredients to almost anything her guests might request." Her laughter faded as Angel disappeared out the gate.

Guilt washed over her about sending her friend in alone, but the last thing she wanted to do was listen to those messages again. At this point, she'd be happy to never hear Scott's voice again.

"I'm going to leave the back door open in here, okay?" Angel called from the house.

"Sure, no problem. Are you sure you don't want me in there to give you a hand?" *Oh God. Please say no, please say no.*

"No way, Gabby. You sit tight and relax. You deserve it."

Did she? She wasn't sure. Sitting out here while her friend went to find God knew what made her feel like a coward. Her hand reached up to rub the collar wrapped around her neck. She needed the strength of Thomas and David right about now, but to involve them in her mess would be insane. They definitely did not deserve this.

"Asshole!"

She laughed when she heard Angel cussing from inside the house. Obviously, she had hit play on the machine. This is going to get ugly. Unable to just sit here sunning herself, Gabby decided she needed to get something done. There were weeds and dead flowers to clean up. That would keep her mind occupied and off what had happened.

Why the hell couldn't Scott just move on and stay out of her life? Why would he come back now after all this time? What could have changed? She was going to drive herself crazy, trying to analyze a man who'd rarely made sense to her. She shook off the thoughts and walked into the garden shed to retrieve her tools. Gloves, a spade and her kneepad were all she needed.

She kneeled at the front of one of many of her rose beds and let the scents and heat of the earth wash over her. Why did the soft smell of loam calm her so? The simple act of being on her knees reminded her of Thomas and David. A smile curved at the edges of her lips. She couldn't keep them out of her mind for long and now wanted to get back to them. Coming home had not been a stellar idea. Gabby pushed her hands into the fitted gloves and reached into the earth, turning it to loosen and allow for more oxygen flow to the roots of her roses. She'd have to remember to get some bone meal out here before she left since it had been a while since they'd been properly fed.

Looking at the position of the sun in the sky, she figured she still had several hours before she would have to leave and head back to Thomas'. It would not be good to be late, and she'd need a shower before going home.

Home.

This was her home, not Thomas' house. She needed to stop thinking like that and letting herself get ahead of the relationship.

Take it slow Gabby, you don't want to make another mistake.

"Oh my fucking God, what a fucking asshole!"

Gabby tried not to laugh at Angel, but it was either that or cry, and she'd given Scott enough of her tears. She'd find her way past this on her own just like she always did with the rough spots in her life. But she'd have to be very careful when she walked back in that house. Thomas was very attuned to her moods and behavior. Yes, she'd have to be very careful.

She pulled at the weeds until sweat trickled down her face and back. Her muscles bunched in her shoulders as she stretched and pulled to be sure and get the roots. God, this felt good. When she'd discovered that she could get more healing out of hard work in the sun and dirt, more so than she ever got with her therapist, she'd cancelled her appointments and quit getting her prescriptions filled. She didn't need antidepressants. She'd only needed to work through the problems on her own with the aid of good old-fashioned hard, sweaty work.

"Oh. My. God. I can't believe the nerve of that dickhead."

Gabby smiled again. Leave it to Angel to hit the nail on the head with one simple statement. She stood and removed her gloves, brushing the loose dirt and debris from her clothes.

"I take it you've finished listening to all of them."

"Hell, yes, and he's lucky he's not here right now, or I'd have him on the ground while I kicked his balls."

Gabby believed she would, too.

"I can't believe everything he said. He really frightened me, Angel. He probably broke into my house."

"Did you find the gift he was talking about?"

She shook her head, "Nothing that I could see, but I was kind of afraid to walk through the house on my own. I don't trust him. He could have done anything."

"Well, I walked every room, and I didn't see anything that looked like a gift." She handed Gabby one of the margaritas she'd carried outside. "Do you really think he broke in? When you got home did you find any signs that someone had been here."

Gabby considered that. She'd had to unlock the dead bolt like normal and turn off the alarm. Nothing at all had seemed different. "No, not that I could tell."

"Maybe, he's bullshitting you. Just trying to scare you."

"Maybe." She took another sip of the sweet drink, letting the frozen slushy sit on her tongue.

"Holy crap, Gabby. What is that around your neck? Is that a collar?" Angel stepped closer, her nose nearly touching it.

"It's a training collar. I just got it."

"Holy hell, I can't believe you didn't tell me. Sit, sit, you must give me all the details and maybe if they're juicy enough, I'll forgive you for holding out on me."

"I wasn't exactly holding out. This is the first chance I've had to come home in days. They've kept me really busy."

Angel's brow arched. "They've?"

"Yes, Thomas and David."

"Well, I'll be damned. That Thomas sure does work fast these days. It won't be long now. Maybe I should have brought the whole bottle of Tequila out here."

Chapter Seventeen

Gabby's heart pounded as she grabbed her bags and things from the car and rushed up the walkway. She couldn't believe how late she was, but she and Angel had gotten carried away in their conversations until almost sunset. She'd missed her friend, and spending that time with her calmed her fears about Scott. That and the alcohol. She'd had to cut herself off, drink some coffee and take a shower before she was comfortable driving herself back to Thomas'. She'd spied both their cars in the garage as soon as she'd pulled up the drive.

Fuck, there was going to be hell to pay for this.

She'd promised to return before they got home from work, and now, they'd beat her home. Hopefully, they hadn't been here long, and it wouldn't be too big of deal. Her pulse raced faster as she turned the knob to the front door. She was as nervous now as she'd been the first night she'd come here. Still, so much had happened since then.

In the foyer, she dropped all of her belongings and flung her shoes with them. She'd put on as little clothing as possible before she'd left her house so she could undress quickly when she arrived. She lifted the sundress over her head, and the cool air inside the house brushed against her skin, tightening her nipples and quickening her sex.

It was actually a relief to remove the dress since they'd taught her to be comfortable in her own skin and embrace the body she had. It was one of the most liberating lessons she'd learned so far.

"You're late." Thomas's voice rumbled from the dining room behind her.

"I'm so sorry. Angel came over, and we were drinking margaritas and catching up and time got away from us." Words tumbled out of her mouth so fast even she barely understood them, but she couldn't stop. "As soon as I realized how late it was, I came as quickly as I could."

Thomas lifted a finger to her lips and quieted her down. "Relax, Gabrielle. You're strung too tight. These things happen. I'm not a complete dickhead."

She wanted to smile, she really did, but instead tears threatened to spill, horrifying her. She quickly cast her eyes downward and placed her arms behind her. A submissive posture that would not only be respectful, but hide her eyes from his all-knowing gaze.

"I'm still sorry, Sir."

"Well, don't be. In fact, I'm proud that you would rush home in your effort to be on time and you undressed the minute the door closed behind you. It's very good progress, I'd say."

A rush of heat crept up her neck and face at his words. "Thank you, Sir."

"We have a surprise for you."

Her head shot up at David's voice to find him standing side by side with Thomas in front of her, a black sash held in his hand. A bolt of fear struck her gut as she contemplated what they were up to.

Hold it together, Gabby. You can do this. This is what you wanted and you aren't going to let your fear of Scott stop it.

"What kind of surprise?" she asked quietly.

"Now if we told you it wouldn't be much of a surprise now, would it?" David's warm smile went a long way in settling her nerves. "You trust us, don't you?"

She nodded.

"Enough to let us blind you and lead you to your surprise?" Thomas challenged.

She swallowed hard, her tongue licking at her lips. "Yes, Sirs. I trust you both."

"I hope so, Gabrielle, because I'd like to take your training to the next level, but we won't get very far if you have doubts about us."

Doubting them was not the problem. It was that damned ex-husband who wouldn't leave her alone that caused her anxiety. "I don't have doubts. I've never wanted to be anywhere more in my life than in this room now with both of you at your service."

David stepped forward, his arm lifting to hold the sash in front of her eyes. "We shall see soon enough. Look at me."

Her head lifted, and his brilliant blue eyes connected with her gaze. Her belief in him was rock solid. She just wished she knew how to ask for a night off, a night to relax and get past this mess she was in.

"Lock your hands behind your back."

Without hesitation her arms shifted, and she grabbed her hands at the small of her back without taking her eyes from David.

"Are you okay with wearing a blindfold?"

"Yes, Sir." The idea actually excited her a little. She was dying of curiosity to see what came next.

David wrapped the cloth around her head, immersing her into the dark.

"Can you see anything?" he whispered at her ear.

She shook her head. A slight tremor of fear shivered through her as she fought to stay perfectly calm. She could do this.

"Gabby, you need to respond verbally to all questions. We can't gauge the extent of your feelings without hearing your voice. It's critical to our job of keeping you safe, comfortable and satisfied."

David stepped away from her, and she immediately mourned the loss of his heat. Silence surrounded her, and she sucked in a breath. Had they walked away, or were they standing there staring at her? She fought the urge to cover herself, knowing full well that if she did, she would be punished.

"Breathe, Gabrielle. Don't be afraid. Remember what you just told us. Think of the trust." Thomas's voice sounded slightly different. Huskier. "Do you still think we'll be able to keep you safe?"

"Yes, Sir." She locked her knees and stiffened her spine to keep from moving too much. She would follow their directions no matter what. It pleased her to please them.

"Good girl."

Cloth rustled, and she wondered if they were removing their clothes as well. With the blindfold covering her eyes, she began to notice some of her other senses sharpening. Here in the foyer of Thomas' house, she could detect the faint lemony smell of the furniture polish. Probably from the sideboard that gleamed by the door. She could hear the water running in the small fountain that sat on Thomas' desk in his office. The tinkling was faint, but she recognized it. He must have left the door ajar.

Fingers grazed against her shoulder, and she flinched. Whoever was touching her didn't stop, they traced along her skin to the curve of her neck and under her chin. When the hand reached her lips it lingered there for a moment, and Gabby stuck out her tongue to get a taste. She sighed wistfully at the texture of a work-roughened hand. Both men were hard workers, and it was impossible to tell which one it was who lingered on her mouth.

She inhaled deeply and thought she caught a faint trace of Thomas' aftershave. A musk that lingered on his clothes and everywhere he went. God, she loved that smell. Was it Thomas who touched her? Her fingers and arms practically itched to move, to do some exploring of her own. When his hand continued its path down the other side of her body until it reached the peak of a taut nipple, she couldn't take it anymore. Her hand blindly reached in front of her and connected with a silk shirt. Oh yeah...Thomas.

Two hands grabbed at her arms and roughly returned them to her side. "No touching. If you can't control them, I could always tie them for you."

A small gasp fell from her lips, and her sex swelled at the sensual image of being both blindfolded and restrained.

"You like that idea, don't you?" His warm breath caressed her ear. "Does it make you wet, Gabrielle? If I reach down and stroke my pussy, what will I find?"

"Wetness." She forced the word out. Her heart rate kicked up, and her breathing turned heavier.

Lips touched her nipple, a chaste kiss before moving to the other and repeating the move. Her back arched slightly, seeking more. God, she wanted him to suck them, pinch them, anything...

"She's already growing impatient."

"Maybe being away from us all day has left her needy."

"Are you needy, my beauty?"

"Yes, Sir."

"Good. That should make tonight all the more fun."

Thomas' hands cupped her breasts and pushed them together. His face dipped between the cleavage, inhaling slowly before blowing out his warm breath across her sensitized skin.

More hands grabbed at her ass, squeezing her cheeks until she cried out. "I can't wait to get a whip on this ass. Or maybe a crop," David threatened.

She was beginning to fall under their spell, their hands and mouths working over her, building her arousal until her skin flashed hot with need.

Thomas changed his methods from soft lifts to the slightly sharper graze of his teeth across one nipple and then the other.

"*Ooh…*"

"You like it when I start to play a little rough, don't you?"

She nodded.

"Good, because we're just getting started."

She lost focus on Thomas' words when David's hands pulled her cheeks wide. "This ass is mine tonight. And I'm going to fuck you there right after you beg me for it." One of his fingers tapped against her tight anus, and shudders of delight rushed through her. Moisture flooded her sex and trickled across the tops of her thighs.

"Fuck, just looking at that berry red tight hole has me hard as steel. Thomas, are you sure we can't play a little first?"

"Nope, not yet. We have to stick to the plan. I want our little beauty buzzing at one hundred percent as she tries to figure out our plans."

"What are we going to do?" She couldn't resist asking the question.

"Oh no, sweetheart. You have to wait and see. Patience is the name of the game tonight."

She blew out a hard breath and tried not to focus on David's finger prodding her hole. If she didn't get her mind elsewhere, she'd be breaking all the rules in record time.

"Do you want me to take you here?" His finger slipped an inch inside when he asked.

"Yes, please." Everything seemed to be so much stronger tonight. Her need, their need, their desire to tease her to death.

"I can hardly wait. I'm going to bend you over and watch your ass greedily suck me in one inch at a time."

Her pussy clenched hard. She needed him right now more than she thought she ever had. What was going on? Why so strong?

She gasped for air, dragging long breaths deep into her lungs. *Don't panic.*

"Calm down, Gabrielle. We can't have you coming quite yet. We have much more in store for you tonight." Thomas's words buzzed around her head as she felt the fog slipping into her mind. His lips covered hers for a long drugging kiss, and she leaned into his body for comfort. Somehow, she managed to keep her hands at her sides and shiver only once when David released her ass.

"It's time."

Thomas pulled his tongue from her mouth and rested his forehead against hers. "You make me wish we could stay in tonight. I need you."

"We aren't staying in?" That seemed to clear some of the fuzz in her brain.

"No, my beauty. We're going out."

"Do I need to get dressed?"

"No, you do not. You're perfect just as you are."

Panic rose inside her. "But—"

His fingers pressed against her mouth as his other hand wrapped around her throat only applying the slightest bit of pressure. "No words. No arguing. Just do as you're told, and you'll be perfectly safe. You still trust us, right?"

Scenarios swam through her head. Her in a crowd at Sanctuary. Them taking her to a play party. Any number of things could happen. One thing she'd learned was that Thomas was the master at creative. She sucked in a deep breath and attempted to calm her racing heart. She'd had a rough day, but unless she confessed what had happened, she had no excuse to not follow their express orders.

"Yes, Sir, I do."

"Perfect." He grabbed her hand. "Just hold onto me and listen to my voice. I'll tell you everything that you need to know."

She gripped his fingers tightly.

"Okay, you don't have to hold on that tight. Relax. Take a few deep breaths. Do you remember your safe word?"

She nodded her head.

"Good. If things get to be too much, you know what to do. But I think you'll enjoy what we have planned for you very much."

He turned her around and led her to the door. The outside air rushed over her, puckering her nipples again from the sudden sensation. Every sound came to her in stereo: The leaves of the trees rustling, some birds nearby, David's shoes walking ahead of them down the path and even faint sound of cars down on the street. She didn't worry at the moment about anyone seeing her. Thomas's property had been landscaped to afford him the maximum amount of privacy, and she knew no one could see her. But what if they could? How would that make her feel? Strangers staring at her body. If they were going out with her wearing nothing but a blindfold and a collar she should probably expect at some point to be in a public place.

A sudden rush of fear gripped at her gut. What if Scott had followed her here? Could he be somewhere watching her now? Panic rose in the form of bile in her throat that she struggled to withhold. Sweat broke out on her brow, and she fought the need to rip off the blindfold and run.

"Can anyone see me like this?" She had to know.

"Gabrielle, you have to trust that I would never put you in a position that could harm you. Neither would David."

"I'm scared."

"I know you are, sweetheart, and that's fine. It's normal to be a little afraid of the unknown, but try to focus on me and David, how we will always put your safety and pleasure first. Your trust and obedience please us very much."

Her heart soared at his words. He was right. She did believe that neither of them would do anything to hurt her. They cherished her, and so far, they'd never given her any reason to think anything else.

Unlike that bastard Scott.

No. She had to get him out of her head. He didn't belong here and had no right to any piece of her. She belonged to David and Thomas, and only, they held those rights.

Then why aren't you telling about this afternoon?

She knew it was wrong but hoped that it would never come back to haunt her. She could and would put Scott and his lame attempts to scare of her out of her mind. She deserved to enjoy this night with her men as much as they deserved her total obedience. She could hear the hum of an engine now and a car door opening.

"Good evening, Sir."

Gabby's back stiffened and her steps faltered at the unfamiliar voice. Thomas's hand tightened on hers in reassurance.

"Evening, Troy. Thanks for coming."

"My pleasure, Sir. Anytime."

The sound of fabric rubbing against a slick surface was her only indication that David may have already gotten into the car. Her legs felt like Jell-o as she imagined the stranger leering at her and her not being able to do a thing about it. Covering herself was not an option.

"Gabrielle, you're about one foot from the entrance to the car so lift your arm and feel the roof to get your bearing." He placed her right hand along the top edge of the car, and she felt for the roof with the other.

"There you go, honey. You've got it. Now, slowly step into the backseat."

With David's words guiding her and her hands feeling the way, she stepped into the car. She gasped when she moved to sit and her ass hit cold leather seats, chilling her.

"I'm proud of how you're handling this. Wasn't sure what you would do when you realized someone else was watching you," David whispered.

"It's not the most comfortable feeling, that's for sure. But I think I'll live."

"Oh, you'll do more than live, sweetheart. We plan to take things to a whole new level tonight, and I'm very excited." He grabbed her hand and led it to his crotch, placing her fingers across the bulge in his pants.

The hard length strained against the material, and the urge to release him overwhelmed her.

"See what looking at you does to me? That and thinking about that ass of yours all night is likely going to drive me crazy."

The seat on the opposite side sank as she guessed Thomas had gotten in beside her. This blindfold was getting on her nerves a little. Not being able to see what was going on around her left her feeling open and vulnerable in a whole new way.

"We're ready, Troy."

"Thank you, Sir."

Thomas's shoulder brushed against her shoulder, and she automatically curled into his heat without taking her hand from David's erection. He'd yet to dismiss her.

"You're beautiful, Gabrielle."

She flushed hotly at his words.

"Thank you," she said.

She heard the distinct slide of a door or compartment opening and ice tinkling into a glass. Thomas was obviously fixing himself a drink, and every sound seemed louder than possible.

After the splash of liquid, the glass was placed in her hand and led to her lips.

"Drink. It will help you relax."

"I-I'm…" she stuttered.

"Don't worry. I have no intention of letting you get drunk. Lots of alcohol and scening never mix well. It's just something to take the edge off until we get to our destination. And…while you do that, I can play with this pretty pussy."

Fingers feathered across her lower lips, teasing the seam where her arousal from inside the house lingered, waiting...

She moved to grab the glass with both hands.

"No, no, no." David grabbed her hand and returned it to his thigh. "I need your hand here, Gabrielle." His hands brushed against hers while he unfastened his pants. She imagined his thick girth as it burst free from the confines of his clothes.

Moments later, he lifted her hand again and wrapped it around his hot and hard erection, even guiding her up and down a few strokes.

"Oh yeah, just like that."

The glass in her hand faltered as she lost her focus. With Thomas tickling the outer edges of her pussy and David using her to jerk him, drinking anything from a glass was the last thing she could concentrate on.

"Gabrielle, don't drop that glass." Thomas warned just as his finger spread her lips apart and delved between the sensitive flesh.

She couldn't think; she couldn't process. The hard cock, the finger in her sopping pussy, the strange car and even the stranger driving were too much. Arousal burned frighteningly high as her limbs began to shake. They were going to make her come like this, and she'd end up spilling her drink across them all.

"I-I can't," she gasped, searching for enough air.

"Yes...you can," Thomas assured her. "What you can't do is come yet. That's for much later. Think about the glass in your hand. Think about Troy glancing at you every few seconds in the rear view mirror, think about where we might be taking you."

Oh God, the torture. He had to stop, or she'd lose it all. She couldn't control it. "Can't control."

"Exactly, you aren't supposed to control anything. Your body belongs to us. We control what happens to it." Thomas swirled through her juices, spreading them from clit to anus before dipping inside once again, but this time with two fingers filling her.

"*Oh*," David groaned.

"I think you're going to make him come. Do you want him to come for you?"

"Yes, Sir, I do."

Thomas grabbed the glass from her hand and slid his finger from her cunt. "Then take him with your mouth and suck him off. Give him that gift."

She quickly turned in the seat and bent her head and swallowed his cock to the edge of her hand. Immediately, her tongue went to work, stroking and licking every inch of the softest skin she'd ever touched. Thomas' hands fitted around her waist and jerked her to her knees so that her ass tilted up in his direction, leaving her completely open to him. His fingers returned to her pussy and thrust inside.

"Hell, woman, you are so fucking wet."

"That's because she likes this. Likes when she gets to suck cock and get her pussy played with. Don't you, Gabrielle?"

She moaned around David's cock and focused on making him come. She couldn't think about Thomas and what he did to her, or she'd be breaking all the rules. Which didn't stop her from pushing back against his hand so that he was fucking in and out of her sex. She was surrounded by need that practically vibrated the car.

For several minutes, no one said a word. Gabby only heard the sounds of fingers sucking in and out of her pussy, David's moans, her slurps on his dick and the constant hum of the car engine. She took more until David pushed at the back of her throat and her gag reflex kicked in. Lifting slightly, she took a deep breath as her eyes watered. Once again, she slowly moved down his length, this time swallowing as he hit the back of her throat.

"Oh shit," David groaned.

She smiled around him and flicked her tongue along his sensitive underside from the root to the ridge of the crown. He pulsed against her tongue. His hand grabbed the back of her head and held her down.

"That's it, baby. Make him come." Thomas' fingers increased their tempo, and she struggled to ignore the friction he created inside her.

When her own desire threatened to overtake her, David tightened his grip in her hair and shouted his release. Pulse after pulse of salty semen filled her mouth, and she greedily swallowed it. His hips jerked, keeping his cock lodged at the back of her throat.

When he tugged at her head, she slowly slid up and off him with a pop and a smile plastered to her face. Thomas had stopped moving his fingers, and she panted for air in a struggle to catch her breath.

"Holy hell, that was incredible." David's fingers cupped her chin, his thumb stroking over her full bottom lip.

The touch sent a quick shiver down her spine and jerked her hips. That tiny move caused her vaginal muscles to clench around Thomas' fingers, and she moaned at the sensation that streaked through those nerve endings.

"I know, baby. You want to come so bad you can practically taste it. And believe me I want nothing more than to give you that satisfaction, when I think you're ready."

Gabby whimpered.

"We've got a plan, and as much as you tempt me, we'll be sticking to it." He withdrew his fingers and wet tears sprang in her eyes.

She was going to die; she just knew it. Why did they insist on torturing her like this? She rested her cheek against David's denim covered thigh and slowed her breathing. Her muscles wound tight, making it difficult for her to move in the small space. With the slowing beat of her heart, she noticed the outside noise and remembered they were in a car, heading down the road with a strange driver in the front witnessing everything she'd done. She braced herself for a wave of humiliation that never came.

She'd loved giving David what he needed, and knowing they were both enjoying this trip so far was all that mattered. What did she care if some man she'd likely never see again had played witness? Thomas and David were here and watching out for her. She trusted them not expose her to anything harmful.

Warm fingers caressed her bottom, before Thomas grabbed her hips and pulled her onto his lap. She snuggled against his chest and listened to the elevated pace of his heart. It was an incredible comfort and turn on to know that he'd been affected as well.

Fingers pushed at her lips. "Clean me, Gabrielle."

Her mouth opened and sucked them in, her own tangy flavor exploding over her taste buds. She wrapped her tongue around them and suckled deeply. Her body still quivered with need, but it had subsided to a bearable level. For now.

"Such a good girl."

David shifted, and she heard the distinct rasp of his zipper as he readjusted himself. Maybe they would arrive at their destination soon.

As Thomas's fingers slid from her mouth, she desperately wanted to see his eyes. In a normal scene, she garnered much of her strength from keeping her gaze connected with his. The intensity and raw power that always radiated from the man made her feel secure and cared for. "I wish I could see your eyes." She'd said the words before she'd even thought to hold them back.

"I know you do, beauty. Rest assured, neither David nor I plan to leave your side for even a moment."

His arms wrapped around her and pulled her tight in his lap, his hard cock pressed against her hip. Her heart constricted in her chest. He needed her to follow through in whatever he had planned, and truth be told he'd not asked her to do anything she didn't want to on a deep down primal level. She liked that he pushed her limits every chance he got. She'd discovered already so many things she would have never known she liked.

"I love your curves." He twisted her in his arms until her back pressed against his chest. "You're so willing to please me. So eager to serve, despite your innocence. It's the most exciting thing I've seen in a very long time."

"I'm hardly innocent," she whispered.

Big, rough hands wrapped around her breasts and cupped them tightly. "In my world, you are as sweet and innocent as they come." He plucked at her nipples, alternating between soft, light pinches and hard, tight ones that took her breath away. Fresh desire stirred between her thighs as more moisture coated her lips. He wanted to drive her crazy, she was sure of it.

Next to them, David shifted in his seat, and she felt his arm brush across her side. A soft gasp parted her lips when his hand trailed along the inside of her thigh from knee to the top of the thigh. She held her breath as he inched closer, until the edge of his nails scraped against the wet flesh.

"I'm not sure how much more of this I can take?"

"You'll be fine," David's low voice reassured.

"I don't want to disappoint you and come without permission."

"Relax, Gabby. You're too worried. This isn't about stressing you out."

"It feels like a test."

"You can't think of it like that." Thomas pulled at her nipples until she gasped with erotic pain. "Your job is to feel. Simply do as you're told and trust in us enough to know what you need. We will see to your pleasure."

"I can't stop worrying."

Two fingers pinched her clit and squeezed. At first, the sensation of pleasure zinged through her until the pressure continued to the point of pain, and not the good kind.

"Do you want us to stop? We can turn around and head back home right now if that's what you want?"

Did she? They'd probably keep bringing her to the edge of orgasm until she managed to let go of her fear, but she wasn't sure she could do it. The sight deprivation was beginning to get to her, and she naturally worried they would take her somewhere and push too far.

David pressed his fingers tightly together until she screamed out. He immediately released the aching bud and fluttered his fingers through her outer lips. She breathed in through her nose and out through her mouth as her pulse throbbed in her sex. One minute, she couldn't think beyond the pleasure or pain they gave her, and the next, she could only focus on what might happen. Thomas was right she needed to let go, but it was much harder than he made it sound.

"You haven't answered me," Thomas reminded her.

She opened her mouth to make him stop, and two fingers plunged into her cunt. Electricity shot through her veins and straight to her core as David finger fucked her.

"Let go of the worries, my beauty. David has two fingers shoved inside you, and you're so wet all I can hear is the sound of you sucking him in and out with each thrust."

Oh God, Thomas was right. The juicy sound filling the car turned her on even more as her heart beat erratically and she allowed herself to race headlong toward the precipice of no return.

"That's it, Gabrielle. Give me what I want. Surrender to the pleasure without worrying about what comes next or who might see you or any other question that is racing through your mind."

She couldn't talk. Her hips bucked, and she fucked down on David's fingers. *Oh God. Oh God.* She couldn't stop it. Sensation rushed through her veins, and the increased pressure Thomas applied to her nipples made her crazy with need.

"Oh, yes. Oh I can't. Oh my God."

"Ah yes, that's it."

He pulled harder on her nipples until the pain exploding in her should have killed everything she felt, but it didn't. Every zing, every pulse increased threefold.

"Come now, Gabrielle. Right fucking now!" Thomas's voice exploded in the car as dots danced in front of her eyes. She pushed harder against the fingers, burying David so deep inside she wondered if his whole hand was in there.

A burst of white light exploded in her head as her muscles tightened and convulsed. Breath whooshed from her lungs as her whole body bucked forward. Her mouth opened to scream, but it was impossible to scream with no breath.

"Jesus."

"Yeah. She had that one coming for a while now."

She barely heard David and Thomas as every muscle in her body clenched and released over and over as she jackknifed into a sitting position. Her wild pants echoed around her as David's fingers slowed to an easier pace. She'd probably be sore from that, but to say it had been mind blowing put it mildly.

"I think we're finally getting to the heart of our pretty little submissive."

"We definitely hit something. Hell, I almost came again in my pants." His hand slowly eased from her quaking pussy, and she heard the distinct sound of him sucking on his fingers and smacking his lips.

"You? You just had your dick in her mouth. I'm going to have bull fucking balls by the time we get there."

The car slowed, pulled to the side and stopped.

"We're here, Sir." The driver spoke with an edge to his voice as well. Obviously, the show they'd put on had gotten to him. Gabby counted to ten in her head, attempting to calm her racing heart but nothing worked. Her body was taut and wrung out, and if they told her to get out and walk now, she was afraid she'd fall flat on her face.

"We're just going to sit here for a while," Thomas explained to the driver.

"No problem, boss. You mind if I go and catch a smoke?"

"Sure, go ahead."

The driver's door opened and closed, and she presumed he'd gotten out.

"You know the poor guy is looking for some place to jack off, don't you?"

David laughed. "Of course, I do. Can you blame him? If I didn't know what we had in store for our beauty, I'd probably be jerking off right now."

"Don't tell me the infamous Master Thomas has lost his cool."

"Smart ass. Just because Gabrielle is the only sub in this car, don't think I'd hesitate to whip your ass if it needed it."

"Very funny."

Thomas snuggled her tight against his chest once again and smoothed his palm up and down her back. She stole strength from that touch and used it to recover from her ordeal. She didn't know what else to call what had happened. Fuzz still wove its way through her mind as she tried to understand this intense vulnerability crawling inside her. She was torn between the need to cry and the need to express her feelings. Emotion swelled until she nearly choked from it. She liked listening to the two of them have a conversation because, if either of them asked her anything serious, she'd end up on her knees expressing her love.

Fresh tears welled in her eyes. This couldn't be love. It would be wrong for her to fall in love with two men. When their relationship concluded, she'd feel twice the pain when they walked out the door—something she didn't feel equipped to handle.

"It's okay, baby. Let it out. Crossing a barrier you didn't even know you had is an emotional experience to say the least. I wish I could say that was the toughest thing you'll experience in your training, but you've barely just begun. We still have a few other bridges to cross."

She sniffled and buried her face in his shirt. He had no idea, and when they found out she was withholding... What would happen then? Would they withdraw from her? There were always more questions than answers.

They sat in silence for a long time. Blindfolded, she had no way to keep track. She listened to their breathing, slow and steady as it lulled her from a state of emotional panic to a calm she desperately needed. They were waiting for her, giving her the time and space she needed until she was ready to get out of the car and follow them to whatever they had in store for her.

Her fingers had been digging into Thomas's arm, something that probably wasn't very comfortable. She lifted her head slightly and released her grip. "I'm sorry, I didn't even realize."

His hands framed her face and pulled her down for a kiss. It was a light, easy kiss that gave her a taste of the gentle man that was but one side of her Dom. She wasn't sure she'd seen the extent of his darker side, but she longed to experience it all.

"Don't apologize. Whatever you need. I'm here for you."

A pang of guilt struck her gut at the truthful ring in his words. So far, he'd asked for nothing more than her trust and despite her intentions she'd only given him half.

"How are you feeling?" David asked gently, his fingers rubbing at shoulder.

"I'm fine now, but I have to admit that was more intense than I expected." She kissed Thomas's lips again, letting her tongue peek out and explore the soft texture and exquisite taste of man. "I'm dying to remove this blindfold."

David laughed and shifted in the seat. "Yep, I'd say she's about back to normal and impatient as ever."

A hand smacked her ass. It wasn't painful, but she yelped just the same. "I'm not impatient."

Both men laughed deeply as Thomas lifted her and handed her over to David who placed her in his lap. The door popped open, and from the sounds of movement, Thomas stepped outside. "I think we're ready to proceed."

David kissed her cheek and slid her across the bench seat until Thomas grabbed her hands.

"Like before, just listen to the sound of my voice and stay close. We'll be inside soon." He pulled her from the car, taking care to duck her head before he tucked her into his side.

Gabby's heart pounded in her chest as the rush of cool outside air rushed over her. It had to be dark by now, but she had no idea where they were or how exposed her still nude body was to the eyes of strangers. The car door slammed behind her, and David plastered himself to the other side of her body as they began to walk across the grass. The cool blades tickled her feet and she had this crazy idea to break free and run naked. She'd had more than one fantasy of being able to do something that. To work in her garden in the nude. Wouldn't her neighbors have a heart attack about something like that? Or better yet, what would the HOA have to say. A giggle bubbled up at the image.

"What's so funny?" Thomas wanted to know.

"It's nothing. This moment just reminded me of a dream I had once."

"You had a dream about being led by two men and walking blindfolded."

"Unfortunately no, I guess my imagination wasn't quite that bold."

"What then? Inquiring minds want to know."

"It's the grass against my bare feet, the scent of roses and honeysuckle. It reminds me of a recurring dream I've had about being in my garden buck naked and being caught by my neighbor who also happens to be the president of our

HOA." She giggled again. "I always thought the look of horror on her face might be worth the embarrassment of doing something that insane."

Both men froze in place, and they had to grip her arms tighter to keep her from falling. She laughed for a minute until she realized no one else was laughing with her.

"I'm sorry, was that silly? Should I be taking this more seriously?"

"It's not that exactly. It's just amazing how things work out sometimes."

She knitted her brows together in confusion, no idea what David referred to. "What do you mean?"

"You'll see." They resumed walking again, leading her carefully once again.

Somewhere in the back of her mind an alarm sounded. Something wasn't right, and she had no idea what it was. "Where are we?"

"Don't worry, Gabrielle. You're safe. We're almost there, and then we'll be instructing you on what to expect."

Now, her stomach cramped with an instinct that told her to run—that all was not well. She tugged at her arms, a renewed desperation to remove the blindfold, but they held her tight, immobile other than her legs, which could only carry her where they led.

She focused on her other senses to listen to the sounds around her for a clue. She heard no cars going by, no people, only a gentle breeze rustling through some trees and bushes, the sound of water babbling from a pond or maybe a small stream and the almost imperceptible faint tinkling of a wind chime from some distance away.

Her nose didn't help her much either. The outdoor smell of fresh cut grass along with a garden of roses and honeysuckle did little to guide her thought processes except to think of her own garden. Wherever they were, whoever took care of this property had the same kind of gardening interests that she did.

Maybe they were going to a private play party at someone's home—another sub like herself? The tingle of laughter and excitement she'd felt just short minutes ago dissipated with the continued sinking feeling that she was missing something very important. The grass under her feet changed to a tumbled brick, which she guessed might be a patio.

A looming sense of dread filled her as she followed them another twenty feet or so and then paused. When she heard the scrap of stone on stone, she knew. *No, no, no, it can't be.* Could they possibly be at her house?

"Where are we?" She tried to hold her voice steady but failed miserably. Scared, she wrenched free from their hold.

"Relax, Gabby. We're going in now," Thomas reassured her with a pat on her arm.

Gooseflesh rose across her entire body as shudders racked her body. This can't be. If they were at her house then Scott was likely watching. Had watched her walk across her own lawn buck freaking naked and wearing a blindfold. Bile rose in her throat and her free hand slapped over her mouth to hold it in. Her body convulsed and tears dripped from her eyes.

"What is it, Gabrielle? Are you okay?"

Metal scraped on metal—a key going in the lock. The knob was twisted, and the door pushed in. The all too familiar scrape her uneven door made across the threshold sounded in her ears, deafening her.

"Oh God. No, no! Please tell me we aren't at my house. Please, Thomas!" Her voice shrieked immeasurably loud even to her own ears. Her heart thumped against her breastbone and full panic took over. She grabbed frantically at her blindfold and ripped it off, blinking at the bright light shining in her eyes.

"Gabrielle, what's wrong? Tell me, god dammit!" The hard edge of Thomas's demand was unmistakable.

She blinked against the burning light until her eyes finally adjusted, and she stood staring at her front door. David stood in front of her, his face creased with worry.

"Oh my God, did anyone see us? I'm not safe. We aren't safe. Fuck, we have to get out of here. Hurry." Words tumbled from her mouth too quickly, she wasn't even sure if they made sense. She tried to pull away from Thomas, to run but he wouldn't let her go. Instead, he pulled her into his arms and carried her into the house. She kicked and clawed at his face and shoulders, desperate to get away. Run. She had to run before Scott found her like this. He would hurt them. Hurt her.

"Gabrielle, calm down. Fuck!" He walked quickly to her couch and dumped her on the cushions. The air whooshed out of her lungs, and she grabbed at her chest unable to breath.

"Jesus Christ, she's having a panic attack." David grabbed her arms pinning them down. "Grab her legs before she hurts herself or one of us."

"Let me go," she yelled. She wanted to hide, turn out the lights, maybe huddle in the corner. Anything other than sit here on display.

"If you can calm down, we'll let you go." David growled at her.

Gabby reached for that shred of sanity she still possessed and willed her body still. Her heart still beat wildly and breath sawed in and out of her lungs but she'd stopped kicking and scratching. "Please, let me go."

Both men immediately released her, and she curled into a tight ball and pulled the afghan draped across the back of the couch over her body.

"You need to tell us what's going on and tell us right now. Why are you so afraid? This is irrational. What the hell are we missing?" Thomas towered over her, waiting for an answer.

As the tears dried on her face and her breathing slowed to normal, her head darted around the room checking to ensure the blinds were still closed and nothing seemed out of place.

"You need to check and see if anyone is in the house."

"What? Why would you think someone is here?" David hesitated and glanced around. "Why the fuck do I feel like we've just been dropped into the Twilight Zone."

"Please, just check. Then I promise I'll tell you everything."

Chapter Eighteen

Thomas walked into the bedroom he assumed was Gabrielle's and checked the closet and bathroom. She obviously took a lot of care in decorating this room and bathroom. Everything was well organized and done in a rich, dark shade of purple. It reminded him of eggplant. She had a king size bed that dominated the space and a stack of books on the nightstand. He hoped she didn't miss reading in bed too much because he didn't foresee her returning to that nighttime activity any time soon, if ever.

He wanted to picture her, lying on the bed, spread out for him, but all he could see was the stark fear in her eyes when she'd started screaming about not being at her house. What the hell could have happened? He sat down hard on the bed, scrubbing his hands over his face. When had he lost control of the situation? He and David had planned tonight carefully, giving her all the time and space she needed this afternoon and they'd both garnered from their time with her here and at his house that she loved the home she'd built here. So what then? She didn't want to taint the space with her kink? No, he didn't believe that for a second. That wasn't the kind of woman she was.

He rubbed his palms along the lengths of his thighs and took one last look around. He wanted to know who the hell she thought was lurking in her house and why. He could drive himself crazy trying to figure out the small mistakes he might have made, or he could confront her and demand answers.

After a quick glance in the closet to confirm it was indeed empty, he headed through the door and down the short hall to the living room where David squatted next to her, rubbing her back and calming her with his more gentle ways. Thomas' first impulse had been to command an answer before she'd even had a chance to calm down. Not because he was a dickhead but because sometimes hysteria needed a firm hand. Luckily, David was the other side of the coin from him and saw reason instead of sheer fear.

"The house is all clear."

Gabrielle blinked up at him. Sadness tinged with fear shining in her eyes. He wanted to take away whatever had done that to her. But what if it was him who'd managed to scare her off. He blew out a rough breath and sat on the couch not far from her head. He needed to touch her, to feel the warmth inside her and feed her his strength if that's what she needed.

"Can we talk now?"

She nodded.

"Good. Now, tell us what happened. What has you so frightened?"

"I came home today to dozens of voicemails. Threatening."

David's face clouded over. "What? From who?"

"My ex. I haven't heard from him in months, and now, all of a sudden he's following me around."

"Wait. He's following you around, too?"

"I don't think I can repeat everything he said. The recorder is on the desk in the hall. You can listen to them for yourself."

"And I will. But answer me something first." He paused, waiting for her full attention. "Why didn't you tell us about this sooner?"

"I-I didn't want to involve you. It's not fair."

"Not involve me? Are you not wearing a collar around your neck? Have you decided you want to take it off? What the hell, Gabrielle?"

David grabbed his arm and pulled him from the couch as fresh tears washed from her eyes. "Thomas, stop. Not yet."

"She doesn't fucking trust us," he managed through clenched teeth.

"Save it. I know how you feel, but first things first. I'll take care of her, and you can listen to the messages. Then we'll decide what to do. Agreed?"

Of course, David was right. It didn't make him feel any better, which wasn't the point right now anyway. He walked over to the desk and lifted his finger, hovering over the button.

"Wait." Gabrielle struggled to a sitting position, holding tight to the blanket around her as if it would provide security instead of him. This was definitely going to be a long night and nothing like he'd planned. Troy had already received his instructions to return the town car to Sanctuary as soon as they'd settled in the house. So they were all staying here tonight unless someone called a cab.

"What is it, sweetheart?" David dropped a soothing kiss on the top of her head.

"I don't want to hear them again. Once was enough."

"How about a hot bath then?"

Gabby looked up into David's face and gave him a tentative smile. Thomas' gut twisted at the innocent expression she carried. They did have some issues to work through, but damn if he had any intention of letting her get away. Somehow, she'd worked her way inside him and he wanted to keep her there.

"That actually sounds good. I'll be fine on my own if you want to stay here and listen with Thomas," she offered.

"Maybe after I get you settled and comfortable first. I'm not leaving you alone until I'm sure you're ready."

"I'm not a child, and this isn't the first time I've dealt with this," she said bitterly.

Thomas' head lifted sharply at her words, a pissed off comment on the tip of his tongue. Luckily, he caught David's signal and squelched the urge to berate her. But she definitely had some serious punishment coming her way as soon as they got this straightened out. If she thought she could shut him out, she had another thing coming.

David led Gabrielle out of the room, and when Thomas heard the soft click of the bathroom door closing behind them, he pressed play. The first message came and the man's voice sounded reasonable and calm, but he had a hunch that after dozens of calls that had degraded quickly.

Letting her recorder continue, he paced to the light switches near the doorway and turned them all off, drowning the room in darkness. From memory, he made his way to the front curtains and lifted the side edge a fraction, only enough to allow him to see out and not catch the eye of anyone who might be watching the house.

He stood there for a long while as the messages continued, and his anger built layer by layer after each subsequent call. Unfortunately, this was not the first time in his life he'd dealt with a man like this, and if he wasn't careful, he'd find himself heading down the slippery slope into his past. As the owner of Sanctuary, he'd seen just about every domestic situation that existed, and this asshole on the recorder was a textbook case of a husband who'd cut his wife loose then when the fresh pussy dried up, came back home, looking to place blame on the woman he'd been married to.

How many men like this existed in the world? Not only did they need to be taught a lesson or two but so did the fucking parents who'd raised them to be like this. His childhood had been majorly fucked up, yet he didn't use it as an excuse to become abusive toward women. He laughed at that thought. How many people had called him just that to his face because of his proclivity to the harder kink? He liked to take risks, and he often used pain to bring submissives to their greatest pleasure.

Not that giving pain didn't give him pleasure, because it did. He didn't love much more than seeing a sub's needy reaction to the kiss of a whip or the fall of a flogger's tails. The marks he left behind gave them both a sense of pride. He'd seen some of that with Gabrielle so far, but they'd barely begun to scratch the surface. Now, they were backtracking. She didn't trust him enough to tell her about these phone calls...to confide her fear...then how would she be able to tell him what she wanted from a Dom or when he'd gone too far? Would she let him push her past the point she could take then never forgive him for it?

He rested his forehead against the cool wood trim of the window, not taking his eyes from the darkness outside. The messages continued, escalating until as he'd feared her ex had begun to seek her out at home uninvited. The bastard was stalking her in the middle of the night and beyond, and more than likely, he was out there right now or would be soon. He didn't sound like the kind of man who would just drop it.

"Did I hear what I fucking think I did?" David spoke from the hallway pass through, hopefully out of Gabrielle's hearing.

"Yes. He's been here. Possibly inside. And he left her a gift. Did she mention anything like that to you?"

"No. We didn't talk about it all. I wanted her to relax."

"Fine, I'll go ask her." Thomas strode across the room and stepped into the hall. David's arm came up to block his path.

"I don't think it's a good idea to confront her right now."

"I'm not trying to confront her. I only want to know what that bastard left here for her," he growled.

David raised his eyebrow. The universal gesture for *yeah right.*

"Don't you want to know? Aren't you curious to know the extent of the danger she's in? I have half a mind to yank her out of that tub and drag her back to my house where I know I can keep her safe."

"Which is exactly why you don't want to go in there right now. If you walk through that door, guns blazing, she's going to stiffen that spine of hers and shoot you down so fast we'll both find ourselves outside on our asses."

Thomas snorted.

"She's scared to death, but I don't think either of us should discount just how pissed off she is."

Thomas turned and leaned his upper body against the wall. A rough breath escaping his lips. "I can't stand by and do nothing. Fuck, man. She's more than just a sub from the club."

"I know. To me, too. Lucky for all of us, this is exactly the kind of thing I do and do well. I'll have that asshole figured out within twenty-four hours and then we can decide what to do. Give me that much, at least. Trust me to do what needs to be done."

What had started as a lighthearted jest had turned down right icy on David's last words. Menace radiated from within and glittered in his eyes. David was right, of course. He was the perfect man for this job. It just wasn't like Thomas to do nothing.

"I have to do something." He pushed off the wall and walked into the living room. "I studied the area outside the front window and so far there's no sign of anyone out there casing the place."

"We're probably dealing with a shithead amateur. Easy enough to handle as long as we get a hold of him before he goes off and does something stupid."

No way would Thomas give anyone the opportunity to get that close to Gabrielle. She might fight him on his ideas of security, but she'd listen in the end because he would make her. Keeping her safe and in his bed were of the utmost priorities. Now, keeping her out of his heart had become another matter altogether. He could try to fight it, but he suspected he'd already lost the battle.

"Is everything okay?"

He turned to see Gabrielle standing in the doorway to her bedroom, a fluffy white robe wrapped around her. He clenched his fingers into fists and tensed the muscles in his legs to keep from pouncing on her. Despite her sweet appearance, he found himself torn between fucking her senseless and bending her over his knee for a spanking that would keep her standing for a week. David must have sensed it as he stepped between them.

"We just finished listening to the last of the messages."

"Thank God. I didn't want to keep them but figured for my own protection I would want the record."

Thomas noticed the slight tremor in her hands before she clenched them together.

"Smart move. These could one day be evidence in case anything were to happen."

"Happen? Like what?" She crossed her arms over her chest.

"Come on, Gabrielle. You know as well as I do that an angry ex can sometimes take things too far."

"I know. But now that I'm calm and some time has passed I feel kind of stupid. He's probably not that dangerous."

"What about the gift he left?" Thomas interjected, tired of waiting for his answers.

She shook her head. "Both Angel and I looked around for anything that didn't belong and so far haven't found a thing. He's probably blowing smoke, trying to scare me."

"Who's Angel?" David looked confused.

"My best friend. Thomas knows her. As soon as I got to the last message, I got scared and ran out of the house and called Angel. She came over, went through the house for me then we spent the afternoon drinking margaritas and calling Scott filthy names."

"You should have called me," Thomas murmured.

Gabrielle opened her mouth to say something then clamped it shut, averting her gaze to the floor. Too little too late as far as he was concerned. She still had a lot to answer for and a lot to learn. Although David was right, now was not the right time.

"So what next, David. You think we should head back to my place?"

"No, actually, I don't. I think we should spend the night here. I'll find the right spot to stake out and keep any eye on the property. I want to see if he does actually show up." He turned back to Gabby. "Do you have a recent photograph of him that I can study?"

She nodded. "Yeah, in the bottom drawer of my desk I have some photos from about a year ago." She pushed past David and avoided even brushing against him before kneeling in front of the desk.

"Are you sure this is the best thing for her?" he whispered to David in a low tone.

"Yeah, I really do. She needs to feel like a part of the solution so anywhere I can use her help I intend to. She needs to face this and deal with it head on."

"Fine." Frustration clouded Thomas' judgment, but he'd keep that fact to himself.

"Here you go." Gabby handed them each a photograph. A small 4 x 6 of a man standing in front of a barbeque grill with one of those ridiculous aprons that said 'Kiss the cook'.

He looked average, with sandy blond hair, dark eyes and a thickening middle. He could have been any middle-aged suburbanite. He had a beer in one hand and a spatula in the other. Harmless. But as Thomas had learned many, many times the hard way, looks could be deceiving. It wasn't all that difficult to hide evil underneath a veneer of civility. At least for a while.

"Perfect. I'm going outside to scope out the area. Am I safe to leave the two of you alone?"

Gabrielle shrugged.

"I won't be punishing her tonight, if that's what you mean."

Her head jerked, her gaze locking with his.

"Don't look so surprised, Gabrielle. As long as you're wearing that collar, you are our responsibility and your inability to be forthcoming compromised us all."

Guilt flashed into her eyes alongside her sadness.

David shot her a knowing look and shrugged his shoulders before quietly slipping out the front door. They were obviously standing together on this issue.

"Look at me, Gabrielle. We aren't getting into this now. You need to know that whatever's happened, we're both behind you one hundred percent. We aren't going anywhere."

Her lower lip curled into her mouth where her teeth lightly nibbled on it. Without her realizing it, that shy and worried move tore down a good chunk of his anger. He really did want to help her.

He sat down on the arm of the couch and reached for her. "Come here."

She took two tentative steps in his direction until his fingers wrapped around her arms and pulled her to him. The sudden urge to touch and comfort her overwhelmed him as she stepped into his arms.

"I'm here for you, sweetheart. Always." He breathed deeply taking in the freshly bathed scent of warm vanilla and that underlying scent of the woman who'd worked her way under his skin.

She could take care of business if she had to, but he didn't want her to. She should be able to rely on his protection and ability to keep her safe when they were together. He tamped down the anger he felt toward her ex, afraid it would taint how he looked at her. In no way did he blame her for that asshole, but he couldn't afford her misreading his reactions.

"I'm so sorry, Thomas. I only wanted to keep you out of my mess."

"Don't you see? We're all together now. What you go through, we go through."

"But it's so embarrassing." She pressed her face into his shoulder, and the wet tears she shed soaked through the fabric of his shirt.

"Don't cry, baby. He's so not worth it."

"It's not him I'm crying about. It's the fact that I've disappointed you."

"Shh." He rubbed a path up and down her spine atop the thick fabric of her robe. "Everything will be fine. We'll talk about it when we're ready. Now is definitely not the time."

She looked up at him, hope glimmering in her eyes. Her hands went to her neck where she traced the path of her collar. "Are you going to take this away from me?"

"Do you want me to?"

"No, Sir. I do not."

Not a second of hesitation in her answer. Good, he liked that.

"I'm not done training you, and I doubt David is prepared to walk away."

"What happens when the training is complete?"

"Let's not worry about that quite yet, okay, sweetheart?" He leaned in, grasping her bottom lip with his teeth. His body ached to be inside her with a force he'd have to temper for now. Frustration and confusion warred within them, and right now they needed to be together. He wanted her to see that nothing going on in her life would turn him away.

"Thomas."

"Yes, babe?"

She reached down and undid the belt around her robe, letting it fall open. Her hips angled closer as she melted into his body. "I need you," she whispered.

A hungry moan sounded in his throat as he scooped her into his arms and carried her down the hall to the bedroom. The light spilling from the partially open bathroom door gave off a romantic glow that bathed the room in a soft, barely there light. He went straight to the bed and laid her out, spreading her robe wide.

"Stretch your arms above you head and spread your legs for me."

She whimpered softly and did as instructed. The bare skin spread before him made her look like a special offering, one that he had to devour quick or die from needing it. He toed off his shoes and yanked at his socks before pulling at the belt looped around his waist. He stared between the strip of leather in his hands and Gabrielle stretched across the big bed, debating the right course. As much as he ached to bind her wrists to the headboard with his belt it wasn't what either one of them needed this time.

He finished removing his clothes, grabbed a condom and moved over her on the mattress. Her soft body gave under the weight of his until he'd aligned himself above her with the head of his cock nudging at her soaking wet sex.

"Jesus, Gabrielle. You burn me alive." Emotions swirled in his head as he looked into her eyes and saw that same churning and confusion. He'd not yet broken through her shields, and still, he felt more for her than anyone else in his life. He sensed his plans to train her and hand her over to David slowly unraveling. If he took her now, like this, with them both burning alive from the emotions of the day, they'd never be the same again.

Fingers brushed his shoulders in a tentative move and sent a sharp shudder of longing from his head to his groin. Wet spots still shone on her cheeks, and he bent to lick them, the slight salty taste awakening his taste buds.

"Tell me everything is going to be all right," she pleaded on a soft cry.

That sound ripped at his gut and tore through what little resolve remained. "It is, darling. I swear it." He pushed an inch forward, her hot moist channel beckoning.

"Make love to me, Thomas, please." Her quiet plea trembled through him, making his limbs shake with the force of holding back.

His mouth pressed down on hers in a possessive kiss meant to dominate the situation as he rolled the condom over his erection and slid inside her to the hilt. He absorbed her moan of pleasure as he pressed into her mouth deeper, his tongue sweeping every inch.

Her tight sheath clenched around him as he slowly pulled from her before thrusting forward once again. Sensations of intense pleasure shot through him from head to toe as he fought to maintain control. She needed him to take care of her, to show her that he cared, and so help him, that's what he'd do no matter what it took. Tonight, her comfort and security were all that mattered, not broken promises or worries about a lack of trust.

No, this feeling, listening to her harsh pants in his ear, the tilt of her hips to meet each push inside her, the contracting muscles of her thighs bracketing his hips, it was all that mattered as he let everything else go for tonight. This woman, his beauty who continued to burrow into his heart against his will, needed him to be her protector and lover. A role he cherished without even realizing it until now.

"Oh Thomas," she moaned.

He kissed his way down her neck and bit slowly into her shoulder until the pain reached her erotic level, and she wailed, a long, loud sound from a place deep inside her. He smiled against her skin and angled his hips so his cock would rub against her G-spot with each thrust inside her.

Quick bite after bite, he trailed down her chest to her breast. He suckled the tight nipple between his lips and laved gently over the tip. Her body writhed underneath him, her climax building under the steady rhythm of his cock shuttling in and out of her. He wanted nothing more than to make her come over and over again until the memories of her day were temporarily forgotten and pleasure was her complete and total focus.

Shifting an inch higher on her body, he created additional friction across her clit with each plunge. Her arms twitched, muscles jerking against the natural need to wrap them around him and hold on tight. That she could still hold onto that modicum of control told him he hadn't taken her quite high enough yet.

Were she tied up, it would be easier for her to fight the bonds without fear of disobeying, but that wasn't the point tonight. Tonight, he wanted to simply give her as much pleasure as she could take.

"Put your arms around my neck."

After a momentary pause, she wrapped herself around him. He reveled in the soft warmth she gave off while he worked her nipple with his teeth.

"Oh God, Thomas I can't…I can't…"

He wrenched his mouth free, pulling her nipple taut. "It's okay, sweetheart. Don't hold back. Come for me."

He pushed harder against her clit until her muscles contracted and she squeezed around his cock.

"That's it, baby. Let it go."

The sting of her nails sinking into his back coincided with the tight fist-like grip she had on his dick. Tense muscles convulsed, her breath catching in her throat. His own heart beat heavy in his chest as the rush of blood roared in his ears. The tight rein on his control slipped a fraction as flames licked at his balls. *So much for control.*

He drove harder, pushing through the tight muscles and creating enough friction to draw her from the tail end of one orgasm into a new harder release.

She screamed into his chest while he pistoned in and out of her at increasing speed. The tingling in his sac quickly changed to surging sensations as his need turned imminent. He glanced to her face and locked his gaze with hers. "You are so beautiful, you're everything and I will keep you safe."

"Thomas..." she whispered. An invitation he couldn't resist.

"Take it, Gabrielle. Claim it." He burned with feverish need as he waited for her to tell him, his pelvis thrashing against her with every thrust.

"Mine," she whispered. "Mine. All mine."

With deep satisfaction, he grabbed her hips and thrust hard and deep, so deep he bumped her cervix. He groaned when his orgasm tore from him and jerked his cock inside her, filling her.

With every jerk, more of his guard against this woman tore away. Before long he would be naked and vulnerable to her in every way. The only shred of protection that remained between them was the fact that deep down she had not given him or David her complete trust and, without that, none of them could move on. He would have to find out one way or another if Gabrielle could close the door to her old life and become the submissive her soul ached for. Every instinct he possessed swore he recognized that in her. From the moment he'd met her at Sanctuary, his mission had been clear. Break down the barriers and show her the woman she could and wanted to be.

Their rough breaths panted in sync as they grappled to recover. If he were a smart man, he'd get up and go into the bathroom, give them the time they needed to put some distance around what happened, but apparently, he wasn't feeling too smart. Instead, he focused on her racing pulse and the sticky heat surrounding them. He'd always loved the aftermath of sex, that sense of satisfaction not only in pleasure but in the woman's acceptance of his domination and her gift of submission.

This was that and so much more. Words he'd thought he'd never voice again sat on the tip of his tongue that. Not until he got all the way inside her could he allow himself to pull out and examine the true depth of feelings for the soft, feminine body underneath him.

He looked into her eyes and caught a glimpse of similar turmoil before he kissed it away with a soft press of lips to her eyes, nose, chin and, finally, her lips.

"Thank you, Thomas." The hoarse whisper of her words caressed his cooling skin.

He grabbed the leg she had wrapped around his hip and rolled them to their sides while staying joined with her. He couldn't bear to not be inside her yet. He wanted her as close as possible so she could feel his ownership and need. She tucked her head into his shoulder when his arms wrapped around her, pulling her close.

"Rest, my beauty. You're going to need it." He smiled into her hair and waited the long minutes it took until her breathing evened into the deep rhythm of sleep.

Yes, tomorrow, we will know one way or another where this is going.

Chapter Nineteen

Gabby woke to the scent of a warm male body wrapped around her from both sides. Not only was Thomas still holding her tight in his arms, David had joined them some time during the night and now sandwiched her tightly between them. A smile flitted across her face at the image they must present like this. She wished she could have a picture of this for her desk. What a perfect reminder at any given moment of what she had to be thankful for the most.

But as much as she liked this position, the call of nature had woken her from a deep sleep, and she needed to move. She shifted her leg from under Thomas as slowly as possible, hoping not to disturb him.

"I take it you're awake," David whispered at her ear.

She nodded without uttering a word, keeping her eyes on Thomas and his sleeping form. He looked so relaxed lying there, so carefree. Very unlike the man he was when awake. He always carried the look of a man who wore the weight of the world on his shoulders—another reason she'd not wanted to drag them into her personal mess.

A fresh pang of guilt swept through her at the memory of the ruined night when her secrets had been revealed. It had seemed like no big deal to not mention it, but hindsight being 20/20, she could see that this path she had chosen to journey with them carried a different set of rules and an entirely new outlook on her role.

Thomas and David's intentions to be aware of and care for her wellbeing at all times filled her with a sense of awe and appreciation far more than she'd expected. She pressed her nose closer to Thomas's chest until the fine sprinkling of hair tickled her face. She could certainly get used to waking up like this.

Last night with him had been the most tender bout of lovemaking she'd ever experienced, and it had taken every ounce of her restraint not to tell him how she felt. That she wanted him. His insistence in caring for her even when she knew he'd still felt the sting of disappointment carried more weight with her than all the words he could have said in a week.

"I need to pee," she whispered over her shoulder.

A soft rumbling laugh vibrated through her back until she too giggled. Thomas stretched and rolled enough to allow her passage.

"Hurry up and come back," he murmured.

A warm hand squeezed her ass cheek, and David moved to give her room as well. She scrambled from the bed and rushed into the bathroom to take care of business.

She hurried in the bathroom, anxious to get back to her men as quickly as she could. Without being snuggled between them, the cool air chilled her skin. Standing at the edge of her bed contemplating which way to jump, her stomach rumbled loudly.

"I take it you're hungry." David laughed.

"Just a little."

Thomas rolled onto his back and scrubbed his face. Gabby nearly swallowed her tongue at the sight. Tanned skin pulled taut over well-defined muscles that flexed as he moved his arms. A flat stomach with that telltale trail of hair that led to a small thatch of dark brown curls surrounding his impressive cock. And what a cock it was this morning. Long, thick and hard as a rock.

Thoughts of breakfast gave way to darker, sexier images of what she could do with his erection. Or more along the lines of what he could do with it. Her sex squeezed with a sudden anticipation. She could feel moisture readying her for anything they wanted from her this morning.

"Ah, darling, you better quit looking at him like you want to eat him, or we'll end up in this bed all day long."

"Is that a bad thing?"

Thomas looked sharply in her direction, heat and something else in his eyes. "No, baby, that is never a bad thing. But first things first, right David?"

David looked a little disappointed, but he acquiesced. "Yeah, the least we could do is feed you to pump up your energy before we ravish you."

They both moved from the bed at the same time, and she was torn between looking at them. Both were perfect male specimens in their own right despite their many differences. Just looking at them reminded her it was time to renew her gym membership.

"You're doing it again."

She blinked a few times to get her bearings back.

"Doing what?" she asked innocently.

"That look of longing in your eyes is doing nothing to make this go down." David pointed at his erection, which he aimed in her direction.

"I would be happy to take care of that for you."

David hopefully looked in Thomas's direction.

"Let's go into the kitchen, and she can take care of you while we talk and cook. I'm anxious to hear how things went last night. I assume since you made it to bed at some point, you've got things under control."

"I do." David and Thomas reached for their pants and put them on in unison.

Gabby looked wistfully at her robe lying on the floor, but Thomas moved in and cupped her chin, turning her head to face him. He kissed her on the mouth, a combination good morning and "I'd like to devour you" kind of touch.

"You won't be needing that robe anytime soon. In fact, the same rules apply here as at my house as long as we are staying here, okay?"

"But—"

"No, no buts. We won't allow any action to harm you or embarrass you. In fact this morning, I want your head thinking long and hard about that trust issue we have."

"I trust—"

"No, you don't. Not fully. But you will soon or this won't work." He released her chin and strode from the room.

Tears threatened, and Gabby's stomach flip-flopped at the hidden meaning in his words. Would he be leaving her if she couldn't prove that trust? *Well, duh, Gabby, of course he will.*

"Don't look so worried, beautiful. Trust means everything to Thomas, and he wants yours, as do I. So what happens next in this relationship is completely up to you."

She opened her mouth to respond, to plead, and he covered her mouth with his. Warm lips nibbled against hers until his tongue probed at the seam willing her to allow him in. It was her turn to give in, to stop talking and feel. His tongue brushed hers, tangled and twirled around her mouth until she moaned with the pleasure of it. Hands reached for her hips and pulled her the hard length of him, straining against his jeans.

When he pulled free from her mouth, regret was written all over his face. She couldn't wait to take that look away, to see him writhing in pleasure when she begged for his cum. And she was prepared to beg if that's what it took.

"Let's go before Thomas comes back in here looking for us."

He grabbed her hand and pulled her behind him giving her a chance to admire the lean lines of his back. There was a long, jagged looking scar at his side, and she wondered how he'd gotten it. She'd have to remember to ask him about that later.

"About time." Thomas sounded gruff, but the smile in his eyes erased any ill feelings.

He'd already found his way around her kitchen and had eggs, bacon and bread lying on the counter. Two of her pans were heating on the gas-powered stove.

"I hope eggs and bacon are okay."

"Are you kidding? That sounds delicious."

Thomas turned back to the stove and added a dollop of butter to the hot pan, making it sizzle and burn. It reminded her of how they made her feel every time they put their hands on her. Completely pleasurable but so intense she thought she might die from the inside out.

David took a seat on one of the stools and pulled her into his lap so that she sat with her back to his chest and they could both watch Thomas cook for them.

His hands immediately cupped her breasts and rolled her puckered nipples between his fingers. So that was how it was going to be. He'd tease and torture her until they were good and ready for her.

"Update me on last night." Thomas cracked the first egg with one hand and deftly dropped it into the prepared pan.

"As soon as I took up a post in the corner of the garden, I got on the phone and contacted two of my guys. One who would compile a complete dossier on one Scott Graham and the other to locate the target and report on his whereabouts."

David didn't pause for a second in his exploration of her body while he spoke. Gabby fought against the distraction to pay attention to what he said.

"Neither took very long. Not only are my guys the best at what they do, but your Scott is a pretty easy mark."

"He's not my Scott." Immediately, she regretted the sarcasm.

"No, he's not, and I'm glad to hear you say that," David said roughly. He stood from the stool and picked her up with him, depositing her on her feet in front of him. He grabbed her arms and turned her to face him.

"You belong to me and to Thomas. Is that still what you want?" Gone were the easy smiles and the happy eyes, replaced with an intensity she'd not seen from David but on the rarest of occasions. "I know, Gabrielle. But I'm afraid you've hit my trigger, as well. Which has nothing to do with Scott and everything to do with your faith. I need your faith, baby."

She nodded, holding herself completely still.

"On your knees, Gabrielle," David commanded.

This time, there was no hesitation. In fact, there was nowhere she'd rather be. She'd do anything to show these men how much she cared for them and loved serving them.

Somewhere in the back of her mind, she heard bacon sizzling in the pan behind her, and Thomas cooking their breakfast.

"Take out my dick, and suck me. Ease me."

Her pussy clenched at the tone of his voice giving her orders and tinged with a clear need. He needed *her*. She lifted her hands and fumbled with the button and zipper of his jeans until she had them open. Eagerly, she pushed her hands inside and around his hips to his ass. His hands went to her shoulders where he grasped her tightly. She gave one tight squeeze to his cheeks before pushing the denim down below his thighs. That glorious cock of his sprang forward and bounced against her lips.

"I like seeing you like this. Eager and willing. But no teasing," he warned. "I'm too far beyond that this time."

With one hand, she cupped his sac, and the other wrapped around the base of his shaft. He pulsed in her hand, a groan close behind.

"You know, I'm glad that our beauty is taking care of you, David, but I still want to hear the rest of the details about last night." Thomas spoke behind her, and she nearly burst out laughing. "Gabrielle, no one told you to stop. So keep going while David finishes filling me in."

"Yes, Sir," she murmured against David's weeping tip.

Both hands increased their pressure as she opened her mouth wide and engulfed the head. Her tongue lapped at the slit, licking up every drop of his salty pre-cum. God, she loved the taste of him.

With slow precision she moved her mouth down the shaft one inch at a time until the swollen tip pressed at the back of her throat, threatening her gag reflex. Her tongue bathed every inch it could reach, paying particular attention to the sensitive veins along the underside.

The hand resting on her shoulder tightened, pressing into her skin. She loved that she had this kind of an effect on him. She liked the idea of making him crazy, of his dick swelling to the point he couldn't hold back no matter what he did and him releasing into her mouth. She needed that. Needed to know that she still gave him the satisfaction he craved.

On her knees giving him pleasure created a sexuality for her so deep, so dark, it made her want so much more. She craved the scene she'd missed out on last night. Regretted that she'd not considered the consequences of her actions. She should have warned herself that being in a training situation with two Doms, learning how to become the submissive they needed, would be addictive. But it was too late for that now.

"One Scott Graham is quite the unimaginative jerk." David spoke hoarsely. Her effect on him was undeniable. "He's not left his house since I put someone on his tail. And according to all the records we could dig up, he goes to work, comes home, watches TV and drinks a few beers then goes to bed. He has a standing poker game with some coworkers once a month, and a couple nights of week, he goes to the bowling alley where one of the waitresses fucks him when she gets off shift."

Gabby froze, her gaze rising to David's. No fucking way.

David's hand wrapped around her head and pulled her onto his dick again. "Did I say you could stop?"

His gruff voice shook her from the daze. Scott had no place in her mind here or anywhere really.

Her mouth surrounded his length, her tongue tracing a path along the underside.

"Oh yeah, there you go."

"Is that it?" Thomas asked.

"No, but our little girl is distracting me with that wicked mouth of hers. Where was I? Right. Waitress. Fucking. We looked into the waitress, and apparently three days ago, she took an emergency leave of absence from work and flew to Florida to be with her ailing mother."

Gabby winced at a sudden loud bang. Thomas slamming her spatula she'd guess.

"I knew it. Textbook ex-asshole psycho bullshit. He doesn't have anywhere current to stick his dick so why not go back to the ex and fuck with her until she gives in and puts out."

"Yeah, pretty much," David groaned.

"So what does that mean for Gabrielle and her safety. Did anyone ever figure out what he did when he was on property?"

"There is no evidence he was here. So either he is a smart criminal, or he was bullshitting her on the phone to try and scare her into answering him."

"Typical."

Gabby tried to focus on their words and hear what they'd learned about her ex, but with David guiding her head if she slowed or stopped, he made it impossible to do anything but pay attention to the task at hand. With every pull on her head or groan that fell from his mouth when she hit a sensitive spot, her pussy heated. Flames licked at the skin between her thighs until it took every ounce of control not to touch herself. Her clit pulsed in time with the throbbing of his swollen cock until she started having serious thoughts of taking things into her own hand with or without permission.

Her gaze cut to David, a stern, desire-filled expression glaring down at her. No, there would be no moves without his express permission unless she wanted to find herself in more trouble than she already was.

"Assessment?" Thomas asked.

"The stalker or the sweet sub with her lush lips sucking me off?"

"I can see for myself how well Gabrielle is taking care of you."

"The situation bears watching, but I doubt much will come of it. I'll keep a man on him, and if he makes a move in this direction we can address it then."

Footsteps against the clean tile floor moved closer. "It doesn't exactly give me the chance to take out the frustration I developed yesterday, but since Gabrielle's safety is our top concern we'll have to drop any desire for payback."

Relieved by Thomas' final words, Gabby refocused and doubled her efforts to get David to come. As much as he needed the release, she ached for his essence, needed the relief of satisfying him on the most basic of levels.

With the hand still grasping his sac, she rolled the globes gently together while applying a steady pressure designed to maximize his sensations. She hadn't exactly come to them a virgin. Giving head was a particular act she enjoyed and had gone to great lengths to perfect her skills.

"Damn, woman!" he snarled, the fire in his eyes spurring her on. "You trying to make me lose control soon? You want me to hold your head tight, my cock deep in your mouth as I shoot my cum down your throat, don't you?"

She moaned in response. Hell yeah, she wanted that so much her pussy wept for it. Her eyes watered not from sucking so hard but as a direct result of the pure unadulterated desire to surrender to the man who commanded her, one of the two holding her heart in his hands like putty.

"I wish you could see this. My dick sliding in and out of your mouth. It doesn't get much more erotic than this."

"Want to make a bet?" Thomas spoke from behind her.

Slowing her pace, Gabby raked her teeth across the slope of David's rigid length until his fingers flexed in her hair, grasping the strands in an erotic bite of pleasure/pain that sent her soaring. His cock throbbed, and his guttural moans filled the room. He was so close. Almost there. A few more seconds and she'd have him.

From nowhere, her arms were pulled behind her back, and David withdrew from her mouth. A cry tore from her lips at the loss. A sudden sense of confusion clouded her thoughts.

"As much as he would love to come down that lovely throat of yours, you haven't earned that right today," Thomas whispered at her ear.

Butter-soft leather wrapped around her wrists, and she recognized the texture and sensation of her hands being cuffed together. What was going on?

She lifted her gaze to David to see his hand frantically working his dick. Her job. Her duty. Her right. Tears sprang to her eyes.

"Eyes down, Gabrielle," David commanded.

Reluctantly, she dipped her head and tore her gaze from his throbbing cock head and imminent explosion. The taste of his pre-cum, that earthy, salty, all-male taste on her tongue created a violent clenching response in her pussy. Empty.

"Please," she begged.

"You do not have permission to speak," Thomas' voice boomed from above her.

"Fuck, I'm going to come." David's harsh cries tore through the room and ripped into her soul as the heated splash of his release struck her breasts. Adrift at being denied, shudders rocked her body as he coated her skin.

She ached to reach for him, to cling to the rock-hard muscles of his legs, but the restraints at her wrists allowed little movement of her arms. David's rough pants faded as he moved away, leaving her to consider the ramifications of what had just happened.

"I know how you feel. Your whole body aches with the need to go to him, to take care of him. Doesn't it?"

She nodded.

"Say it out loud."

"Yes, Sir."

"But right now, you can't. Not because your hands are bound. That's not the real reason, is it?"

Gabby hesitated, tried to focus on the question. She knew what Thomas wanted and was afraid to give it. To admit it would mean she'd been wrong all along. She *was* wrong, but saying it out loud made it real.

Thwap.

A loud pop sounded in her head, followed by a sharp little sting on the flesh of her right butt cheek. Nothing too painful but he certainly had her attention now. Although what the hell he'd wielded it with she had no idea.

"Answer me."

"No, it's not the reason," she whispered, her voice cracking.

Thomas knelt in front of her, his faded jeans tightening across his muscular thighs. She started to lift her head and froze. She'd not been given permission to raise her eyes or speak first. While he stared at her intently, she could only wait as patiently as possible. Her knees ached a little from the hard tile in the kitchen, but she found it a comfort, a dull pain she wanted to endure for the sake of the lesson she needed to learn.

"Why are you here?" He dragged a crop across his thigh and into her view.

She blinked in surprise. "What do you—?"

Thwap.

Another strike with the crop, this time to the outside of her thigh. Despite the fear of rejection, of having these two men walk out because she hadn't given them what they needed, her pussy spasmed and fresh desire trickled to the tops of her thighs.

"Why are you here, Gabrielle? You're wearing a training collar that you eagerly accepted, and I want to know why. What is it that you need?"

The sharp edge in his voice startled her. Not because it was anger. It had a different quality, something she couldn't quite put her finger on.

"I...I..." She didn't know how to put it in words. "For years, I have ached with a need I never understood."

"Do you understand it now?" His hand reached up and tucked a lock of hair behind her ear. An unexpected thoughtful gesture that made her eyes water. She didn't want to keep crying all the time, but she didn't know how else to express it.

"I need freedom." No, that didn't make sense. She was bound and liked it. She felt vulnerable yet more turned on than ever before. Scared and excited all at the same time. "I need freedom to explore what I've hidden so long is what I mean."

"Keep going," he urged.

"I have fantasies I don't understand. I've discovered pain enhances my sexual arousal, and I've learned that pleasing you or pleasing David gives me a sense of something special." She shook her head. "It's so hard to put into words."

Thwap.

Gabby sucked in a sharp breath at the burst of pain across the top of her thigh. The sensation jolted through her in a direct line to her clit. It hurt. Yet her pussy wept harder, clenching for attention. The need for Thomas to bend her over and take her overwhelmed her until whimpers fell from her lips.

"No excuses, Gabrielle. I won't have them." He stood and walked around her until she could no longer see him. "You can't be afraid to tell me what you need. I wont allow you to be embarrassed. I know how to get you exactly what you need, but first, you have to be willing to tell me what it is."

"I'm sorry—"

Thwap. Thwap.

Heat spread like wildfire through her ass with each new touch of his damned crop. Where had it come from? She wanted him to stop. She needed him to keep going. Confusion clouded her brain.

"What do I need, Gabrielle?"

The question stuck in her brain, repeating over and over. What did he want? He said he wanted to please her, to fill her needs. But there was more.

"Me to obey?" she asked tentatively.

"Well, that is important under the right circumstances, but no, Gabrielle, that is not what we are getting at here. Think basics. You've admitted you need freedom to be the woman you crave to be. So what do I or David need? The most important thing in all of this."

She didn't want to say it.

Thwap, thwap, thwap.

"Focus, Gabrielle. Think about the pain running through your ass right now. The pulsing in your clit it's created." He leaned close to her ear, his chest draped across her back. "If I put my fingers in your cunt, what will I find? Are you dripping wet and dying to be fucked?"

"Yes, Sir."

"And why is that?"

"The pain feels good."

"I know that baby, but why? Why does the slap of my crop feel good to you? How do you know I won't go too far and really hurt you?"

"No, no, you'd never."

"Why dammit?"

"Because I trust you not to," she screamed. "I trust you to give me what I need whether I know it or not." She struggled for breath, her heart racing. "Because I serve you and I serve David. I belong to you."

Tears streamed down her face as uncontrollable sobs rocked through her. It was the truth, and she could see it with an amazing clarity. She trusted them because they deserved it...needed it, and it was her right and duty to give it.

"Look at me, baby." David had come to squat in front of her, and his fingers touched her chin and lifted until her gaze met his.

"Trust means giving us your all, in and out of the bedroom. Do you understand?"

"Yes, I do. And I'm so, so sorry."

"No, no more apologies. We believe you." His fingers swiped away the tears before he produced a tissue that dealt with the fact that her nose ran and she could do nothing to stop it or clean it herself.

When he finished mopping her face, he leaned forward and pressed a chaste kiss to her lips. The soft and warm sensation soothed her, but it wasn't enough.

"David?"

"Yes, my beauty?"

"Kiss me. Please."

The light in his eyes changed, darkened with a renewed lust to match her own, before he sifted his fingers into her hair and pulled her to his lips.

No more soft and easy. His tongue pushed into her mouth and prodded and tasted every inch it could reach. Her head swam from the heady taste and the warm hands now caressing her back. Thomas had put the crop down and explored her skin with hot and rough hands. When his fingers slid between her cheeks, she went mad with the need for more.

Wrenching her mouth free, she panted. *Oh God, Thomas, please, please.*

"Are you teasing her?" David murmured.

"Of course I am." His fingers gently grazed her slit, barely touching her and definitely getting nowhere near her clit. "Put your forehead on the ground." Thomas rumbled behind her.

David shifted to her side and eased her forward so she wouldn't lose balance. In this position, her bottom opened and cool air swept across her pussy lips. She'd been spread wide for Thomas.

There was a quick zip and rustle of clothing, and before she could exhale, Thomas' cock began pushing inside her.

"So damned wet. So damned perfect."

"Thomas…Sir," she wailed.

"Take me," he demanded.

She moaned at the delicious, dark, slide of his cock filling her. Never in her life had she felt this complete. With her body burning from the inside out, David began to idly toy with her nipples. Every touch, every thrust, sent her senses into overload. Her breath caught in her throat.

"You're ours. Never forget." David's warm breath bathed her skin.

Gabby's resistance fractured. Tears rolled down her cheeks, and her body began to convulse.

Oh. My. God.

Chapter Twenty

"Angel, over here." Gabby waved over her best friend to the tiny table she'd chosen in the alcove. She had so much she wanted to share with her friend, and some of it not necessarily appropriate for public consumption. Luckily, their favorite outdoor cafe offered a few tables tucked away from the others for couples or whomever to have the extra privacy they might need.

This cafe was actually part of a twenty-four hour bakery here in the North Art district that she'd grown to love. Not too many places in town offered a place to come and chat with friends in the middle of the night, and it served the best pastries in the South. It was like experiencing a little taste of Paris every time she came in.

When they'd opened the cafe alongside the bakery, she and Angel had eagerly shown up on opening night to check it out and had ended up making it a long time favorite.

"I'm so sorry I'm late." Angel kissed her cheek and squeezed her arm before she sat down in the seat across from hers. "You know how Jeff is sometimes."

"I do. He may be a demanding Master who likes to keep you busy, but I think you love it."

"Oh without a doubt." Her friend smiled, but somehow the expression seemed tight, quite a bit off from her usual perky self.

"Is everything okay?"

"Of course, why do you ask?" Angel picked up her water and took several swallows before putting it down again.

"I don't know. For a second there, you seemed different."

"No, really, everything is great."

Gabby shook off the strange feeling and picked up her menu. They had methodically gone through every dish offered in those first months and had quite a few favorites, but since they'd not been coming here as much as they used to, she'd become a creature of habit. Maybe she'd do something different today and order from the specials. Her world in the last couple of weeks had been completely turned upside down, although for the better.

"So what brings you to this neck of the woods? Aren't you staying at Thomas' house these days, what with Scott harassing you and all?"

Gabby nodded her head. "Yes, I've been at Thomas' house every night, but I've started coming back to my house during the day for work. Plus I really miss my garden." As much as she'd been curious about Sanctuary, it hadn't taken long for her to remember why she loved working from home. Fortunately, she'd easily verified the discrepancies in Thomas' books, and he'd immediately brought in an accounting team to take over the recordkeeping on a permanent basis. David's firm had tracked down the missing accountant, and official charges were now pending. The efficiency with which Thomas worked made it hard for her to believe he'd really needed her services. She half believed he'd used it as an excuse to keep her close. Not that she'd minded. Things had a way of working out perfectly...

"What about Scott?"

"He's gone."

"'Gone' gone? How'd you manage that?"

The waiter stopped by, and Gabby waited to answer her friend. They both ordered the soup of the day with a house salad and fresh bread. The friendly waiter smiled, took the menus and assured them the wait would not be long.

Leaning close to Gabby so no one would overhear, she spoke softly. "Apparently, David's firm had him investigated, and it seems he'd gotten bored while his new girlfriend was out of town. The next time he called, I challenged him on it, and he confessed. He apologized, and I let him have it for scaring me like that. Since then, I haven't heard a word."

"Just like that?"

"Yep, just like that."

"What a putz. I really hope it's for good this time."

"God, you and me both. Although…"

"What? Are you hoping to get back with him? What about Thomas?"

Gabby rushed her hand to cover her mouth before she spewed water all over the table. "Oh God no! Nothing like that at all. Ever. Let's just say that incident managed to change my relationship with Thomas and David tremendously." She couldn't suppress the silly grin she knew covered her face. She was in love and didn't care who knew it.

"Oh, now, you've gone and done it. Spill. I want all the details."

Gabby's face flushed despite the cool breeze sweeping through the cafe. She had nothing to be embarrassed about, but still. Just thinking about it brought back vivid memories of the day in her kitchen. It had been the hardest thing she'd ever done and the most exhilarating. She doubted that would be the end of it. Thomas and David seemed eager to push her boundaries.

"Well, that day I found all those messages…"

"Yeah."

"Well, little did I know that very evening Thomas and David had planned out a scene for me and would take place at my own house."

"Uh-oh."

"Yeah. Well, as you can imagine when I found myself blindfolded and in my own living room, I freaked. I was genuinely scared of Scott and what he might do if he was spying on me and found me naked between two men."

"You were naked? This just gets better and better."

Gabby shook her head. "You have no idea. I learned a few lessons that night, and they weren't all fun and games."

Angel leaned in. "Girl..."

"Yeah, just like we discussed, I didn't tell Thomas or David about the calls from Scott, but when I went all crazy psycho girl on them in my house, I had to tell them, and they were hot. Hell, pissed is more like it. I'm still kind of surprised I wasn't disciplined right then and there."

"Me, too. Thomas is known for being pretty strict with his girls."

Gabby paused. Girls. That didn't sound right coming from Angel. She shook it off as a meaningless comment and continued.

"Well, long story short, the next twenty-four hours were a whirlwind of anger, fear and so much fucking I'm surprised I was able to get up and walk out of there."

Angel burst into a fit of giggles.

"What?" Gabby held up her hands. "What did I say?"

"It still sounds weird hearing you, Miss Prim and Proper when we met, say fucking."

That familiar heat of a blush crept up Gabby's neck, and she hid her face in her hands.

"No, don't be embarrassed. It's an important part of your training. It's just new for me since we haven't spent much time together lately."

"I know, and I'm sorry about that. I've gotten a couple of really nice accounting contracts that have kept me scrambling during the day and let's just say keeping up with two men is quite a job."

"Well, in a few weeks, things will probably slow in that department, right?"

Gabby cocked her head. "What do you mean?"

Angel looked so intense, if Gabby didn't know better, she'd think the grim line of her lips and clenching of her jaw were anger.

"Thomas. If things are going as well as you say they are then he's almost done, and he'll probably leave soon."

Gabby's head reeled. "Leave? Why would he do that? Where would he go?"

Angel covered her mouth with her fingers. "Uh...I...uh...never mind, I don't know."

Gabby reached across the table and grabbed her best friend's hand, fear twisting in her gut with a powerful force. "Angel, what is it? What are you not telling me?"

Tears welled in the corners of Angel's eyes. "Nothing...really...I'm so sorry. I didn't mean to bring it up."

"Angel, stop being sorry and tell me. You're my best friend. You've seen me at my worst going through the divorce with Scott. I trust you completely."

Angel nodded her head.

"Here you go, ladies. Your salads and fresh baked bread. Can I add some fresh ground pepper for you?" The waiter pulled a long pepper grinder from his side apron pocket and hovered it over Gabby's bowl.

"No, thank you." She forced the words past the lump forming in her throat.

"And you miss." He moved to Angel's bowl.

"Yes, please." Angel watched him twist the knob several turns before holding her hand up for him to stop.

"Anything else I can get you ladies?"

"No." The word rushed from Gabby's mouth with more force than she'd intended, and the waiter threw her an odd look.

"Okay, let me know if you need anything." He rushed away.

Angel had picked up the salad dressing container and began drizzling the oil over her greens. It took all of Gabby's strength not to knock it from her hands and demand an answer.

"Mmm, this is delicious," Angel moaned around her first forkful.

Gabby refused to touch her food, her appetite quickly dissipating. "Angel, enough. Tell me what's going on, right now."

Angel sighed and laid her fork on the linen napkin at her elbow. "Fine. But Gabby, I thought you knew."

"Knew what?"

"You're not going to like it."

"Stop stalling and spit it out already. It sounds like it's something I need to know."

"It's about Thomas. He's a trainer. I think I told you that. He likes to train subs."

"Yeah, I've heard that about him. So?"

"Gabby, that's all he does. He trains them. He hasn't kept a sub for himself in years. Every so often a prodigy, like you, comes along who he deems worthy of training. Something you should be grateful for because he is very particular."

She so didn't like where this was going.

"Once the girl is chosen, he finds another male Dom to work with him. To help train you. Someone he thinks you'll mesh with and vice versa. Whenever you reach the point of being a successfully trained submissive, he backs out, leaving you and the other Dominant alone to cement the long-term relationship for yourself. It's his thing. Matching up new submissives with the right Dom in order to avoid anyone getting hurt or worse on his watch. He's known at Sanctuary as the Dominant matchmaker."

Gabby shook her head. "What? No, no that can't be right. We have a relationship. He never said anything about leaving not even when I told him I loved him."

"Oh Gabby, you told him that you loved him?"

"Yes, he and David both. They love me."

"Did they say they love you back?"

"Yeah...uh...I think so." She tried to remember, but nausea had set in full force and she wanted to throw up. What had she gotten herself into? They'd put so much emphasis on trust, surely, they wouldn't lie to her.

"You don't remember?"

Gabby struggled with her memory. They'd been lying in bed after sex in the kitchen, the living room and the bathroom floor. In fact, she'd thought they were going to initiate every room in her house before they were done. They'd snuggled together in the middle of the bed with David facing her in the front and Thomas spooning her back. She hadn't meant to say the words, but as her eyes had started to fall and the warmth and goodness surrounded her, she'd been unable to help herself. David had looked at her for a moment before pressing his lips to hers and said he loved her, too. But what about Thomas? He'd mumbled something at the back of her neck, but now she couldn't remember what it was. Had she dreamt it? Moments later, she'd drifted off more alive and happy than she'd ever been in her life.

Being owned and loved and cared for had made the last week exquisite and one she'd never forget. Thomas enjoyed and needed pain on a level similar to hers, and David demanded her obedience in everything but was always quick to nurture her when she needed it. She'd come to believe it was the perfect combination, and there was a real possibility of something long term.

"Angel, this can't be right."

"I'm so sorry, Gabby. I never thought I would be the one to tell you."

"I have to go see David now. He'll tell me what's going on." She threw down her napkin and pushed back her chair.

"Gabby, wait. You can't go anywhere in this frame of mind. You need to calm down."

"I can go where I want and when I want, and right now, I want my Dom."

Angel sat back in her chair. "I hope you're referring to David because Thomas is going to break your heart."

* * * *

Outside the restaurant Gabby rushed across the street to her car. She yanked on the door and nearly fell on her butt when it didn't open. She fumbled with the keys for a few seconds before finally locating the right one amidst all the stupid store shopper cards. Why the hell did she need all this stuff? She just wanted to get in the fucking car.

The lock popped, and she wrenched open the door and slid in, throwing her purse into the backseat. Her hands shook when she tried to start the car, and she rested her forehead on the steering wheel.

Calm down, Gabby. It's all a mistake; you have nothing to worry about. She breathed deeply in and out of her nose, willing her racing heart to calm so she'd be able to make the few blocks to David's office.

Finally calm enough to go, she turned the ignition and put the car in gear. She'd talk to David, and everything would be fine. Angel was confused. Angel was...hell, Angel was...she didn't know. Mistaken maybe. Confused. What a nightmare.

Luckily, it was still early in the day, and this part of town was fairly quiet traffic-wise. She drove the four blocks to his office and maneuvered the small car into a parking spot on the street right in front of the building entrance.

Without her usual glance in the mirror to check her makeup, she pulled herself from the car and marched into the building. The sparse lobby offered little to a stranger who came across the sparse structure. No tables, no couches, not even a front desk to welcome visitors. The offices located inside were discreet, not wanting to advertise their services so there were no signs announcing the company names and their location. She fished into her purse and pulled his business card from her wallet. The typeface simply stated David's name, the address of his office, including the suite number and a phone number. She gave a thought to a call first, but no, she wanted the element of surprise so she could see his face when she asked the questions. It was the only way she'd feel one hundred percent confident of his answers.

That old familiar warning went off in her head as she made her way to the elevators. Trust. She'd given it, promised it in fact, and at the first sign of any question, she'd stopped giving them the benefit of the doubt? No, that's not what this was about. She did trust them and, with all her heart, believed that Angel was somehow mistaken.

The elevator dinged and dumped her onto the 4th floor. She compared the card to the numbers on the wall and walked the thirty feet or so to David's office. Instead of a company name, there were three silver engraved plates across the door that simply listed the names of David and his employees. They really took this privacy thing seriously.

Unsure whether to go in or knock she waited, transferring her weight from one foot to the other while she considered. Too anxious to delay another second, Gabby rapped on the door with her loose fist. Her heart pounded in her chest, and her stomach still threatened to heave with nausea. She needed to calm down or this wouldn't go well. She needed answers, but she had also learned to tread carefully down the trust road.

She was free to speak her mind, but it would be her actions they'd use against her if she went to far.

She knocked again.

The door opened, and Trey appeared before her. She'd seen him a time or two when he'd come to the house, but dressed in a tuxedo, he caught her off guard.

"Oh hey, Gabrielle, come on in. You don't have to knock. We all have our private offices so feel free to walk in anytime."

She swept past him and surveyed the room. No reception desk in here either, although they did have a small couch and coffee table with some old business magazines placed across it. From the looks of the dust covering them, this room didn't get much action.

"David's back in his office just finishing a conference call. You can go on back if you want." He pointed to the corner office, indicating for her to go ahead.

"Why are you all dressed up? It's not every day I'd expect to see a security man in a tux."

"There's a formal collaring ceremony at Sanctuary tonight. A good friend of mine is the Dom, and he's asked me to take part."

Gabby raised her eyebrows. "Take part? That sounds official. What will you be doing?"

"Uh...I...I'm her gift."

That caught her attention. "Her gift? Dare I ask or is it none of my business?"

Trey looked at her with a sly smile. "You can always ask, but that doesn't mean you'll get an answer."

"Fair enough."

"But in this case, I don't see the harm in it. It's a big ceremony, and many will be in attendance. In fact, I assumed Thomas and David would be bringing you."

Gabby shrugged. Thomas loved to surprise her so she understood when he didn't tell her things in advance.

"The submissive tonight has earned a special gift from her Master beyond the collar. He has set up one of her fantasies in particular."

She nodded. She got it now. The sub hadn't yet been with two men and had grown curious. She laid her hand across Trey's forearm. "I understand completely."

He winked back. "Yes, I believe you do. Well, I'm going to go get out of this tux before I mess it up for tonight. Go on in. David should be done by now."

"Thanks, Trey."

She focused on the door and took a deep steadying breath. Time to get her answers.

The door was already ajar so Gabby pushed it open enough to slip inside and closed it behind her. David must not have heard her because he'd not moved from his chair where he said holding his head and massaging his temples. Automatically, she wanted to go to him and brush his fingers aside so she could touch him and soothe him. Whatever it took to ease his suffering.

At the last second before she moved, she remembered why she was here, and he looked up and caught her gaze.

"Oh hell, isn't this just the perfect surprise." David stood from the chair and walked across the room to her. "You are just what I need right about now." His hands caressed her cheeks and rested along her jaw line, pulling her slightly forward for a kiss.

At the modest pressure against her lips, her back stiffened and she turned her head a fraction.

"What's wrong?" David tightened his grip on her face and turned her to face him, forcing their gazes to connect. Harsh lines creased his forehead in question.

"I...I just had lunch with Angel."

His face softened. "Did it not go well, sweetheart?"

She tried to fight back the tears already threatening her. Breaking down had not been an option she'd considered when thinking of what to say, but sure enough her vision blurred slightly from the sheen.

She shook her head.

"Do you want to talk about it?" Those strong fingers she loved on her body dropped from her face, and he settled on the corner of his desk.

"Yes, we need to talk about it, but I don't know what to say or where to start."

"How about the beginning?"

No, rehashing the entire fiasco wasn't what she had in mind.

"Is Thomas really planning to hand me over to you and leave?" she blurted. "Angel said that's what he does. Train a submissive alongside the Dom he has chosen for her, then once the training is complete he leaves them to each other."

She watched David carefully, waiting for the look of shock to cross his face at any second. He wrinkled his eyes and nose, but in a gesture of genuine confusion not shock. He wasn't shocked at all.

Backing away from the desk, she covered her mouth.

"I thought you knew."

Gabby shook her head. No. No. No. Please this was not happening. More steps back in the direction of the door.

"Gabrielle, stop. I need to explain."

"No, I can't. Don't want to hear it." She turned and rushed the door.

When she thought he'd let her go, hands wrapped around her waist and pulled her back into the room. "No running away. We need to talk about this."

"I don't want to talk." Anger fueled her now, and she was ready to get the hell out of this office.

A smack to her bottom got her attention, and she turned to him wildly. "Don't. Don't go there."

Fire flamed in his gaze. "I will go there any time I damn please because it is my right to do so. Unless you remove that collar or utter your safe word, you'll do as I say." He pushed her into the chair, facing his desk and bent close. "And right now, you are going to listen."

She glared at him, her safe word hovering on the tip of her tongue. Even her collar, that she hadn't given a second thought to until now, seemed tight on her throat. The demand in his eyes warned her that now would not be the time to threaten or defy him. Not unless she was ready to walk away forever.

"Breathe, Gabrielle. Maybe, if you calm down, we can figure out what's going on."

"Don't you already know?"

"Well, I knew what Thomas was like when I got involved if that's what you're asking, and I was okay with it."

Her mouth opened ready with a stream of what she thought about that.

He held up his hand to halt her. "Let me finish. I know Thomas very well, and from the moment, I met you I truly thought you were different. I've never—and I mean never—seen a sub able to work through his control like you do. After one day with the two of you, I recognized something different and began to believe that this situation would be nothing like the ones before it."

"I don't like being set up without my knowledge."

"Maybe you shouldn't jump to conclusions."

Reason. Fuck, she didn't want to listen to that right now. Being pissed kept her on guard, and she could wear it like an armor to get through this.

"We should go and talk to Thomas. I've never actually asked him what his plans were. I preferred our relationship grow organically and see what happened. There are never any guarantees in life as well you know, and finding the right person to fill both your darker side and your vanilla life is not an easy task."

Her stomach lurched at his words. Was he saying what she thought he was? He'd already told her he loved her, and she'd been afraid to think beyond today. Tomorrow would be here soon enough, and she didn't want to make any more assumptions.

A vision of three of them flooded her mind as the emotion she felt for them both overwhelmed her. She'd grown to want and need them both. How could she be ripped away from one of them and still have things be the same?

Fuck, she'd gotten herself into the mess of all messes this time.

"Don't throw away the hard-won trust quite yet, Gabrielle. Thomas deserves a chance to answer to your friend Angel's accusations."

He was right. It didn't make her feel any better, but he was right. "Fine. I'll talk to him." She jumped from the chair and headed for the door. "You coming?"

Chapter Twenty-One

David shifted in his seat, once again trying to find a comfortable position to drive this godforsaken car. Why had he agreed to drive her over to Sanctuary in her ridiculously small car? Whoever said a Mini could accommodate even a tall man like him could kiss his ass.

He peeked at her from the corner of his eye to see she still sat leaning against the door and looking out the window. It was as if she was doing whatever she could to get as far away from him as possible. Since they'd argued over which vehicle to take, she'd not said a word. The silence in the car rubbed against him like sandpaper. Gritty and rough.

She drummed her fingers on her leg, the window, the seat, anywhere she could reach. He didn't know for certain what Thomas would say when they confronted him, but for her sake, he hoped his hunch was right. Thomas not telling her his plan felt like a betrayal to them both, and if he had been planning to leave, he might be tempted to kick his ass himself.

He steered the car onto the narrow lane that would lead to the very private Sanctuary property here on the edge of the state line. He loved this moment when he turned into the wooded acreage and he left the city behind. It had always given him a sense of freedom from the constraints of daily life by the simple change in environment.

When the lane opened into the oversized parking lot, he wasn't surprised to see lots of cars already here. The ceremony tonight would draw a large crowd especially with the promise of a public scene, and they'd be busy getting the place decorated and set up for the party.

He'd only been to one other formal collaring ceremony, and it had been a small intimate affair with less than a dozen guests. The sentiment and meaning in that often forgotten formality charmed him. He'd like to do that for Gabby. He could picture her, maybe in an outdoor ceremony with only their closest friends. But she was right; without Thomas, it would feel incomplete.

Never before now had he considered sharing a woman in a poly relationship with another man. It wasn't all that common in the lifestyle. Generally, a Dom would take on multiple submissives and build a family in that manner. David could think of only one other relationship he knew of like this. He'd enjoyed learning that he and Thomas complemented each other perfectly, and both brought something different to the table. When Gabrielle had professed her love, he'd been more than eager to share the sentiment.

With the first glimpse of her smile and the fire in her eyes, he'd known he was a goner. And getting all those lush curves underneath him had been the icing on the sweetest cake of his life.

Now, everything was unraveling, and there didn't seem to be a damn thing he could do about it. If Thomas broke her heart today, he didn't know what he would do or how they would recover.

They exited the car together, and Gabrielle didn't wait for him before entering through the back door with her key. Frustrated, he reined in his emotions and braced himself for the worst.

The outer office was empty, and the only sounds were the distant voices coming from the ballroom in the middle of the club. Gabby headed for Thomas's office door, which was slightly ajar.

She reached for the knob and froze. She spared a glance in his direction, and the fear and disgust in her gaze chilled his blood. Something was wrong.

She lifted her finger to her lips to keep him quiet, and he joined her at the door.

"Sir, please, I have done everything you've ever asked of me. I've been a good sub to the Master you loaned me to and have been waiting patiently to return. Can I please come home now?" a woman said on a sob.

"Angel, you know better than this. I've never lied to you or misled you in any way. Why would you think this?"

Uh-oh. Was this Gabrielle's Angel? He needed to get her out of here before she heard any more. He wrapped his hand around her arm and pulled her in the direction of the door.

"Let go of me right now," Gabrielle seethed.

When he didn't immediately drop his hand, she jerked from his grasp, her strength surprising him.

"Please, Sir. Tell me what I've done to deserve this lengthy punishment. I'll do anything to make it up to you. I love you."

A tiny gasp sounded from Gabrielle at Angel's last three words, and David hung his head in resignation. Thomas had a lot of explaining to do.

Before David could stop her, Gabrielle pushed opened the door and walked inside.

To David's dismay, Gabrielle's friend knelt in a formal submissive position in front of his friend, her hands behind her back and her head bowed in respect. To see them together like this in Thomas's office sickened him. What exactly was going on here?

"Yes, Thomas, Sir, please tell us all why she's being punished. We'd like to know, too."

Gabrielle's voice sliced through the silence, and both Thomas and Angel jerked in her direction.

"This is all your fault," Angel shrieked. "You've turned him against me." She sprang from the floor, and before anyone could react, she leapt onto Gabrielle, catching her off balance and knocking them both to the floor. The sickening crunch of Gabrielle's head connecting with the corner of the table ripped through the room as he and Thomas sprang into action.

He jerked Angel from atop Gabrielle and tossed her in the direction of Thomas. Nothing mattered to him but Gabrielle. He had glimpsed the blood on her face when he'd lifted her friend, and his heart jerked painfully in his chest. His knees slammed into the floor, and he gently rolled her onto her back.

The blow had knocked her out cold. His fingers pushed against the baby soft skin of her neck to check for a pulse. When he found it beating steady and strong, he heaved a sigh of relief. Brushing the blood dampened hair from her face, he searched for the source of her wound.

"Is she all right?" Thomas pulled the table out of the way and dropped to her other side. He imagined the terror on Thomas's face mirrored his own, yet he couldn't conjure an ounce of sympathy.

"Get away from her, and go call an ambulance."

David found the gash at her hairline, and while he guessed she would need stitches, it didn't look life threatening. He hoped. He ripped off his shirt and pressed the cloth to the still bleeding wound to try to stop the flow of blood.

"We need to get her to a hospital."

"We could take her," Thomas insisted.

"No, you need to stay here with *her*." David nodded to the now sobbing ball of woman curled on the floor several feet away.

How had this day turned to shit so quickly? "C'mon, Gabrielle baby, can you hear me? Wake up now so I can take you to the hospital." Blood still oozed from her gash, and her face had turned pale white far too quickly. If she didn't wake up on her own soon, he'd have no choice but to call an ambulance.

"I'm calling 9-1-1. We can't take a chance with her. She has to be all right." Thomas picked up the phone, and David listened to him state the emergency with half an ear. Thomas was right. She had to be all right.

"Please, Gabrielle, don't leave me. I don't think I could take it. I love you, sweetheart." He bent and gently placed his lips over hers.

"The ambulance will be here in less than five minutes. Someone needs to wait outside and direct them in."

"I'm not leaving her. I'm not *ever* leaving her."

"I'll do it. You stay with her," Thomas whispered, the sadness evident in his tone.

"What about that one?" David pointed to Angel still sobbing relentlessly nearby.

They exchanged looks before Thomas rushed over to the other woman while dragging his phone out of his pocket. He ordered someone within Sanctuary to wait out front and direct the ambulance personnel to his office when they arrived.

Precious minutes ticked by, and still, Gabrielle didn't wake up. He'd stopped the flow of the blood as best he could, but with her hair matted and half her face tinged pink, she looked like a victim bleeding out.

"In here." He heard someone directing the paramedics and the rush of feet running into the room filled the air.

One of the men crouched next to Gabrielle on her opposite side. "I've got it, Sir. You need to remove the cloth so I can see what I'm working with."

David moved his shirt and gave the man some space as he inspected the gash.

"Has she regained consciousness at all?"

"No."

"How long has she been out?"

"Maybe fifteen minutes."

"Okay, she's going to need some stitches, and without her conscious, we're going to have to take her to emergency."

Another paramedic moved in with a board and ushered David out of the way. He hated the fragile appearance of his Gabrielle. As if she would break at any moment, they transferred her carefully to the board and strapped her on.

"Okay, gentlemen, we're taking them in."

"Them? That one wasn't hurt. She's the attacker, and the police should handle her."

The EMT shook his head. "Sorry, Sir. She's completely incoherent. She'll have to be checked out by a doctor first."

"I'm going with you."

The paramedic shook his head. "Sorry, Sir, that's against regulations. You'll have to follow us in. From a safe distance please," he added at the last second.

As much as he wanted to argue, David didn't want to waste any time. When they ushered both women out of the office, he went to follow.

"Wait." Thomas stopped him with a hand to his shoulder.

"You'll need this." He produced a white pullover with an M emblazoned over the left breast. David took it quickly and shrugged into it as he stalked from the club.

"I'm going with you, David."

"Take your own car."

Maybe not giving Thomas a chance wasn't fair. But with Gabrielle being loaded into an ambulance because of something related to him, David didn't give a flying fuck about hurt feelings.

* * * *

Hours had passed before they'd finally let David into see her. He'd worn a path in the floor outside the room they'd put her in, keeping him away from her. They'd tried to keep him outside in the waiting area but had finally relented when he wouldn't give them a minute's peace.

He'd been told she'd regained consciousness in the ambulance on the way to the hospital. He'd sagged in relief at the news, but the hours waiting had strung his nerves taut until he thought he'd snap at any moment.

Thomas waited at a distance, patiently leaning against the wall. They'd not spoken for a good long while, and it was probably for the best. Until he saw with his own eyes that Gabrielle was indeed going to be fine, his rage at the situation would continue to simmer just underneath the surface.

"I brought you some coffee. Thought it might help."

David looked up at the nurse who'd taken pity on him and had tried to give him as much information as possible.

"Thank you." He took the offered cup, and the heat in his hand did feel good. He tentatively took a sip testing the temperature. The first slide of hot liquid down his throat warmed his insides and relaxed a few of the tense muscles in his neck.

"What's taking so long? When can I see her?"

Before she could answer, Gabrielle's door opened, and the doctor walked out. "You can see her now." He frowned. "It's none of my business, but well, you seem like a good enough guy. She doesn't really want to see anyone, but the only way she can go home tonight is if someone drives her and stays with her for the next twenty-hours."

The fact that she wanted no one cut him deep. He didn't know what Thomas was up to, still didn't, but damn it, he needed her.

"I'm serious about this. I need your word that she won't be left alone. Her head is concussed, and she should stay, but she won't have it. So she's relented to allowing you to take her home."

"Oh no worries there, Doc. I'll be keeping an eye on her, whether she likes it not."

Thomas pushed from the wall and walked toward them.

"One other thing." The doctor hesitated. "She is reluctantly allowing you in but was adamant that no one else accompany you." He tilted his head at Thomas who'd stopped midstride at the words.

"I understand. You have my word."

David watched the doctor and the nurse walk away, regret weighing heavy in his chest like a piece of lead he couldn't dislodge.

"She needs to understand it's not what she thinks it is." Thomas spoke quietly, reserved, sad.

"Isn't it, Thomas?" He turned to face his friend, the sadness tearing at his gut. "Angel told her everything today."

"Angel sees things that never existed. Things I didn't even know she harbored until today. I need a chance to explain."

"That's not going to be up to me."

He pushed through Gabrielle's door and stepped into the darkened room. She faced the far wall, but even in profile, he could see her eyes were open.

"Hey, babe." He tried to lighten his tone.

"I don't have a choice."

David moved closer to the bed. "You don't have a choice about what?"

"I have no one to call. No one to bring me home and stay with me. It's the only reason you're here."

"What about your parents?"

"There is no one. No parents, no sibling or cousins or aunts or uncles. No one."

Her harsh words broke his heart. Not only did she not want him, but his baby was alone in this world. How had he not known that? Every fiber of him ached to cuddle her and tuck her into his body. He owed her his strength, especially now.

"I'm sorry." He didn't know what else to say.

"Me, too."

"Maybe once we get you home and comfortable, we can talk about what happened. I think we both need some answers."

She turned and looked at him, her gaze full of sorrow. "I don't want to talk anymore."

"Gabrielle, don't do this. After everything we've established, don't shut it down now."

"You need to understand something, David. I don't care. I don't want to talk to you or Thomas."

Just then the door behind him pushed open, and the nurse bustled in pushing a wheelchair. "Time to spring—"

The looks on their faces must have clued her in. That or the tension so thick in the air one could slice it with a knife.

"I don't think I'll be needing that." Gabby pointed to the chair.

"Sorry, hon, hospital policy. Do you need some help or can you manage."

"I...uh..."

"Don't move," he commanded.

"I don't need to be ordered around."

He walked to the edge of the bed, threw back the covers and scooped her into his arms. Unable to resist, he nuzzled her neck, rubbing the white leather with his nose, and moved his lips to the shell of her ear.

"As long as you wear that collar, I have every right to demand, order and expect your cooperation," he whispered low for her ears only.

A deep shudder passed through her and vibrated into him as her soft sweet gasp brushed over him like a lover's caress.

He stood and faced the nurse with a big ass smile that seemed to put her at ease. "I think she's ready to go now." He sat Gabby gently in the chair and retrieved her shoes from the foot of the bed. He knelt in front of her and slipped them on her feet one at a time while she struggled not to glare at him.

He chuckled despite himself. His beauty was quite a little spitfire, a trait he loved about her. But if she thought she'd get a chance to easily shut him out, she was sorely mistaken.

Chapter Twenty-Two

God, they'd only been home a few hours, and the man was driving her up the wall. She wanted to rest and be left alone, and he wanted to bring her stuff every other minute.

Whether his actions were fueled by guilt or not, she had no idea, and thinking about it made her head throb even more. In the blink of an eye, she'd gone from a blissfully happy submissive to two men to once again alone with not even a best friend to turn to anymore.

Which one hurt more, the loss of Thomas or Angel, she couldn't say. Something had fractured inside her, and if she examined it too close, she might lose herself in a complete and total breakdown. Much like her friend had.

She turned into the pillow, willing the tears not to flow. She was sick of all the damned crying. After hours and hours of it, how could she have any left?

Her best friend had lain claim to Thomas, Thomas had lain claim to no one and David, well, she didn't know if she could give to him without thinking of Thomas every moment. Where one began, the other continued until the three of them had become a cohesive unit that worked.

And if the constant pain in her chest was any indication, the sudden loss might be more than she could bear.

"I've brought you something to eat."

Gabby rolled her eyes. "I'm not hungry."

"I didn't ask if you were hungry. I would, however, like to know if you are feeling nauseous or light headed or experiencing any sharp pains."

Did the ache in her chest from her heart being ripped out count? "I'm fine. Just want to sleep."

She listened to him place the tray on the bedside table he'd set up once he'd gotten her in the bed. He fussed worse than the nurses did. What part of she wanted to be left alone did he not understand?

"If you're not nauseous then you need to eat something. It's been a long time since lunch."

She wasn't going to bother telling him that her lunch had gone uneaten either. It had been more than twenty-four hours since she'd eaten, and that was fine with her.

His body walked into her line of vision, and she squeezed her eyes shut. "Please, David, I just want to be alone."

"Open your eyes, and look at me."

Reluctantly, she did as he asked to find he'd squatted down to her eye level. His beauty still took her breath away, and seeing the worry in his eyes triggered the impulse to comfort him. He wanted her to let him in, and eventually, she would. She wasn't stupid. She knew she wouldn't be able to deny him for long. She believed in his feelings as much as she did her own, although her instincts had failed her miserably when it came to Thomas.

"I'll give you as much room as I can, but it probably won't be what you're hoping for. I can't stay away from you, no matter how hard I try. I need you."

No way was she getting any words past the lump in her throat. When would she learn that life sucked?

"You eat some of the soup, and I'll give you some peace and quiet for a while." His fingers brushed her cheeks, wiping the stray tears still clinging there. "You shouldn't cry. One way or another, things will work out."

God, how she wished she could believe in that. Giving in, she pushed to a sitting position and allowed David to place the tray over her lap. The scent of her favorite vegetable soup wafted from the bowl. Mmm...comfort food. Maybe David was right, and the food would be just what she needed.

"How'd you know this was my favorite?" She grabbed a spoon and took a bite, savoring the warm liquid sliding down her throat.

David smiled. "You had three times as much of this kind than any other in your pantry so I took a wild guess."

"Guess that's why you're the investigator around here. That incredible sixth sense of yours." She smiled even if it was a little tight.

"Careful there, or I might think you've been faking all evening."

Not faking, but in a sudden moment of clarity, she realized ignoring him while he was here in her house wasn't going to work. He knew how to push every one of her buttons, and the need she'd let bloom and grow wouldn't be suppressed again that easily.

"Just being a realist."

"Well, I'll take that for now. Eat up, and I'll get you some more pain meds and water."

Minutes later, Gabby stared at the bottom of the empty bowl. She shrugged and pushed the tray away. Her eyes felt gritty, and already, the exhaustion of her ordeal was moving in. She curled back under the covers, trying to get warm.

"Good girl with the soup." David lifted the tray from the bed and set it on the table next to them. "Now, take this then you can get some sleep."

"I'm so cold." She shivered and swallowed down the pills, chasing it with the water before handing it back to him.

"Cold, huh? I can probably help with that." He pulled back the covers and slipped in behind her.

A thought of protest hovered but died quickly when she got the first taste of his warmth as he curled against her backside. One more night wouldn't hurt. Tomorrow she would have to send him away, but for tonight, she could fall asleep with his fingers caressing her skin, comforting her.

David's magic hands massaged her muscles from her shoulders and back to the backs of her thighs. Her breathing slowed, and she let some of the worries fall to the side. When his fingers slipped underneath the band of her panties, her skin flashed hot and warm with a rush of arousal she couldn't act on but certainly could revel in. Here in his arms, she felt safe. Her shoulders relaxed, and she faded toward sleep.

Her last thought was about Thomas. David clung to her, but her arms were empty...

Chapter Twenty-Three

Two weeks later, Gabby found herself right back where she'd started. Alone. David had reluctantly agreed to give her the space she needed, and thus far, she had refused all contact with Thomas. She'd returned to her old routine of work and gardening but had started trying her hand at gourmet cooking.

She'd lost some weight, which didn't bother her at all, but she worried that her lack of desire for eating wasn't a healthy move. So she'd finally decided to put her herb garden to work on a regular basis, and along with the Food Network channel, she'd begun to create some amazing dishes.

Her appetite hadn't improved, but she did a lot of sampling when she cooked or baked and figured that was better than nothing.

"I always thought you a goddess, but seeing you like this makes it a definite."

Gabby jumped up, startled. Her hand clutched at her heart even after she realized that it was only Jeff, Angel's former Dom, who'd wandered into her garden.

"Holy crap, scare a girl, why don't you."

"Oh, Gabby, it's so good to see you. I wasn't sure you'd want to see me though."

"Of course, I do." She moved into his embrace and snuggled against him like the teddy bear she'd always thought he was. "I've missed seeing you."

Try as she might, being in his embrace brought every emotional thought she'd tried to suppress racing to the surface. For the first time in days, she cried—not slow gentle tears she tried to hold back but a torrential flood that would not be restrained.

She sobbed into his chest as his hands stroked up and down her back, comforting her.

"Let it all out, sweetheart. You deserve it."

"And what about you, Jeff? Who takes care of you now?" she sniffled.

"Oh don't worry about me, hon. I can take care of myself. I've had plenty of practice."

"That's not what I mean."

"I know, Gabby. Don't worry. I came here to discuss it, but I think you needed this far more than I realized."

Her tears fell harder, and Gabby simply clung to him for support until the moisture dried up and the dry heaves shook her shoulders. When her cries died out, she pushed from Jeff and took a few steps back. He wasn't her Dom, but just being in his arms reminded her of what she missed so much she ached from head to toe.

"I am so sorry. I didn't mean to fall apart like that. I'm so embarrassed." She cast her eyes down and let her hair tumble around her face, imagining what a mess she must look.

"Stop it."

His firm tone captured her attention, and she raised her head to look at him.

"You have nothing to be sorry to me for. I understand how you feel. Betrayed. Whether we understand it or not, whether it's true or not, the perception of being betrayed by the ones we trust the most is one of the most devastating thing we can experience." His hand reached for and cupped her chin. "You've turned away from your Doms, which is your right, little one, but going cold turkey hasn't left you with a clear mind."

"But I—"

"Don't interrupt. It's not polite." His eyes sparkled with mischief.

Gabby compressed her lips and tried not to smile.

"You know I'm not talking about sex."

Oh God, she didn't want to talk about sex with Jeff.

"That blush is so cute. One of the many traits I knew Thomas would love."

"You knew? I don't understand."

"Well, that's what I came here for. To check up on you as well as have a talk. A confession of sorts. Maybe then you can find the solution you need."

"I'm a little confused."

Jeff paced over to her pond and stared down at the Koi aimlessly swimming in the small body of water. For a minute, she could have sworn she recognized the look of resignation crossing his face. No, it had to be a trick of light. Although...

"How is Angel?"

He turned and looked at her, surprise written all over his face. "Not very good, I'm afraid. They say she's suffered a complete mental break from reality. That her obsession and beliefs are singularly focused, and she's unwilling to even consider anything else."

"It's Thomas," she whispered reverently, afraid to say it too loud.

"Yes, she fixated on Thomas a long time ago, more than I ever knew. How she managed to hide it from me for this long is beyond me. She and I have been through some emotional scenes over the years, and not once, did she ever falter. It's troubling to say the least."

"Did Thomas train her?" Finally, she'd voiced the question that had been plaguing her for days. That kind of devotion didn't come from nowhere. Not usually. Yes, she believed there'd been an emotional breakdown, but more often than not, it originated with a broken heart.

Jeff sighed, tunneling his fingers through his hair until some of the strands stood on end. "Thomas and I trained her together."

Oh God.

The truth was as bad as she'd thought. Nausea rolled through her stomach, forcing her to turn away from Jeff. She'd wanted to believe everything was a lie or some other truth would exist that would make it all make sense. Not this. Definitely not this.

"So everything Angel said was true." Not a question anymore, a simple statement of fact.

"There's a little more to the story than what you're thinking. An explanation that should come from Thomas. But you haven't given him a chance to explain, have you?"

"I don't want to hear that the man I trusted with everything I am thought so little of me. That everything we did and everything he said was some sort of act. Don't you understand? To hear Angel say what she did clawed into me, if I have to hear Thomas say it as well, I might not survive."

"I don't want to belittle the pain you feel, but don't you think you're being a little dramatic? Not to mention making a lot of assumptions?"

Anger pulsed through her as she listened to Jeff.

"Can you tell me I'm wrong? That Thomas didn't do the same thing to me that he did to Angel?"

"Dammit, Gabby, listen. He didn't do anything to Angel. We offered to train her together, and we both told her what the outcome would be. I was fairly new to the scene, but I didn't want a gem like her to pass me by because of my experience. So Thomas offered to work with us both. Hell, he wasn't sure it would work because he'd never tried it before. But I pushed him to help me, even called in a favor he owed to get it done. Little did we all know it would become his only way. But he has his reasons for not taking on a sub of his own."

"What? What reason could he have for misleading me?"

Jeff shook his head. "Some things have to come from him."

Exasperated, Gabby flopped down onto her chaise. She'd wanted a simple life. She'd carved out a nice independent professional life, but personally, she'd wanted something entirely different. But submission couldn't be based on lies or half-truths. Everyone had to be open.

"Gabby, I encouraged Angel to send you to Thomas. I've known him a long time, and I saw in you the woman who could be different for him. And I still believe I was right. If he never told you that you were being trained for David then I think subconsciously he didn't want to do it. But we both know old habits die hard, and admitting that you're in love, even to yourself, is not an easy thing to do. Especially not for a man like him. You need to talk to him."

Her hands rubbed at her face. "I love them both."

"I know you do."

"Then you see my dilemma?"

"No."

"I can't take one without the other."

"Then tell them that. You owe it to yourself to at least try."

"You don't think it's weird?"

"What? That your submission is tied to them both?"

She nodded.

"You opened your mind to the reality once then you got scared. Stop thinking like a vanilla woman and only consider what matters here." He pointed to her heart. "You learn pretty quick in this lifestyle that there is no one way or right way that fits all. We all have to find what works for each of us and embrace it."

Maybe. Her head pounded with possibilities and confusion. She couldn't see how to make things right.

Jeff reached behind him and pulled an envelope from his pocket. "Here."

She hesitated. "What is it?"

"An invitation to Rick and Diane's collaring ceremony. They wanted me to be sure you had this."

"What? I thought they did this a couple of weeks ago." Yeah, on the day...

"Nope. Poor Diane came down with a horrible case of food poisoning, and they've been trying to reschedule ever since."

"When is it?"

"Tomorrow evening and you will be there. Is that understood?"

Her heart pounded in her chest. This was at Sanctuary, and she'd have no choice but to face Thomas and David both.

"I...I..."

"No, Gabby, I'm serious. You will be there if I have to take you there myself."

The firm set of his mouth and the look in his eye gave her no doubt that he would drag her there by the hair if he had to. She knew what kind of Dom he was, and she wouldn't put it past him to hogtie her and deliver her to Sanctuary by force if that's what it took.

"You will be there," he commanded.

"Yes, Sir."

Jeff patted her on the knee. "That's the good girl I know and love. Just go, and don't worry about what will or won't happen. It'll all work out the way it's supposed to."

"I hope you're right."

"I'm almost always right." The words came out light, but Gabby didn't miss the fleeting moment of wistful longing written across his face.

"What will you do now?"

"Hard to say. Like you, I feel betrayed and only time will tell if we can all get past it."

She stood and wrapped her arms around him, wishing she could take his pain away with hers. "I'm sorry for you too, you know?"

"Thank you."

One of his fingers touched to the collar she still wore at her neck. "From the first day I met you, I knew you needed a collar. I wasn't sure any one Dom could be what you needed them to be, and now, I see why. You needed two. This is right for you, and you must know that, or you wouldn't still be wearing this."

She didn't know what to say. She'd stared at herself in the mirror for hours trying to get the nerve to take it off. She'd given herself every pep talk she could think of and still nothing. He was right. She wasn't ready to give up just yet.

"Now, go get ready because you have a ceremony to go to in a few hours."

She squeaked. "It's today? But you said... Are you kidding?"

A broad grin crossed his face.

"Oh my God, you did that on purpose."

"Would you expect anything less? Giving you time to talk yourself out of it was not an option. I'll just see myself out."

She considered biting his head off, but instead, she swallowed her words and a little bit of her pride.

"Thank you, Jeff."

"Don't thank me quite yet. Tell me how you feel later when I see you at Sanctuary." He turned and walked through her gate whistling while he went.

Why did she get the sinking feeling that he done more than manipulate her into going to the ceremony? What else had he done? But more importantly, what the hell was she going to wear?

Chapter Twenty-Four

Thomas stared at the phone, contemplating. He'd already tried so many times to see her, and so far, she'd refused. The first week, he'd agreed that she needed some time and had accepted her requests not bother her, but the last seven days had grown unbearable until he'd decided come hell or high water that damn woman would talk to him this weekend.

He'd discovered, to his own surprise, that he couldn't even sleep in his bed without her. Hell, he didn't want to. Even David had moved back to his old room while Thomas had taken to the couch. When he could sleep. Most nights, he prowled the rooms seeing Gabrielle everywhere.

Now, she wouldn't come out of her house. David had described her broken, and all Thomas could see was history repeating itself. He scrubbed his face, wishing the memories would die. He needed to be whole.

No more waiting. One way or another, her time was up. Tonight after the ceremony, he'd drag David with him to her place, and they weren't leaving until she heard him out, until she told him to his face whether or not she would still wear his collar. His feelings had gone far beyond a simple training collar. He wanted forever.

Tap. Tap. Tap.

"I don't want to be disturbed before the ceremony," he answered gruffly.

"I'm sorry, I didn't mean to disturb you," a familiar voice sounded from the doorway.

No.

Thomas whipped his chair around to confirm that, yes, Gabrielle had come to him. His beauty.

He tried to form words, to keep things light, but holy hell, she was a vision. Beautiful curls surrounded her face. Her eyes were cast downward, drawing his focus to her clothing. His mouth went dry, and he fought not to swallow his tongue. She wore a pink corset cinched so tight her waist nipped-in several inches and her breasts swelled from the cups, threatening to spill out. A small flared skirt made of delicate pink lace covered her hips, stopping at mid-thigh. The outfit highlighted her shapely legs showcased in the highest fuck-me heels he'd ever seen her wear.

In the time it had taken to appraise her outfit, his dick had gotten half hard and his heart had tripled its beat.

"You are not disturbing me. On the contrary, I've never seen a more beautiful sight."

He stood and walked around his desk, barely controlling the urge to gather her in his arms and thank her for returning. He needed to play this cool, not scare her away. As grateful as he was to see her, his dominant side still wanted to turn her over his knee and spank the fire out of her. Under normal circumstances, he would have demanded her attention before now, but these weren't exactly normal circumstances. He'd not been particularly forthcoming about his past, and the fact that it came wrapped up in her best friend's betrayal made it even worse.

He didn't blame her for not talking to anyone. But nobody said he had to be rational at all times. And seeing her like this, standing innocently in his doorway with his collar around her neck, he wanted nothing more than to assert his ownership once again.

"I wasn't planning to come."

"I'm really glad you did, although David hasn't arrived yet."

"I know. I came early on purpose."

"Oh?"

"I'm afraid."

"Why?" He held back, letting her wander into the room. He needed to keep some space between them so she could ask what she'd come to find out. "I don't want to hurt you."

"No, I don't believe you want to, but that doesn't mean it won't happen. Seeing you here, standing so close to where you and An—"

She stopped, and it dawned on him that confronting him here in his office was making it worse.

"Would you like to come outside on the balcony? I promise I'll be good and let you say what you need to before I try to ravish you."

"Not funny."

"Wasn't meant to be."

Her gaze drilled into him, watching him like a hawk. So far, she wasn't giving an inch, and that thought filled him with pride. He didn't want her to be a doormat. She needed to be able to stand up for herself and demand what she wanted when the time was right.

The standoff continued. He rigidly held his place, and her back stiffened with each passing second. The tension in the room mounted until he thought she might turn and run. To his surprise, she relented and headed toward the balcony doors and out into the night air.

Thomas sucked in a few deep breaths and exhaled slowly. He would contain himself. He had to. He suspected if he pushed she would succumb to him, but that would not be the true submission he wanted. It had to come from her.

When he exited his office and out into the starless night, he realized he'd not turned on the fountain lights yet. He could still make out her faint silhouette against the railing, but not being able to see the expressions on her face or the way her gaze devoured everything around her would never be acceptable. He walked to the switches on the wall and made some adjustments until the soft lighting accompanied by the whispered tinkling of the water filled the air around them.

For a brief moment, a smile upturned the corners of her mouth as she realized what he'd done then she quickly schooled it away.

His little girl wasn't giving in without her answers.

He stepped to the railing, keeping a respectable distance between them. He followed the direction of her gaze into the gardens below where the landscaper had been instructed to hang new white lights in many of the trees to light a path that wove around the house and into a few private and not so private alcoves for outdoor scenes.

The grounds were protected from the view of outsiders, but here inside the house, a couple balconies as well as many of the upstairs bedroom windows served as viewing areas. He could envision he, David and Gabrielle in one of the alcoves. She loved the garden, and it suited her so well. What better place to spend a beautiful Carolina evening such as this.

"It's beautiful out here."

"It makes me think of you."

She eyed him suspiciously.

"Seriously. Ever since that night in your backyard, just about any garden in the city reminds me of that night and how much you love your outdoor space. I may not have handled these new landscape changes myself because, let's face it, I probably have a black thumb, but everything new you see down there was direct inspiration from you."

He angled his body to hers and held out his hand, hoping she'd take it. She looked at his hand then raised her gaze to his before finally sliding her small hand into his. He needed some contact. He ached for it. He wasn't sure he'd ever be able to pinpoint the moment he'd fallen in love with her, but his subconscious had probably known from the beginning that he wouldn't be handing her over to David.

"Why do you only train submissives for others?"

The sudden question kicked him in the gut and knocked the wind out of him. She'd skipped everything he'd thought she'd ask and had gone straight for the jugular. His mouth opened on instinct to disagree to deny that it was all he did, but dammit, she'd been torn down by the scene with Angel and they both deserved the truth.

"Because I'm afraid." He turned away and settled his gaze into a vacant spot in the darkness. He couldn't see her response, didn't want to see the hurt in her eyes.

"Of what?"

She wasn't going to back down until he'd ripped open the wound and revealed it all. He owed her.

"I let myself get too involved when I knew better. I was brought in as a trainer." God, if he closed his eyes, he'd still see that young, innocent face of his past. A beautiful blonde who'd been new to the scene.

"She was a new submissive with no training, but she was so young, too young. I was thirty at the time and knew, I mean my gut screamed at me that she was just a child. So much so that I'd asked for I.D. from the man who'd brought her in. Her license said twenty-one, which I didn't believe, but she convinced me she was of age and I wanted to believe her. Something about her touched me, and I wanted to train her. The man who would be her Dom had to leave the country for a month, and he wanted someone to help her learn while he was gone. Back then, I'd already developed the reputation as someone to go to for that kind of help."

He paused for a moment, gathering the memories a little at a time. From the corner of his eye, he saw she watched him carefully and waited for him to continue.

"I was up front with her about everything that would happen, specifically explaining things about D/s in great detail. We took the month, and I taught her as much as I

could, even including some of the aspects of the lifestyle
that were favored by the man who would be her Dom."

"Did he not come back for her?"

"Oh he did, and when he'd taken her, I felt like a piece
of me had gone with her. She had cried and told me that she
had fallen in love with me. I understood how she felt. She
had come to mean as much to me as well."

"Did you tell her?"

He shook his head, the shame of it welling fresh inside
him. "She wasn't mine."

"What happened?"

"She acted out, went crazy wild a few times with her
Dom until he finally released her. By that time, I'd gone
out of town. I needed to get away for a while, get my head
on straight."

He'd played the "if only" game so many times with
himself. If only he'd been here, if only he'd told her the
truth, if only he'd not let himself get attached...

"By the time, I got home she'd disappeared and had
become a part of one of the biggest manhunts this county
had seen in a long time. Everyone wanted to know what
had happened to her."

"She just disappeared?"

"Without a trace. And the moment, I set foot off the
plane I was hauled into questioning and interrogated for
hours. Her parents believed I had kidnapped and
brainwashed her, and if it had been possible, I'd have been
charged with statutory rape and thrown in a dark cell never
to be seen again."

A soft gasp sounded next to him. "Statutory rape?"

Thomas hung his head, unable to say the words. The
nightmares had kept him from sleep for what seemed like
years. He'd turned away from the lifestyle, unable to trust
his judgment, and he'd let his life crumble around him.

"Oh God, Thomas, I had no idea."

"Of course, you didn't. That's a part of my life I
wished I never had to share."

"But it wasn't your fault."

"Wasn't it? I'd known. On some level, deep down, I'd known she was too young."

"Was she ever found?"

He shook his head. He doubted they ever would.

"For five years, I searched for her. I existed only for that. For two years after I gave up, I hid in the bottom of a bottle of Jack until Jeff looked me up when he'd passed through town. He dragged my ass here and put me to work. He owned one of the bars uptown back then, and eventually, I worked my way out of my fear and became his manager. When this place came onto the market, I bought it. I had no idea what I wanted to do with it, but it called to me and I came. One thing led to another, and here we are today."

"I'm sorry, Thomas."

"I didn't tell you so you'd feel sorry. You asked and I needed to be honest."

"Fine. If you want to be honest, then what about Angel? What about me? Were you just going to hand me over to David like you did Angel to Jeff?" Anger sparked from her eyes. He'd definitely lit her fire on that one.

He yanked on her hand and pulled her against him. "Angel knew the deal going in, and Jeff reaffirmed it every step of the way. He has owned her from the beginning. She hid her feelings from us all, not giving any of us a clue of what went on in that head of hers. I cared for her as any friend would, but I never felt love."

She struggled against him, trying to push him away with her hands on his chest. Thomas tightened his arms around her until she quit struggling. He'd given her what she'd come for, now, he needed something.

"Look at me, Gabrielle."

Ever so slowly, she tilted up her head.

"I won't lie. I did weigh my options and considered whether or not you and David would work better without me."

"Let me go. I don't want to hear any more."

"No, that's just it. I'm *not* letting you go. I need you more than anything I've ever needed in my life. You're wearing our collar, for cripes sake. If you wanted out, you would have taken it off."

"Don't presume to know my thoughts," she whispered between clenched teeth.

Her anger turned him on. He'd pretty much been hard from the moment he spied her in his doorway, but here, like this, fighting what they both knew to be inevitable made him so hard it hurt. He dipped his head and nipped her lips at the same time he flexed his hips and pressed his dick against her cleft. He'd bet, despite her protests, if he slipped his hand under her skirt, she'd be soaking wet.

"What makes this time different than all the other times you've done this? How can I believe you?"

God, what did he have to do to convince her? She looked at him through dark inky lashes, her lips slightly parted and her warm breath blowing little puffs of warm, sweet air across his skin with every pant.

She tried to hide desire, but he wasn't buying it. His teeth gently grabbed at her bottom lip and suck it into his mouth. When he let it go, he leaned into her, his forehead resting against hers.

"I need you, Gabrielle. Of all the things I've tried to teach you these weeks, nothing is more important to me than you knowing how much I need you. You and David together have brought something to my life that I'd forgotten was missing."

He released her arms and stepped back. He'd said what she needed to know and now it would be up to her.

"I need you, Gabrielle."

Tears hovered at the edges of her eyes, wetness she valiantly fought back.

"I don't know, Thomas. I just don't know." She backed up a few steps toward the door.

"Quit running away."

She paused. "I'm not running. I promised Diane I'd help her get ready when she called me this afternoon, and I don't want to be late. In fact, I don't suppose you know anything about that phone call do you?"

Yeah, but he sure as hell wasn't going to admit it out loud. He'd conspired every which way to get her in here tonight, and he wasn't a damn bit sorry.

"Yeah, that's what I thought. So, I'm going to help Diane." She turned and took a few steps before stopping again. "Oh and Thomas, thank you for being honest. I know that wasn't easy."

He nodded. What else was there to say? He'd laid it on the line, and now, it would be her decision whether she would stay with them or not. God help them all if she took off her collar and walked away.

He watched her stride through his office and out the door. Letting her go would be the hardest moment of his life. He turned back to the gardens and breathed deep, marveling at the different scents wafting up from the newly redesigned outdoor space. A few couples had wandered outside with one already taking up a scene in one of the more public alcoves. A large breasted, big-hipped woman had been bent over the bench, and her Dom used his crop to mark her ass. The breeze carried sexy screams up to him on the particularly hard strikes.

He smiled. He wanted Gabrielle like that. Open and willing...

"Was that Gabrielle I saw rushing out of here?" David appeared beside him.

"Yeah."

"What happened?"

"She walked out obviously."

"What the hell did you do? I thought you were going to open up, to tell her the truth."

"I did."

"What did you say?"

He turned to David. Why he'd never told one of his best friends the truth escaped him now. Shame probably. Jeff had found out on his own, but for David to know, he would have had to confess and he'd never wanted to talk about it. He still didn't. The look of horror on Gabrielle's face when he'd explained it all would be something that would likely haunt him for a while.

He had eventually come to realize that while he'd fallen for the inappropriate girl, her disappearance and revelation of age was not his fault. He'd done what he could to ascertain the truth from her, and she'd managed to fool him. And now Angel. Thomas sighed. Was he doomed to keep repeating the mistakes of his past no matter how hard he fought against them?

Now, he'd have to tell the story to David and take the risk that he might not understand. Might not be willing to forgive.

"Take a seat. I have a story to tell you."

Chapter Twenty-Five

"It's a special day at Sanctuary, and I'm glad to see so many of you have joined Rick and Diane to celebrate this momentous occasion."

Gabby watched Thomas up on the stage welcoming everyone to the ceremony. She'd not realized he would officiate, but somehow, she should have known. He was dressed in head to toe black, from the silk shirt to the form hugging slacks that showed off a physique she adored.

Listening to his voice now reminded her of the first night she'd met him. Was she even sitting in the exact seat she had then? The dark room had been decorated with hundreds and hundreds of candles that gave off plenty of light with a romantic glow. She closed her eyes and allowed the deep, silky voice to roll over her. He'd drawn her in that first night, just like this. Had it only been weeks since then? So much had changed. She'd changed. Yet simply sitting and soaking in his voice still had the same effect on her. Her sex dampened in anticipation, and her clit throbbed in tune with the strong timbre of his voice.

She'd managed to hide her feelings from him, but his story had broken her heart. So many mistakes from multiple sources had culminated in a broken man. He'd used that painful life lesson to not only overcome the tragedy but to help people avoid the same mistakes as well.

She wasn't stupid. She'd read online stories from submissives about their horrid missteps before either giving up and suffering on their own with their needs unmet or worse getting hurt both physically and mentally. The fact that she'd had Angel and Jeff to watch out for her as she'd explored meant a great deal to her, giving her a safety buffer that eased her transition into the lifestyle. And thanks to them, she'd met Thomas. Despite Angel's deception, Gabby still felt grateful for the time she'd gotten to spend with Thomas and David. Even if it didn't end well...

"We've come together to witness these two people making a commitment to each other. One they know they must make."

That sentence resonated within her. When she'd left her husband, it had been because she had a journey she knew she had to take. It had eaten her alive from the inside out until she'd been unable to hide it another minute. Automatically, her hand rose to touch her collar she'd been unable to remove. To rub the leather in remembrance. That voracious need to never hide who she was again was what had her wearing it no matter where she went. If anyone had a clue as to the real meaning then so be it. She was proud to be owned, to belong, not matter how temporary it would be.

Temporary.

Distaste for the word roiled through her.

"This commitment is without end. It is immeasurable, cannot be seen, touched nor felt by anyone but the two of them. It is a locking of heart, mind and body that strengthens them into one."

Thomas nodded at Rick and left at the rear of the stage. Rick looked great in dark pants and red shirt. He had that serious look on his face she'd come to know as his trademark, but his eyes looked different, lighter, excited.

In his hands, he held a simple black leather crop. She hadn't had a chance to ask anyone what the ceremony would involve so she didn't know what would happen once they got started. The chairs were separated into two sections with an aisle down the middle much like one would expect at a wedding.

Rick faced the crowd and lifted his hand, and the crowd around Gabby surged to their feet. Going with the flow she stood and turned in the direction behind her to see Diane, blindfolded and breathtaking being led into the room by two collared subs. The sheer black robe she wore hid nothing from the crowd, and her excitement was evident with the hard tips of her nipples pressing against the see-through fabric.

Gabby had helped Diane with her up do and the simple band she wore to keep it up with only a few strategically placed curls hanging free. Ebony elbow-length gloves shone in the candlelight, lending an elegance to an outfit that was little more than lingerie.

The cleansing ritual before the ceremony had been an exciting turn of events she'd not expected. It had surprised her to find her panties damp as she'd watched Diane's body cleansed and shaven by the submissives chosen for the momentous occasion. After the bath, her legs had been spread and her entire body oiled with a sweetly fragranced oil that Gabby figured had to have some sort of aphrodisiac in it. Diane had writhed and moaned as the women pulled at her nipples and fingered her cunt. When she'd begun to beg for permission to come, they'd stopped their ministrations. It was then one of the older women had produced a large, black latex butt plug. Gabby's gasp had drawn their attention, and they'd smiled at her before the plug was slowly inserted into Diane's anus. She'd moaned long and loud until the toy was fully seated.

When Diane had been helped to a standing position, Gabby had been excused and told the ceremony would begin momentarily. Now, she couldn't hold her curiosity and wondered if the toy had remained in place for the ceremony. There were no tell tale signs in the way she walked, even with the spike heeled boots that laced to just below the knee.

The women led her onto the stage and formally offered her to Rick. He nodded to the women, and they peeled the sheer robe from her shoulders and left her nude except for the boots and gloves.

"Present yourself, " he commanded.

Diane leaned slightly forward and, with her gloved hands, reached behind her and pulled the cheeks of her ass apart, revealing to the assembled crowd the wide black base of the butt plug vivid against the cream of her pale skin. The guests clapped their approval, and the knot in Gabby's belly loosened a fraction.

Moments later, Diane released the flesh, and the women helped her kneel on the fur rug at Rick's feet. The women moved off stage and took their seats in the front row with their respective Doms.

"Do you come to me of your own free will?"

"Yes, Sir, I do."

Rick reached for the blindfold covering her eyes and pulled the scrap of black fabric from her face.

He then pulled out a leather collar and held it above her head for all to see. It was a simple black and silver link braid with a small O ring in the front. He withdrew a tiny silver padlock from his pocket and threaded it through the link at one end of the collar.

"By giving this collar, I offer my vow to do everything I can to be worthy of you. I promise to hold you and keep you safe, to push you when you need it and to give you the freedom you need to soar, to love you and honor you. I acknowledge the respect I have for your needs and desires."

His strongly spoken words rang true for everything Gabby felt. What would it take to have that very freedom he spoke of?

"I acknowledge the ultimate level of trust you offer and accept the responsibility of the safekeeping of that trust. I will never violate that trust or threaten to violate it."

Oh God. Those words.

What had she done? By hiding from David and Thomas, did she keep demonstrating a lack of trust in them? It wasn't true. She knew that, now more than ever. When the relationship between her David and Thomas had developed into more, Thomas had faltered while dealing with his scars. But nonetheless, he needed her.

He needs me.

"I will always work at remaining open minded. In times of trouble, I vow to be supportive and caring always remembering that this is a loving relationship between two caring people."

Gabby felt the first splash of tears land on her cheeks.

"Most importantly, I will cherish the gift of submission you have given me. This collar is a symbol of two halves becoming one and is the outward sign of what everyone in this room already knows. You are mine, and by wearing it, you are safe to be everything that you are or will be. Do you accept this collar as it has been presented?"

Her breath caught in her throat as she waited for Diane's response. She'd been to countless weddings and never had a ceremony had such an effect on her.

"Yes, Sir, I do." Diane's voice sounded strong and clear. "I accept your collar freely and without restriction. I agree to honor our relationship above all others and seek to fulfill your needs and desires as you allow. I want nothing more than to be there when you need me. I promise to communicate honestly and openly and keep nothing from you."

Tears streamed harder from Gabby's eyes as her heart broke all over again. She wanted, no needed, to give this kind of devotion to David and Thomas. Their missteps aside, they were good men, and she would be honored to be chosen by them.

"I will strive to be the soul mate you've desired and will not dishonor you in any way."

Gabby had to bite her lip to the point of pain to stop her wail from slipping out. Had she learned anything at all these weeks? What must the people here think of the way she'd been acting?

"I will wear this collar with pride, knowing that you love me, cherish me, respect me and hold me above all others. In return, I promise to love, honor, respect and obey you with no limits."

Gabby covered her face with her hands in a lame attempt to muffle her sobs. Thoughts of leaving the room pushed at her, but interrupting the ceremony would not be forgiven.

Rick wrapped the collar around the bare expanse of Diane's neck so the O-ring rested in the hollow indentation of her clavicle and threaded the lock through the loose end.

"By wearing this lock, I express the finality of my commitment and surrender my body to your control as long as it is closed." Diane's voice hitched on the last word, and Gabby wished she could see Diane's face, the love she knew would be shining there.

"With the closing of this lock, I accept the depth of your passion, devotion and trust and provide a safe haven for you to express all that you desire knowing that I accept who you've been, who you are and all that you will be."

The click of the lock snapping into place vibrated through the room and for the first time Gabby noticed many of the other attendees in tears as well.

When Rick bent down and cupped Diane's face to his, he whispered words meant only for the two of them before claiming her with a kiss that made Gabby's toes curl. The crowd erupted into applause, catcalls and general cheers until they broke apart, and Rick helped Diane to her feet. He turned her to the guests, and Thomas appeared on the stage to present them as Master and slave.

Gabby wiped furiously at her tears, hoping no one had noticed what a fool she'd made of herself. Thankfully,

David and Thomas were at the front of the room, and she'd sat out of their line of vision.

She was about to make a run for the exit when the black curtains at the back of the stage opened up and the spotlighted St. Andrews cross came into view. The wood gleamed, luring her to stay and see what happened next. Obviously, Diane was about to participate in her first public scene as Rick's collared slave.

He led her to the cross and quickly fastened her wrists and ankles to the attached cuff and chains, leaving her spread and ready for whatever he wished to do. To her surprise, when Rick stepped a few feet away, the bottom of the cross lifted, and Diane became suspended at a slight angle giving everyone in the room a bird's eye view of her pussy and the black plug still in place.

Without hesitation, he smacked the crop he'd been holding against the flesh of her ass, and she cried out loudly. Gabby crossed her legs and rubbed her thighs against her slightly swelled clit in an attempt to stop the throbbing that had begun when Diane had first been restrained.

The desire to be in her friend's place nearly overwhelmed her until she searched the room for David and Thomas. She couldn't find either one, which meant little with the crowd gathered. Rick and Diane had chosen to allow quite a few people to be a part of this intimate scene. How would she feel if David and Thomas asked her to do something similar?

Part of her was scared to death to imagine a crowd gathered around where they would see every part of her exposed for their pleasure, but she couldn't ignore the fact that her pussy had flooded with moisture. Her body involuntarily jerked on every strike against Diane's lush and now very red ass. The last had been a direct hit to the base of the plug, and the woman had begun to beg and sob for release.

Gabby needed this. After today, Gabby would never again be able to deny how intrinsic that need had become. If David or Thomas were sitting with her, she'd be on her knees her head bowed, pleading for her own relief.

In fact...

She grabbed her cell phone and typed in one simple word.

Help.

She pressed send and hoped David had his cell phone with him. Less than a minute later, she looked up to see both David and Thomas standing by her side. The dangerous look in their eyes mirrored the anxiety she felt as her hand pressed against her sex.

"Come with us. Now."

Chapter Twenty-Six

"I didn't want to interrupt the ceremony," she whispered.

"You're fine. Both parties are too involved in the scene to notice who comes and goes at this point."

Gabby glanced at the stage to Rick's fingers pumping in and out of Diane's pussy as her cries of ecstasy and need soared through the room. Gabby's clit throbbed more at the sight, but David was right, they didn't care anymore who saw or who didn't. Their focus was entirely on each other as Diane surrendered to his will.

Thomas curved his arm around her waist and pulled her in the direction of the exit.

"Let's go." He spoke so close to her ear the warm air of his breath tickled her skin, and her sex clenched as if there was a direct line between them.

"Yes, Sir." Lost in the charged atmosphere around her, she walked along side him helpless to ease the ache in her body. Each stride pulled the corset tighter against her bare nipples, and his hand at her waist heated her skin until she thought he'd leave her with a brand.

At the lounge, David and Thomas ushered her into one of the corner booths, which simply consisted of a horseshoe shaped seat with no table in the middle.

"We should probably talk," Thomas muttered.

She nodded her head, but talking had nothing to do with the buzz of need slicing through her body and fuzzing up her head. She'd much rather they being doing stuff to her.

"Gabrielle, what happened in there?" Thomas looked at her questioningly. He still held her around the waist, their bodies touching from shoulder to knee.

Automatically, she curled into his warmth, the desire to be as close as humanly possible driving her. She took several low breaths to calm her racing heart and gathered her wits. "I was thinking about everything you told me when the ceremony started." She peered up at Thomas through damp eyelashes. "There's so much unfairness and misunderstanding in the world. Then when Rick began his vows, all the pieces I've been struggling with finally clicked into place, and I realized how wrong I'd been." She sucked in more air. "I never should have shut either of you out."

Strong fingers caressed her chin. "It was critical that you come back on your own when you were ready. Being without you these weeks may have begun to drive me mad, but I'd do anything to ensure you have what you need." Thomas' lips pressed against her mouth, a soft kiss that tingled her nerve endings until he parted her lips with his tongue and delved deep.

He tasted of his favorite mints and sexy man. That unique taste reminded her of wild, untamed sex and incredible restraint all wrapped up in one. From her other side, hard hands wrapped around her waist and cupped her breasts.

"Are you sure about this?" David whispered in her ear between nips at her neck.

Gabby moaned into Thomas' mouth and pressed back into David's warm body.

"I'm going to take that as a yes." He squeezed her breasts in a tight grip, edging closer the line of pain.

Once again sandwiched between two dominant men, their hands and mouths worshipping her body, Gabby wanted to scream. How she'd lived without this for a few short weeks was beyond her. This was what she wanted in her life more than anything.

With a reckless and wild combination of gentle touches and hot demand, they worked her in perfect harmony. Where one left off the other picked up until she couldn't think. Couldn't breathe.

Abruptly, Thomas pulled away from her. His molten lust filled gaze connected with her. "Tell me again."

"I made a mistake."

"We all made mistakes," Thomas admitted. "What else?"

"I don't want to take off my collar. It means too much."

A slow smile crossed Thomas' face. "No one asked you to, although I think we should make it more permanent. But first…"

Gabby swallowed. "Buts" made her nervous. Especially with these two.

David cupped her chin and turned her to meet his gaze. "There's a little matter of trust we still aren't clear on."

She bowed her head. "I know. I've been just as guilty about hiding."

"You have. How do we know you won't go running at the first sign of trouble again?"

A heated flush swept through Gabby. "I can't promise I won't ever mess up, but I can promise that my intentions are pure. I will accept any punishment you see fit to give." She wasn't sure how to explain that she'd grown emotionally attached. That by coming back to them, she was essentially putting her heart in their hands. "I won't let you down, Sirs."

"Please stand, Gabrielle." Thomas grabbed one hand and David the other, both helping her to her feet.

"You'll still have to serve us both."

Her heart soared. She smiled. "Gladly."

"Take off your clothes."

Gabby jerked at David's command. They were in a public area of Sanctuary. Fear, excitement, dread, arousal—her emotions spun out of control. They were testing her resolve.

With trembling hands, Gabby obeyed. She untied and unlaced the corset she'd worn to the ceremony and shimmied her way out of it. Then she unwrapped the simple skirt and revealed the fact she wore nothing underneath. The sharp intake of breath from Thomas fluttered in her stomach. She now stood bare and vulnerable in front of her Doms where anyone who walked in the room would see.

"Give me your wrists." Thomas leaned forward and wrapped her offered hands in thick leather bands that were buckled together. Gabby remained silent while David watched Thomas raise her arms over her head and attach the cuffs to a chain suspended above her she'd not noticed.

"Sir…" Her voice shook.

Thomas stepped forward and brushed against her. "What? Are you not willing to take what we give you?"

A heated blast of lust flashed through her. The edge to his voice demanded her submission. Gabby tamped down her panic and met his gaze squarely. "Yes, Sir. I am." Fear be damned. She trusted them plain and simple.

Thomas leaned forward and whispered in her ear. "Your new safe word is *trust*. Keep it in mind."

Thomas eased back onto the seat. "Linda. Lights, please."

To her shock, a bright wash of spotlight flooded over her. She squinted against the harsh light and held her breath. They'd essentially stripped her bare, placed her on display and ripped away the last of her inhibitions. Gabby remained silent, knowing in her heart she needed this test of her submission. If she didn't desire to give them what they wanted, she had no business being here.

Neither man moved. Their eyes devoured her. Twin hungry gazes swept across every inch of her body, setting flame to her need. Gabby stared back at the two men who'd captured her heart and mind in such a short amount of time. They were as different as night and day in appearance and demeanor, yet both were dominant men who expected her compliance in every way.

Could she live with that kind of commitment? Nothing less than complete trust would satisfy them.

Hell, who was she kidding? Of course, she could. A month ago maybe not. But she'd changed. They all had. That realization allowed much of her fear to dissipate, need rising in its place.

"Are you ready for the next step, Gabrielle?" Thomas leaned forward and swiped a finger along her slit.

A rush of sensation sizzled over her. Her head fell back as she widened her legs for him.

David chuckled. "I think you have your answer."

"I need a crop."

Gabby whimpered, moisture flooding between her thighs. Those words set off a thousand butterflies scrambling in her belly. Her breasts ached for their touch, her pussy throbbed for their attention and they were going to crop her instead.

"Is this punishment?" She wanted to understand.

"Consider it a release. A release from the hurt of the past. Our clean slate."

Gabby shivered and moaned softly. She wanted that more than anything in the world.

Thomas picked up the crop Linda offered him and studied Gabby carefully. Perspiration broke out across her skin. He flexed the instrument and snapped it back into place. "This will be perfect."

Thomas disappeared behind her, and David took his place at her front. "We've missed you wildly, beautiful."

Her breath caught. "I missed you, too. Every single day."

"No more fears?"

She shook her head. "None. All I have now is love."

David's eyes widened, and a groan sounded from Thomas. "You please us more than you know. Surrender to us forever. Be our beauty." David mesmerized her with his words.

"Forever," she whispered, her heart exploding with joy.

Thomas leaned into her back and brought his lips to her right ear. "Thank you, my love. That means the world to us. Now, get ready."

About the Author

Eliza Gayle lives a life full of sexy shape-shifters, blood boiling vamps and a dark desire for bondage...until she steps away from her computer and has to tend to her family.

She graduated Magna Cum Laude (which her husband translated into something very naughty) from Park University with a dual degree in Human Resource Management and Sociology. That education, a love of the metaphysical and a dirty mind comes in handy when she sits down to create new characters and worlds. The trick is getting her to sit still.

...Join her in her world at her website at www.elizagayle.net The door is always open and the next red hot adventure is just a page away.

Also available from Resplendence Publishing

Bottom's Up by Eliza Gayle

Snooping is risky business...sometimes it pays off in unexpected ways.

Jenn has been in love with her best friend since college and despite their years apart she is determined to at least find out if he has any interest in her. When the opportunity opens up in the form of a job interview in his hometown, she jumps on a plane with a plan to see what happens.

Riley walked away from Jenn after college to explore and understand the dark side of him that harbored needs he knew she was too young to understand. They kept in touch and after years of exploration into his kinks, he's decided the time for hiding the truth from the woman he loved has come to an end.

When Jenn finds a BDSM book and a flyer for a local sex club in his condo, she is both shocked and intrigued. Riley catches her red-handed snooping through his things and dares her to give him and his lifestyle a chance. Two days to explore her potential submissive side and see where it leads.

With no hesitation and barely a thought to how far he might go, she jumps at the chance to prove she's the woman for him, even if it's just for the weekend.

Kidnap and Kink by Brynn Paulin

Be Careful What You Wish For...

Jenna Marks has a secret fantasy, to be kidnapped, tied up and seduced. When she confides her secret to her best friend on a dare, she never imagines her wish might come true.

Rob Colvin, owner of The Dungeon, has had his eye on Jenna for months, but he didn't think Jenna would be into the things that make him hot. When he overhears her secret, he knows he's going to be the one to deliver her fantasy— one weekend of her submission to him, her mysterious and masterful lover.

Guardian's Challenge by Bronwyn Green

No good deed goes unpunished...

When Neeve returns to the kingdom of Maelgwn to help a friend, she finds herself face to face with the man she ran from nine months ago. Before she fled, she'd promised a year of service to the Guardians of the Temple, and now that she's back, Asher, the Chancellor of Maelgwn intends to claim the remainder of that time.

For almost a year, Asher has been searching for his consort, Neeve, who vanished without a trace. He wants her back where she belongs. In his bed. And a year won't be nearly long enough. When the pair ends up on a diplomatic mission, with another guardian accompanying, Asher finds his plan to claim her sidetracked by duty and torn by the obligation to share her with the other man for the duration of their task.

With hearts and the future at stake, Asher and Neeve must find the power to believe, trust and love one another, not just for the moment but forever. But that might be more than either is able to give.

Mr. Smith's Whip by Brynn Paulin

Librarian Olivia McKinnion's life rarely changes as she oversees the Brandywine community library and archives, but when Colin Smith takes up residence to research his latest book, everything changes. She's heard whispers of Mr. Smith's whip and his dominant ways—whispers that make her tremble with need for her secret wishes to be fulfilled. And more than anything, she wants Colin to show her the darker side of sex, bent over his knee and begging for more.

Infernal Devices by Abigail Barnette

All Steamed Up: Book One

The Two Aces. Victorian London's most salacious secret, the club is a place where erotic fantasies are played out among clockwork automatons and aether powered machines. Where nothing is off limits and the pleasures are as wicked as the imagination will allow...

Permilia Deering goes to The Two Aces looking for the sexual excitement that she knows she will not find with the man to whom she is affianced, notorious cold-fish Wallace Sterling. On her first visit to the club, she meets the Ace of Spades, a masked stranger who drives her to heights of passion she's never dreamed possible—and makes her seriously reconsider becoming a mannerly society wife.

When Wallace Sterling first glimpses his fiancée standing outside The Two Aces, he assumes she's uncovered his secret identity—the Ace of Spades. But Permilia has no idea that her intended is living a double life, and Wallace worries that he'll be out of the picture once she gets a taste of what the Ace of Spades can offer her...

Las Vegas by Demi Alex

Determined to spread her grandmother's ashes from the top of the Eiffel Tower, Angel embarks on a cross-country trip to Las Vegas. It's not France, but it's all her budget will allow. Too bad the screened observation deck hinders her plans, and when she attempts to slip her hands past the wire, the local authorities cuff her wrists.

With the last of her money used to pay fines and court fees, a complimentary food voucher leads her to a casino pub for a bite to eat. There, a late night proposition arises. Baring her breasts for a bit of cash seems simple enough, but three intriguing strangers change the odds and raise the stakes.

Angel discovers she doesn't need Lady Luck when she's got the Luck of the Irish. Laying all her cards on the table, she bets on a passionate night with Liam, Brody and Ryan. But come morning, the guys up the ante. The jackpot is tempting, but staying with the three men is the greatest gamble of her life and requires that she go all in.

Will Angel fold and leave Las Vegas as she arrived? Or will she add her heart to the pot and meet their ante?

Possessing Eleanor by Tessie Bradford

Eleanor Lewis is perfectly content with her comfortable, quiet, relationship free life until she finds herself on all fours at the feet of Jackson Royce. Eleanor is stunned by her instant and intense attraction to the power and confidence radiating from the devilishly handsome building contractor. He scrambles her brain and heats her body to the boiling point.

Jackson always trusts his gut instincts. The ultra sexy woman sprawled on the floor is a sexual submissive. How intriguing that the all-business, sensible shoe-wearing office manager has absolutely no idea. The moment he takes her into his embrace, he vows to possess her mind, body and soul.

From their first sizzling encounter, through a whirlwind courtship, Eleanor discovers being possessed by a man who loves her absolutely is what she had been searching for all along.

Transparent Illusions by Melinda Barron

Freelance writer Saffron Tyler needs work. When she offers her journalistic skills to Steele Publications, they suggest that she spend two weeks as a submissive at Fingertip Fantasies, an exclusive BDSM resort that caters to the ultimate fantasies of any customer willing to pay for the high-end service. She's been tasked to come back with a titillating exposé guaranteed to enthrall the readers of Steele's underground magazine, *Salacious.*

But when Saffron arrives at the resort, she realizes nothing is as it seems, from the fact she doesn't know where the resort is located, or anything about the man she is submitting to—except she's to call him Master, with a capital M.

What starts out as an undercover assignment soon becomes so much more. Immersed in the lifestyle, Saffron finds herself no longer acting the role of the submissive, but actually wanting to be the perfect sub her Master believes she can be. When all is said and done, will Saffron take her experience and her story and never look back? Or will she choose to stay with the man who commands her mind, body, and soul.

Heart of Ice by Brynn Paulin

Kai is perfectly unhappy with his life. Cast into a role as shop boy and forced into marriage to save his family, he sees nothing good in his future. In fact, his betrothed, Gerda, seems to hate everything he enjoys. Especially winter and his attraction to dominating his partners. His prospects look grim...until the Snow Queen arrives.

Wyn has spent her life alone, living vicariously through those who love winter. When she learns of Kai's predicament, she knows she must save him. If only she could save herself. She craves his dominance, but there's one tiny thing standing in their way. No human can touch her without experiencing chilly agony. And that might bring any relationship to an icy death.

Find Resplendence titles at the following retailers

Resplendence Publishing
www.ResplendencePublishing.com

Amazon
www.Amazon.com

Barnes and Noble
www.BarnesandNoble.com

Target
www.Target.com

Fictionwise
www.Fictionwise.com

All Romance E-Books
www.AllRomanceEBooks.com

Mobipocket
www.Mobipocket.com

1 Place for Romance
www.1placeforromance.com